John Hanrahan was born in 1939. He did his secondary
studies in a minor seminary. After completing his
theological studies, he was a priest from 1965 to 1970.
After leaving the priesthood, he lectured in literature
at Royal Melbourne Institute of Technology for twelve years.
Since 1984 he has been a freelance writer and reviewer.
He is married with three beautiful children.

O
EXCELLENT VIRGIN

John Hanrahan

A novel in stories

William Heinemann Australia

First published 1990 by
William Heinemann Australia
22 Salmon Street, Port Melbourne, Victoria 3207

Edited by Jackie Yowell
Designed by R.T.J. Klinkhamer
Author portrait by Leslie Thompson
Typeset in 10/12 Schneidler by The Type Gallery
Printed in Australia by Australian Print Group

National Library of Australia
   cataloguing-in-publication data:

Hanrahan, John.
   O Excellent Virgin.

   ISBN 0 85561 334 3.

   I. Title.

A823.3

*I dedicate this book
to the memory of my father,
Jack Hanrahan, 1910–1985.*

*He taught me to love books
and showed me
by example
his ways
of loving people.*

*And to three of his grandchildren,
Brigid, Michael and Sheena.
'Moira', in particular, I dedicate to Brigid,
because it really is her story
of 'the falling sickness'.*

Acknowledgements

I am entirely to blame for this book. But I would like to thank some of the people who gave me encouragement and support.

My wife Helen has unstintingly supported me through many travails. She and my children, Brigid, Michael and Sheena, have not only suffered graciously through the writing of this book, but have also warmly encouraged it. I owe more than I can say to their patient and accepting love.

Ludmilla Forsyth brought to this project her unfailing friendship, her generous enthusiasm and her daring critical insight. Her wanting this book helped me make it. By insisting with grace and flare, she kept reviving my faith.

Teresa Pitt, Jill Taylor, Tony Lintermans and Jane Arms believed there was a book in there somewhere and gave generous encouragement.

My friends at Heinemann, Louise Adler, Maryann Ballantyne, Carol Benetto and Susannah McFarlane have been always supportive, nursing a neurotic writer into print.

Jackie Yowell is that rare human being – the creative, meticulous, warm and imaginative editor – who brought her caring professionalism both to the book and to the writer.

I thank all these people most sincerely, knowing that words are not enough. But they are a start.

And I thank, too, all those reading and writing friends who have shown me in so many ways that fiction is an important form of truth.

Some parts of this book have had another life elsewhere and they are reincarnated in a different form in this book. I thank

ACKNOWLEDGEMENTS

the following editors: Julian Gitzen and John Powers of *BIALA* ('Melchisedech of the Mulga'); Bruce Pascoe of *Australian Short Stories* ('The Insiders' and 'The Service of the Bishop'); and Mal Morgan who edited *La Mama Poetica*, published by Melbourne University Press ('Hello, Grandfather, Goodbye').

O most excellent, most glorious, most holy and ever inviolate Virgin Mary, Mother of our Lord Jesus Christ, Queen of the whole world and Mistress of every creature; thou forsakest no one, thou despisest no one, thou sendest away disconsolate no one who comes to thee with a pure and lowly heart; despise me not for my countless grievous sins; neither forsake me for my exceeding iniquities, nor cast me not away, who am thy servant, from thy grace and love...

From *The Raccolta* or *Prayers and Devotions, enriched with indulgences*, authorised by the Holy See, prayer no. 307.

Every sin that a man commits is outside the body, but the immoral man sins against his own body. Or do you not know that your members are the temple of the Holy Spirit, who is in you, whom you have from God, and that you are not your own? For you have been bought at a great price. Glorify God and bear him in your body.

Now concerning the things whereof you wrote to me: It is good for man not to touch woman.

Saint Paul, 1 Corinthians, 6:18 & 7:1

Therefore, fair Hermia, question your desires;
Know of your youth, examine well your blood,
Whether, if you yield not to your father's choice,
You can endure the livery of a nun,
For aye to be in shady cloister mew'd,
To live a barren sister all your life,
Chanting faint hymns to the cold fruitless moon.
Thrice blessed they that master so their blood,
To undergo such maiden pilgrimage;
But earthlier happy is the rose distill'd,
Than that which withering on the virgin thorn
Grows, lives, and dies, in single blessedness.

William Shakespeare, *A Midsummer Night's Dream*.

Contents

1945

one

Our Little Hiroshima at Home

*H*E SURPRISED ME a few times that year, my father. It was 1945. I remember – it was some time in August – holding the receiver of our new phone as close as I could to our cabinet wireless so that dad could hear Ben Chifley tell us peace had come in our time. That day dad was out at the Conway farm, doing a grocery round and the Conways had a phone but no wireless. I remember stretching the phone cord, I don't remember what Chifley said. I was nearly five years old. But I do remember my father being emotional. That was new for me, but it wasn't the first surprise of that year.

We lived – at that time only four kids and mum and dad – close huddled at the back of the Boolingalap General Store. It was a typical country store, built about the time of a previous war. We sold everything from gumboots to nighties, from boiled lollies to English comics like *The Champion*, with its great stories of soccer heroes and the defeat of bullies in the upper fifth. We sold Havelock and Log Cabin tobacco and, in those hard times, even tobacco in jars, and tea bagged from the box. When I was ten we moved to Wangaratta, and later I lived in Eden and in Balwyn, but I remember the days in Boolingalap were a lot of fun, mainly. Sometimes the parish priest, Father Dolan would come, usually to buy petrol without coupons, but sometimes he stayed to eat my mother's scones, and then we were very proud.

On Friday mornings, before we went off to Saint Patrick's school, dad would harness Sonny to the creamery van, a wagon that could have had a role in the westerns we watched at Boolingalap Mechanics Hall before we went north to

Wangaratta. Our relations thought we were a bit funny, leaving Boolingalap for the big city, but Father Dolan gave us his blessing. It was sad leaving our horses and some of my cousins. My favourite horse had been Sonny. Sonny was a six-year-old, half-draught stallion who hated harness. He kicked getting into harness, he kicked getting out. When he was bored or irritated, he kicked bits out of the stable wall. Dad loved him.

Boolingalap was twelve miles out of Ballarat, on the Melbourne road. My first surprise came one Friday afternoon when all four of us kids were watching dad and Sonny doing their unharnessing performance. As dad explained to us how lovely it was to escape the madness of the Melbourne road, Sonny threw his head up and kicked out at every unbuckling. Dad dodged, and smoothed his neck, and kept saying, 'There's a good fella, you've earned a feed and a drink.' Sonny had once broken dad's leg and, though we didn't want it to happen again, we enjoyed watching the possibility.

Cousin Bern turned up, after visiting one of our many relatives in Ballarat. Cousin Bern always wore a blue suit and a yellow cardigan. In the top pocket of his suitcoat there was always a green Conway Stewart fountain pen, lined up with four nicely sharpened HB pencils. Cousin Bern was dad's cousin, and about forty. His father had died when he was a kid, his mother just the year before, and he had taken to speaking of himself as an orphan. Bern lived on a farm. 'My wife Beth' and 'my sister Beth' worked it, lumping bags of spuds and bales of hay, while Bern worried about the coming of the Japanese and the potato inspector.

'G'day, Joe. Ought to get rid of that horse. I'll take the useless beggar off your hands for three quid, thereabouts.'

'Best horse I've ever had, Bern. Besides, what would you do with him?'

'My wife Beth would sort him out in no time, you know. She's a wonder behind the plough.'

'He's a real goer, Bern. Not for sale.'

'Well, I'd go four quid. My sister Beth, there's nothing she can't do with horses. Nothing. Mind you, I'm a pretty dab hand myself, but I never seem to get the time, these days, know what I mean?'

Cousin Bern nearly always turned up with some treat for us kids. Usually he brought Peters' dixie ice-creams, 'the health food of a nation', and usually pretty soggy by the time Bern remembered to get them out of the grey Plymouth. This time, however, he reached into his pocket and produced American chewing gum. Any chewing gum was a luxury. Our shop sold Wrigleys: four pieces in a pack for a penny. But like the boiled lollies and broken biscuits, they were for paying customers only, such as the rich young men who gathered round the shop after Sunday mass and drank soft drink straight from big bottles without spilling much. Father Dolan didn't approve of them and sometimes preached against them.

So when cousin Bern produced American chewing gum, all four of us kids were delighted. We'd heard of it from kids who'd actually been to Melbourne but we'd never actually seen it. Even the Duke of Gloucester, stopping off quickly on the way to Melbourne, had given us only boiled lollies. The four of us received Bern's offering in silent wonder. It was like going to communion, but more fun.

Dad had returned from putting Sonny in the stable and we could hear Sonny having what was, for him, a quiet kick at the stable wall.

'Come on inside, Bern, and we'll have a cup of tea.'

'That'd be nice. Can't stay long, though. My wife Beth's cooking my favourite, Irish stew, and my sister Beth's been grading the spuds and I've got to check on that. But I've got something special for you, Joe.' He gave dad a stick of spearmint.

'Well, thank you, Bern, that's very nice. But give it to the kids.'

'Well, suit yourself, Joe.'

Bern was clearly offended and I helped him out by taking the stick of spearmint before it was buried forever in his coat pocket. Bernadette cut the American gum into four almost equal pieces. Father Dolan turned up just as she finished and grabbed the piece on the end, laughing kindly at us. It turned out, after a big debate, that the bit he had taken was to have been mine.

My next surprise came on the day of the Boolingalap races. Excited at my first day at the races, I entered the racecourse also a bit frightened. Bernadette was in charge of me. Before we went in, she pointed to a sign: 'Trespassers will be prosecuted'. She told me how severely wicked Roman emperors and English kings and queens had prosecuted us Catholics and urged me to behave myself. I wouldn't have dreamt of misbehaving at the Boolingalap races. What with dad being secretary, two of my uncles trainers, and four of my cousins amateur jockeys. I was going to be a jockey when I grew up.

I spent a good deal of the day in the tin shed that was the secretary's office. Trainers, and even jockeys, came and went and they treated dad with a respect that I thought belonged only to Father Dolan.

After the third race, a trainer came in wearing his hat and looking fat and red, as many of the trainers seemed to.

'Why the hell, Joe Hannigan, isn't Heavenly Lady in the race book for the last race?'

Dad looked through the race book, then through some papers on his desk, which was also my aunty Meg's kitchen table.

'She was entered in the first race. Nothing else.'

'But the six furlongs was just a pipe-opener. I've been getting her ready around the farm for the ten furlongs, and bugger it all, I could win some money on her. She's already won a Corinthian at Molongip.'

'Well, she'd have to improve a bit. She ran dead last in the first race, or was the jockey just holding her up?'

'Well, she's going in the last, you can take it from me.'

'She's not going in the last. You didn't fill in the papers.'

The trainer paused, then moved closer and spoke more quietly. 'Actually, Joe, she's owned by Father Dolan. She just races in my name.'

'I'm sorry, Brendan, you know the rules. So does Father Dolan. Seeing he's a racing man.'

'Well, I'm going to stand here until you tell me she's in. Or do you want me to go and get Father Dolan?'

'You can bugger off, Brendan Dougherty. And so can Father Dolan. I'm the boss, at least on this racecourse,' dad pronounced, entering family folklore.

It was an each way bet who was more surprised, Dougherty or me. He backed out of the room and I backed further into my corner. I had never heard my father swear before. And about a priest's racehorse! I was pleased and surprised.

The other time dad surprised me was also in August. It was August the sixth, Bernadette's birthday. She turned thirteen that day. That night was also Bill McBride night. Bill came to tea once a week. I always stayed awake on Bill McBride nights. Bill was interesting, partly because he was the only Protestant we knew, partly because he kept canaries and let us feed them, but mainly because we firmly believed in his tragedy. It was part of our faith that Bill McBride had once been married, that his wife had got off what we called the shanghai from Ballarat, and had wandered into the pine plantation opposite the Boolingalap station and disappeared forever. That night, I listened to talk about spud crops, about what we and the Americans would do to the Japanese, about playing Forty-fives in the Mechanics Hall, about what was going on between my cousin Damien and Loretta Ryan, about the death of John Curtin, who was still mourned in our house.

At about ten o'clock, when I was supposed to be hours asleep, there was a thundering knock at the front door of the shop, which was not unusual, as farmers kept their own hours, especially if they needed tobacco or petrol. I heard dad come back into the kitchen and say, 'Just three Melbourne blokes on the way back from the Ballarat races. Need some petrol, be back in a minute.' I could hear Mum and Bill discussing whether Loretta would have to get married, which was a pretty funny idea. Suddenly there were crashing noises. I jumped out of bed and ran into the shop. Dad was lying on the floor in front of the counter. Two men, standing beneath a sign that said *A right place for everything, and everything in its right place*, were kicking him in the ribs. They wore brown suits, with waistcoats, and snappy hats.

A third man in a blue suit was watching as if he liked it. He threw his cigarette butt among the lemonade bottles neatly arranged against the front window of the shop and said, 'You poor country bastard, when we want petrol, we get it. This time we're not even going to bother to pay.'

There was blood seeping from my father's mouth, but he could still talk. 'You've got to have petrol tickets just like everybody else, and I'm going to get them from you.'

Bill McBride was standing on the counter next to the scales. He picked up the two-ounce weight and got one of the men in brown right in the forehead. Mum was coming up behind the blue man with a brand new shovel in her hands. Bill jumped down from the counter, now with an eight-ounce weight in his hand. He thumped the second man in brown on the shoulder.

It was a bit like a school tableau. There was dad outstretched, surrounded by boiled lollies and tobacco and broken glass. He was lying on a couple of shattered packets of Bushells tea. One man in brown was wiping blood from his forehead with a white hanky and looking as though he wanted to cry. Bill was standing over the other bloke with the weight poised over his skull. Mum stood behind the man in blue, her shovel raised, looking as though she'd had a bit of practice donging blokes from Melbourne on the head. I was still standing behind the counter with my pyjama pants about my ankles. I was always careless about my pyjama cord. We never did much night travel in pyjamas, as we used the enamel chamber pot and not the outside dunny after dark.

I travelled quite a bit that night, however.

Mum and dad were magnificent, standing strong in the tea leaves and the crushed lollies. I always looked up to them, even when – later on – they sort of had to look up to me a bit.

Dad still had blood coming out of his mouth and his nose looked awfully crooked. 'Stop it!' he yelled. 'They don't know what they're doing. They're drunk, they don't know what they're doing.'

I thought mum and Bill both looked a bit disappointed. I know I was.

Armed with the weights and mum's shovel, Bill escorted the foreigners to their black Buick. Mum helped dad into bed. Bill came back with all the petrol tickets they had and eighteen quid 'to cover costs'.

Back in the shop, I sat on the counter, waiting to be hustled to bed.

Bill talked as he swept up. 'Never been to Melbourne, but I've never trusted a bloke from Melbourne since Daniel Mannix took it over.' As he tried to sort tobacco from broken glass, he added bitterly, 'And ever since John Wren took over Collingwood, things have got worse.'

But then, Bill was the only Protestant I knew.

I rescued two handfuls of boiled lollies which I sort of shared the next day.

I never saw any other violence in Boolingalap, except cousin Matthew giving me a blood nose behind the shelter shed, but that wasn't the same. And I was at Creswick the day Sonny kicked down the stable door and broke dad's leg again. I remember that day because the kids from Saint Michael's, Creswick, turned up to play cricket and we turned up to play footy. We won the toss and footy it was. We lost the game though. Timothy O'Mara, who was our captain and who had his front teeth knocked out, blamed the Hannigans, especially me. He said all Hannigans were useless at football and Michael Hannigan was the most useless. Even more useless than my three sisters. He was probably right, but he may also have been annoyed because I was the one who knocked his teeth out. When we got home, dad was in hospital and mum had sold Sonny to cousin Bern for eleven pounds.

That was a day I remember but it wasn't as unforgettable as August the sixth and the foreigners from Melbourne. I also remember Father Dolan asking us to pray for the boys who had flown over Hiroshima and Nagasaki, but I don't know if he had much luck. We never had much time for foreigners and foreign words in Boolingalap.

1947

Hello,

Grandfather,

Goodbye

I WAS THE LAST GRANDKID to see my grandfather alive. Just for once, I stood out from my sixty-four cousins. At Saint Patrick's school, thirty of the fifty kids were Hannigan grandchildren, so classes were called off on the day of the funeral. I wasn't too impressed myself, as this denied me my full day of skiting about the last meeting with an old man of whom we were all a bit scared.

It had been a typical July day in Boolingalap. Even in the afternoon, mist sat round the top of the mountain. Occasionally small clouds scampered across the sky as if running for home. On the green hills that had reminded my great-grandfather of Ireland, sheep and cows stood reproachful against the wind.

I had saddled Dolly, the family pony. That was the easy part, for Dolly was quite cheerful about being saddled. Then she challenged you to get a bridle on her head. It was, as my father said, one way of putting the cart before the horse, but the game pleased Dolly and Dolly was not to be denied. I'd drag Dolly alongside a big rock that stood next to the vegie garden. My mother would stand on the rock with the bridle. You got to ride Dolly if my mother's patience triumphed over Dolly's head-flings. Once the bridle was buckled, Dolly would repose into her imitation of a statue. The ritual was for my mother to give her a hefty belt on the rump with her stick for stirring the copper. This was a day of good omens. Dolly consented to the bridle after only twenty minutes and deigned to move after the fourth whack. So it took me only three-quarters of an hour to cajole Dolly up the hill to the old family house where my grandfather lived with my two bachelor uncles.

My turning up on a horse pleased my grandfather. Tractors were starting to noise their way across his sons' farms. I think he welcomed Dolly more than me. But I loved the old kitchen, a vast room completely separate from the rest of the house. Even in summer the open fire burned, with the blackened water fountain always hanging over it. It was quiet now in this kitchen, as my grandfather tapped his pipe on the hearth and asked me occasional questions about school and home. The huge deal table had been the centre of life for my father and his thirteen brothers and sisters. Here, too, were taken many decisions important to the life of the parish.

My uncles were out in the twenty-acre paddock harrowing the spuds. I liked to sit and watch the fire, watch the smoke curl from the pipe of the man whose father had fought alongside Peter Lalor at Eureka. I explained my problems at school with Sister Athanasius and with fractions. He nodded at my world and I remembered his, fondly old in family story.

My parents had packed away their card-playing days as part of their almost frivolous, nudgingly sinful past. But I knew from aunty Meg that my father's family, grown larger and busier with cousins, had played ferocious Forty-fives. The parish priest had presided over the rules. I knew the card evenings, and had lived through many hands, though I had never dealt a card in my life.

With that priest too, my grandfather had plotted strategies for greyhounds. Those greyhounds had ripped across the paddocks after the blood of real hares, all raced in my grandfather's name, though the best of them had actually belonged to Father Mulvaney. Some Sundays, Father Dolan would preach against the evils of greyhound racing, and therefore against his predecessor. For himself, Father Dolan preferred racehorses. Grandfather definitely preferred grey-hounds and Father Mulvaney. On his amiable days, my grandfather would stop in front of a picture of Father Mulvaney's champion greyhound, Michael Collins, which hung on the wall next to the Sacred Heart. My grandfather would always say, always surprisingly, 'Had the fun of Cork in those days, we did. A man could have a worse job than being a parish priest. Though for the life of me, I don't know what we're going to make of you, a boy with no farm and four sisters now, and probably another one on the way.'

I didn't know what any of that meant.

My grandfather had lived into an irascible peacefulness, but I knew all the arguments that had died behind him. Young Daniel Mannix had been right about conscription, De Valera had been half right about Ireland. I knew the family arguments and disputes and competitions. My father and his brothers had ridden against each other as jockeys at country race meetings. My father had ridden sixty miles on his bike to settle an argument about the highwater mark on Lake Burrumbeet.

I loved the silences with my grandfather, and felt uncomfortable only when he moved in duty to ask about my sad-horsed present. I hoped he would decide on a walk past the hawthorn hedge to the main road, with a tour through the house on the way back. I loved, and I think he did too, pausing before the ship in the bottle, before the piano long silent, before the glass-doored bookcase, with Lawson and Dickens and Ogilvie and Paterson and *Every Housewife's Guide to Home Health*, before a browning photo of my aunty Meg, wearing the regalia of the Queen of Boolingalap and surrounded by her attendants, disappointed cousins. Aunty Meg stood on the other side of the Sacred Heart. Her usual regalia was an apron and a loud voice, which she wore in mothering the thirteen children younger than her, particularly the boys.

We did take our walk that day, and it was full of comfortable silences. My grandfather, pausing on his walking stick and looking with disfavour on the cars racing along the main road to Melbourne, worried about whether it was too cold for me.

Then we drank sweet black tea from the enamel mugs that I insisted on, because they seemed both historic and grown-up, though they were generally used only for spud-diggers.

It was time to go and he followed me out of the kitchen. He talked to Dolly and she seemed to listen. 'There's a good girl, There's life in you yet. We old ones've got to stick together. I hope the boy's good to you. You deserve it, don't you, old girl?'

I mounted from the fence, while he held the bridle. In sorting out the reins, I dropped the switch that I always carried for Dolly. She usually went home at a gallop, but sometimes had to be persuaded that home was where we were heading. It was the first time that I realised how bad my grandfather's sight was. Leaning on his stick, he fumbled on the ground while I gave him instructions about where the switch was. I almost became impatient with him as he groped on the muddy ground. Finally he handed me the stick. Dolly knew that day that it was hometime and she was galloping towards the road before I could say goodbye.

My grandfather was dead next morning.

I lived some months in the glory of being the last cousin to talk to my grandfather. Spring came, as usual, uncertainly. It must have been mid-December before we took to lying in the horse trough after school. I was in a frolicky mood that day. My cousin Damien, who was fifteen years older than me, worked in my father's store. He had been delivering groceries to the farms. He unharnessed Ben, our beautiful bay, half-draught gelding and brought him to the trough for a drink. As I lay in the water and Ben slurped at the other end, it seemed almost compulsory to splash Damien as he stood there in his red face and fireman's braces.

'You cheeky little bugger. You think you can get away with anything.'

He was right, of course. I did feel cheeky in my green woollen togs, newly acquired from a cousin a couple of sizes bigger than me. But they were my first togs.

'I don't know how you can still be so smart when you left our grandfather to die.'

I didn't know what he was talking about. Dolly had galloped off; my grandfather had gone back to sit by the fire. He always went back to sit by the fire.

'You just galloped off and left him lying on the path. He had to wait for Pat and Frank to find him. Fat lot you cared, you cheeky little bugger.'

I was still sitting in the horse trough when dad brought Dolly out for a drink an hour later. Dolly jibbed at drinking in my presence. I had been thinking of my grandfather lying on the path to the empty kitchen. I splashed my face to wash away the tears and the memory. When dad said I looked sour, I blamed Sister Athanasius and fractions. But Dolly wouldn't drink till I got out of the trough.

1954

three

Beneath
the Hanging Tree

*T*HEY DISAPPEARED from his life, both of them, one Sunday evening in the mid-winter holidays. After tea, Roy McDougall went for a walk. On his own, and down the seniors' avenue, to make matters even worse. And he was gone for good, more or less. Brother Bernard, he just up and died.

It was the last day of the holidays in the junior seminary, a secluded boarding school for future priests run by the Marianite Order. On this morning, the boys were enjoying their usual Sunday sleep-in. Roy McDougall, always cheeky and dangerously different, pretended to sleep on after the six-thirty bell, beyond the shouted invocation, *May the Blessed Heart of Mary live forever in the hearts of all men.* Kevin Milton, who was pious, yelled out 'Eternally! Forever! Amen!' and bounded out of bed and onto his knees before anyone else sat up. Roy McDougall, who was not pious, definitely, and who didn't even own a saint's name, pretended to sleep on. Michael Hannigan, who was partly pious, but wanted to be holy, got out of bed very slowly. He didn't yell the prayer, he didn't kneel down. He sat on his bed, a parcel of clothes in his lap: singlet-inside-shirt-inside-jumper, top two buttons of the shirt undone, with the tie loosened but knotted inside the shirt collar. He sat till the rush to the washroom had almost emptied the dormitory. He dropped his clothes to the floor, whipped off his pyjama trousers, and shoved them under his pillow, wet as they were.

It was freezing in chapel at seven o'clock. Father Kennelly, who was Father Prefect of the boys, gave his morning talk

[24]

walking up and down the aisle, sweating. He talked about prayer and purity, and the need for them if the boys were to become good missionaries in South India. God and Father Provincial, who controlled all Marianites in Australia, had not seen fit to send Father Prefect to South India, but he thanked God now that he was training boys who would one day be priests in South India. Or the Solomons, though the boys knew that Father Prefect had a preference for South India, where there were no women who went bare-breasted. Father Prefect became a bit agitated when missionaries from the Solomons turned up with their boxes of slides.

Michael Hannigan was much inspired by images of these missions to far-flung souls. One day he would come back to this junior seminary, famous among the Marianites for his preaching; and he would introduce to eager schoolboys his rows of dark smiling converts. And like Brother Bernard, one of the few Marianite laybrothers lucky enough to be sent to serve the priests serving the people of South India, he would become an expert on Hindu temples. Laybrothers never studied much theology, and never said mass or performed the sacraments. But they became holy by washing floors and serving soup for priests and noticing lots of things unnoticed by priests.

'And, boys, I want you to notice what Saint Paul says in today's epistle.' Father Prefect wiped the sweat from his glasses and held them up to the light. 'We are not to commit fornication. Or adultery. And I've been meaning to mention that the junior toilets have been left very dirty. Even when cleaning the toilets, think of God looking down on you. Or his Blessed Mother. Or me. And tomorrow, on your day of prayer and recollection, I want you to put aside all thoughts of worldly things like soccer, and think only of the vocation that God has given you, to be His priests forever.'

Father Prefect, unsure about the purity of glasses held towards Heaven, wiped them again. Then he knelt at the altar rails and paused in a shudder of prayerfulness. 'We will now say that loved prayer that our Father Founder commanded us to say every day.' The boys went through the prayer with a devotion that ranged from arabesques of piety to slouches of boredom. Roy McDougall scratched an ear and counted holy cards. *O most excellent, most glorious, most holy and ever inviolate Mother of Our Lord Jesus Christ, Queen of the whole world and Mistress of every creature...despise me not for my countless grievous sins; obtain for me forgiveness of all my sins, and the grace of fear and the love of thee; health likewise and chastity of body...*

During the mass that followed, Roy reorganised his holy cards in his missal, and then promptly went to sleep when they sat down for the offertory. Michael sometimes liked to frighten himself by wondering if Roy really had a vocation. After the consecration Michael's attention wandered to the two small brass angels, screwed either side to the top of the tabernacle. He realised with horror that the angels were bent devoutly in prayer, with their backsides turned towards Father Prefect saying mass. Yesterday, when they had been cleaning the altar brass, Roy had turned them round the wrong way for a joke, and had forgotten to turn them back. He nudged Roy and whispered, 'Hey, look at the angels'. On the other side of him, Kevin turned and asked with excitement, 'Where?'. Kevin had a vocation, definitely.

After breakfast, the juniors walked down their avenue. Some raced ahead, to be first to shatter the ice in the puddles. Roy and Michael dawdled behind.

'Been called up again, I have.' Roy spoke with pride and worry.

'What's it this time? Talking to the seniors again?'

'I dunno. Probably. I'm not sure but.' Roy picked up a piece of brown ice and sucked it. He came from Cairns and was enjoying his first winter of frost and chilblains in the mountains west of Eden.

'Why is it, why can't we talk to the seniors at all?' Michael was asking a question that puzzled him eternally.

Roy was stomping on the ice of a virgin puddle.

'Probably because we're too cheeky,' said Michael, answering himself.

'It must be funny, you know, being in third form,' said Roy, throwing a stone at a willy wagtail. 'There's six seniors and two juniors in third form. Must be funny, not being able to talk to kids in your own class.'

'Maybe it's the ones who shave who get made seniors.' Michael wanted to explore the philosophy of the matter.

'I bet it's sex, I bet that's what it is.' Roy spoke with authority.

'Why should it have anything to do with sex?'

'I'm not exactly sure, but I bet it's got something to do with sex. Everything else does.'

'You're nuts.'

'Hey, you two!' yelled Dominic Lynch, who was the fourth-former in charge of the juniors. 'You know the rules. *Nunquam duo.* Even you two know what that means: Never two. Never, so come on and catch up.'

'Actually,' said Roy, moving in a slow-motion hurry-up, 'I think Father Prefect's called me up for talking to Brother Bernard.'

'You're nuts. He's a laybrother, he's very holy.'

The bell broke into their talking and summoned them to their second Sunday mass, complete with flowing gothic vestments, rather than the dull sandwich-board vestments of every day. Celebrant, deacon, sub-deacon, a bevy of altar boys, clouds of incense and storms of singing. It was believed to be fun.

As always, Michael endured rather than enjoyed high mass. He loved listening to plain chant, but hated being forced to sing it. He bumped through the notes as erratically as a wallaby through a bushfire. Afterwards, he hurried to the study to write his weekly letter home to Wangaratta, so he could get to his approved holiday reading, *For the Term of His Natural Life.*

Dear Mum and Dad,

I hope this letter finds you as it leaves me. Pretty well, in fact. Last night some of us had goanna stew, from a goanna we killed in the bush. Thank you for your letters, Majella, Bernadette, Philomena, Teresa, Brigid and Sheena. Your running writing is coming on really well, Sha.

I'm glad that you ran into Father Mulligan at the races, dad, and Brother McDermott at the bootmakers, mum. I'm glad the parish and the Christian Brothers are proud of me. Yes, I'm looking forward to saving hundreds of souls too, no, make that thousands.

I'm glad Father Mulligan thinks that the Marianites have the most interesting missions in Australia. I guess it may be a chance to travel. It hadn't occurred to me. I'm surprised and pleased that Brother McDermott intended to put me in the under-thirteen footy team this year. Last year I only got two half games with the possibles. I never made it to the probables.

Today we have our first game of soccer. We have switched from rugby, because Father Prefect doesn't think it is a proper game for future priests. Father Prefect thinks that soccer is a more Ccatholic game than Australian Rules, which some boys want instead of rugby. But Father Prefect has pointed out that we will be able to coach soccer in South India and the Solomons. We must do all we can to help the natives.

I'm glad that Bernadette got over her appendix OK. Fancy Mrs O'Flynn's dog having six pups. Give my love to Oscar. We have a dog here, part Alsatian, named Aloysius, but not as smart as Oscar. Give my regards to Majella, Bernadette, Philomena, Teresa, Brigid and Sheena. You know, I have the most sisters of anyone in the school. Do we plan on getting any more? Kevin Milton says he is. I will enclose a pamphlet on vocations to the

*Missionary Handmaidens of Mary, the MAMs, our
Order of nuns. I found them stacked away in the loft with
the costumes for* Charley's Aunt.

*Don't worry, mum. I understand perfectly about your not
being able to come on visiting day, what with Bernadette's
appendix, and the Redemptorist missioners and dad doing
overtime. I'll check with Father Prefect, mum, if you are
allowed to come up some other time, apart from the official
visiting day. But I wouldn't want to overdo things and
there's always next year.*

I remain,
>   *Your loving son in the Heart of Christ and His
>   Mother,*
>>   *Michael.*

*PS Next time you see Brother McDermott in the boot-
makers, mum, tell him thanks.*

*PPS Father Prefect asked me to tell you not to mention
how Essendon are going. I hardly even think about football
these days.*

*PPPS Father Prefect has asked me to mention that it
wasn't really goanna stew, mum. Brother Bernard was
playing a trick on us.*

*PPPPS Too bad about John Coleman. He gets a bad time
from fullbacks. I will pray for him.*

*PPPPPS Next year it is 150 years since the Venerable
Giovanni Buongiorno had his vision of Our Lady of the
Snow and founded the family of our Order in Sicily.*

Michael folded his letter in the way Father Prefect had
shown them. He looked up to see Roy standing in front of his
desk, his freckled fingers twisting and twining, his red hair
glowering above his red face.

'I've been to see Father Prefect, he warned me...'

'You got Dominic's permission to talk to me?'

'Damn Dominic! Father Prefect warned me about "particular friendship" . '

'Father Prefect is always warning against "particular friendship". You can't damn Dominic. Particular friendship with who?'

'I can only tell my friends.'

Michael could see Roy's anger disappearing in the slipstream of his smile, but he was offended. 'Well, in that case,' and he turned his attention elaborately back to his letter.

'You're a dill, Michael,' said Roy affectionately.

'Michael Hannigan, shut up! Roy McDougall, sit down! Or I'll send you both up again. You'll both miss Sunday dessert again.' Dominic stood up as a snigger shuffled through the room.

There was quick silence. Dominic Lynch seemed to enjoy getting kids put off dessert, though Michael suspected it was because he was a bit scared of them and was trying to show that he was the boss.

That afternoon the seniors walked the seven miles into Eden, where they were allowed to have some fun walking along the beach and visiting the church. The juniors stayed home to play their first game of soccer. Father Prefect umpired with a rule book in one hand.

Brother Bernard, his grey hair streaming in the wind, prowled the boundary. 'Come on, boys! The students at Our Lady of the Snow College, Trivandrum, South India, could play better than this. Off-side? That wasn't off-side, Father Prefect. You're getting your off-sides mixed up, Father Prefect. You're putting all the wrong people off-side!'

Roy McDougall scored a goal and was later sent off for play unbecoming to a future priest. Kevin Milton, trainee martyr, offered to go off in his place. Michael Hannigan was so cold and bored at full-back that he found himself thinking of Marilyn Monroe. When he raced the ball up the field to the praise of Father Prefect, he wondered if Father Prefect would have been quite so pleased if he'd known he was praising a rush against Marilyn Monroe.

After the game, Michael and Roy sat at the foot of the stairs, taking off their football boots, reluctant at the prospect of an icy shower. Besides, Dominic had not come back to chase them up.

'Not as good as rugby,' said Roy.

'Not as good as Aussie Rules,' said Michael who came from Wangaratta. 'You know what? A Christian Brother once gave me six cuts for playing Rugby League. And it was with the Catholic scouts!'

'Yeah, pretty rough weren't they, the Christies? That's one thing about this place, no more cuts. I was dying to get away from the Christies.'

'Brother McDermott – I ever tell you about him?' Michael looked around and lowered his voice. He banged the mud from between the stops of his boots as he spoke. 'Well, I hated him. I'd've done anything to get away from him...'

'Well, maybe you did but.'

'I don't know what you're talking about.'

Roy was attempting to head the soccer ball, but making frequent contact with his nose. 'Friend Mick, I really believe you don't. You're a drongo, mate.'

'Hey, we're not supposed to use words like that.'

'What's wrong with "drongo"? My dad says I'm a "fair dinkum drongo".'

'No, you know what I mean. We're not supposed to use words like "mate" and "friend", you know perfectly well. They can lead to particular friendships.' Michael knew he was right, but he sounded off-note even to himself.

'What's so bad about particular friendships, that's what I want to know. Come on, you're so smart, you tell me. Come on, smarty.'

'Well, you know, they can lead to bad sorts of things. You know, I mean...'

'Come on, you don't know, do you?'

'I bloody well do know. I know as well as you.'

Swearing would bring even Roy to a stop. Michael grabbed his footy boots and scuttled upstairs, just as he saw Father

Prefect coming along the path. From the landing, he heard Roy being cross-examined. 'Have you seen Dominic or any of the other seniors? You two weren't nunquam duoing, were you?'

That evening, study took place in a heavy stillness. The seniors had not yet returned. Father Prefect hovered in and out of the study as if expecting to catch them hiding in the desks. Michael read *For the Term of His Natural Life*, but perfunctorily, unable to get as involved as usual in the lives of the men and boys of Port Arthur. Roy was summoned again by Father Prefect. Soon after, Brother Bernard came into the study, an unusual event. He looked around, then came over to Michael.

'Have you seen Roy?'

'He's up with Father Prefect, Brother.'

Brother Bernard looked grim. He said, more to himself than to Michael: 'I hope he isn't making a mistake with that boy.'

Just before six o'clock, there was a scurry of seniors up the stairs. At ten past six, when the whole school assembled in the big study for Father Prefect's evening talk, some of the seniors rushed in during the invocation to the Holy Ghost. Michael felt the excitement of the innocent about to enjoy the punishment of the guilty.

Father Prefect did not take his usual place at the teacher's desk. He walked up and down in front of them. 'I am sad, boys. This is a sad day. Today, as a special privilege, I let the seniors go for a walk into Eden. The seniors, whom I ask the juniors to look up to. The seniors, who are supposed to set an example. They come back late. They took a short-cut and they got lost. At least, I hope they took a short-cut. They say they took a short-cut. But worse – and boys I am shocked, I am amazed – worse, they went to the milk bar. No permission, they just went to a milk bar. And worse, worse, they were seen standing on the street, the main street, talking to a group of girls. How do I know this?'

Father Prefect stopped pacing. Sweat was running down his forehead, down his five o'clock shadow. He wiped his face and his glasses. He wiped his neck and then stuffed his white handkerchief inside the back of his clerical collar.

'How do I know this, you ask? I know this, to my shame, from Father Mulcahy, the parish priest. To my shame. To our shame. And worse, when I went round to the fifth-form study, to the empty fifth-form study, I found this.' Father Prefect held up a book, an orange Penguin, *Pygmalion* by George Bernard Shaw.

'Against my better judgement, I let this book come into this school. I even read this book, because it is called Literature. I suspect Literature. It is usually dirt written by atheistic socialists who are unfaithful to their wives. But I let this book into the fifth-form bookcase, after I had wasted my time reading it and stapling up the offensive bits. What do I find? I find the book unstapled, that's what I find. Someone – maybe, God help us, even more than one boy in this school – but someone, has been deliberately, consciously, flagrantly reading about a young person, a female, a girl of the opposite sex, in the bath. Yes, that's what I said, in the bath.'

Father Prefect rocked back on his heels and closed his eyes. 'In the bath, that's what I said.'

Father Prefect opened his eyes and seemed surprised to find the boys still there. 'This, boys, is the path to Hell.' He waved *Pygmalion* at them. 'It is men like this who would destroy the God-given vocations of girls – boys – like you. To draw them back from the path to Hell, the seniors will go without dessert for a week. To focus their minds on God and His Blessed Mother, there will not be the usual Sunday talking at tea. We will start the new refectory book.'

Father Prefect was clearly going to say more, but he was stopped by a salvo of sneezes. He reached into his pocket for a handkerchief and couldn't find one. He left without saying the concluding prayer to Our Lady. At the door he tried to wipe his nose with his knuckle. He looked surprised at a piece of snot dribbling down the cover of *Pygmalion*.

During tea, Dominic took his place at the rostrum and

began reading the life of Saint Aloysius Gonzaga, by CC Martindale, SJ. Father Martindale had been particularly impressed that this patron saint of youth never looked a woman in the eye, not even his own mother. While Dominic read, the juniors ostentatiously enjoyed second and third helpings of dessert, bread-and-butter custard. Michael had lost his appetite on the first course, the usual Sunday night fare of a tureen of stale bread, soaked in warm milk and topped with raisins. When he refused the bread-and-butter custard he felt he was letting the side down. Kevin had none because, as was well known, he was doing a novena of no-desserts for the defeat of Communism. Roy had ploughed through three helpings with a sad-faced resoluteness.

After tea, a stern Dominic herded the juniors for a walk down their avenue, Our Lady's avenue. They could see the seniors milling uneasily beneath the Hanging Tree, an old elm that stood between the fathers' house and the school buildings. It was called the Hanging Tree, because De Valois, who had owned the main house ninety years before, had hanged himself from that tree. Some said it was because his daughter had eloped with a Catholic.

Roy McDougall grabbed Michael Hannigan by the shoulder as the others headed down the avenue. 'Mike. I've got something to tell you. Come with me.' He went behind one of the cypress trees that lined the avenue.

'Roy, we'll be in trouble for nunquam duoing again.'

'Not me. Never again.'

'Don't tell me you've reformed?'

'No, dope. I'm going.'

'Where? Where on earth are you going?'

'Home, you dill. I'm going back to Cairns.'

'You'll never get there.'

'I got away from there, I'll get back there. First, I'll hitchhike to my aunty's in Wollongong.'

It was all beyond Michael's universe of possibilities. He

started shredding a branch of cypress to keep touch with the earth. 'You mean you've lost your vocation?'

'I never had one. Who does when they're twelve?'

'I got mine when I was ten.'

'Well, anyway, I got no time for arguing. I just want you to give a message to Brother Bernard in case I don't see him. I might try to catch him in his room.'

'Roy, you can't. You know Father Prefect would kill you. He'd throw you out.'

'He can't throw me out if I'm not here, can he?'

'No, no, I guess not,' said Michael, still not believing.

'Anyway, tell Brother Bernard... well just tell him that I had to go, that I couldn't... Hell, just tell him whatever you like, so long as you tell him I've gone.'

Voices up the avenue indicated the juniors were returning.

'Good luck, Mike. See you, mate. You can say a prayer for me if you like.'

Roy was suddenly gone, leaving Michael Hannigan to trail behind the chattering juniors, unnoticed, unnoticing.

As usual, Brother Bernard was waiting for the juniors in the floodlit courtyard outside the chapel. He provided ten minutes of fun before night prayers and the Greater Silence, which moved sweetly through the buildings each evening. Tonight he startled them by producing a strange whip and pretending to chase them with it. It was made of about ten strands of leather, over two foot long, joined together at one end. Each strand was interrupted by a series of fierce knots.

'Never seen one of these before, eh? You will, one day, at least some of you will. You lucky little devils!' Then he would make another pounce and mock hit. By the time the bell rang for night prayers, the pretence had gone out of the hits and Brother Bernard was landing solid thwacks across the shoulders of slower boys.

After night prayers, Michael Hannigan had to do a job he hated: to collect the written projects from the juniors and take them across to Father Prefect's room in the fathers' house. This meant walking through the dark silence past the Hanging Tree. In his relaxed moments with the boys, Father Prefect would tell them stories of De Valois' body swinging for three days in the tree; of the workman who, forty years later, had shot his head off beneath the same tree.

Michael hated this walk through the listening night. He ran, arriving breathless at the fathers' house. He dumped the books, walked sedately along the cloister and burst again into a run as soon as his feet hit the lawn, his eyes on the welcoming lights of the dormitory a hundred yards away. Just past the Hanging Tree, he almost died.

'Hey, Mike. Stop!'

Terror was made flesh in his juddering heart. Terror became anger became surprise became pleasure.

'Roy. You're back!'

'I never went yet.' He headed off towards the seniors' avenue, across the already frosting grass.

Michael followed reluctantly. Something was still wrong. Michael looked up to the unhelpful stars, then kept following.

Roy stopped at the top of the avenue. Even in the dark, he looked older. 'It's all right. You don't have to talk to Brother Bernard. I've already talked to him. So it's OK. You don't have to worry.'

'You didn't go...'

'No, I didn't go to his room. Though he asked me to – the other day he did.'

'Why for heaven's sake?'

'He wanted to tell me about India. He knew I wanted to go there. He had pictures of the god Krishna and the shepherd girl Radha, the god Vishnu and some hero bloke called Arjuna or something. He reckoned we were getting the wrong ideas about sex and stuff.'

From habit, they started walking down the avenue.

'Well, when did you tell him you were going?'

'Down the juniors' avenue, when you were at night prayers. He scare me.'

'You mean that whip thing?'

'No, don't be silly, he didn't have any whip thing.'

Somewhere to the left, a wallaby scuttled through the bush. They walked on in nervous silence.

'You know, he wanted me to go to his room. I think he wanted me to do things.'

'Whadya mean? Things?'

'Well, you've got a dick, haven't you?'

'We weren't talking about dicks. We were talking about things.'

'Poor Mike, you don't know anything about the problems with dicks, do you.'

'I do so. I damn well do.' They walked on in silence. Michael broke it. 'I wet my bed.'

'Hell, Mike, you know even less than I do.'

'You think you know so much just because you're nearly fourteen.'

'Look, I'm not going to argue. I've already had one argument tonight.'

'You didn't argue with Brother Bernard? Gee, Roy, you didn't, did you?'

'Yeah, you could say that. You could say we had a hell of an argument. Gee, Mike...'

Roy stopped and leant over the rail of the small bridge. Suddenly, Michael realised that sobs were shuddering into the silence. He stood in the middle of the avenue, in the middle of a bedevilled world. Roy sobbed himself into silence.

'Got a hanky?'

Michael handed Roy his grubby handkerchief.

'One thing, Mike, I would never harm Brother Bernard. It got just a bit funny about dicks and things.'

'What the hell are you talking about?' Michael felt a winter chilling the blood of his world. Roy was being very evasive, and very solemn.

'Mike, I want you to do me a favour.'

'Of course. But I haven't got a clue what you're talking about.'

'It doesn't matter. Just listen. I pushed him and he fell over. At the top of the juniors' avenue. I want you to make sure he's all right.'

'You come too.'

'No, Mike. I gotta go. Honest.'

'Why?'

'I just have to go.'

As if to prove the point, Roy jumped off the side of the bridge and disappeared under it. He came back quickly, carrying a gladstone bag.

'I'm sure he'll be all right. I'd just like you to check, that's all. You're not scared are you?'

'Me? Hell no.'

'That's all right then.' For a moment he cheerfulled back into the old Roy. Then he held out his hand solemnly. 'You better get back, Mike. Dominic will be sending out a search party. See you, Mike. Don't forget to slip in a prayer. I used to wet the bed too. Don't worry. You get over it. You get over most things.' Then he walked off into the night. Michael stood on the bridge, fearing for him.

He never saw Roy again.

He stopped crying when he reached the Hanging Tree, where he dried his eyes and stood sad with fear.

At the top of the juniors' avenue, he tripped over the body of Brother Bernard.

The next time he actually looked at Brother Bernard again, the old man was lying in his open coffin two days later. The community was keeping vigil before the coffin all through Tuesday night. Being juniors, Michael and Kevin had one of the early shifts.

The candles around the coffin threw shadows on Brother Bernard's peaceful face. Brother Bernard had a closer shave, a neater hairdo, than he'd ever had in life. There was discolouration around the right temple. As Father Prefect had explained, Brother Bernard had hit his head on a stone when he was felled by a heart attack. Entwined in his fingers were the rosary beads that had been a gift from the soccer team in Trivandrum, South India.

Michael Hannigan prayed for Brother Bernard, for Roy McDougall, for the mission in South India, before he fell asleep, kneeling down.

1964

*M*oira

*H*E MET MOIRA outside the monastery, in a branch office of God's love. She was sent into his life because he was a devout but incompetent footballer. It happened this wise.

Always keep your eyes on the ball, that's what God asks of his team, Brothers. Christ was a team player. Brother Hannigan thought of Father Superior's advice as he watched a neat drop-kick coming towards him in the forward pocket. The kick came from Brother van der Haar, who in three years out from Holland had learnt to kick a drop and bowl an outswinger as if he had been born properly in Victoria. Father Superior often used him as an example of the catholicity of the Church.

This time Hannigan was going to mark it. It was the last quarter and the opposition, the Missionaries of the Sacred Heart, were six goals ahead. So far he had dropped five marks, kicked two points and three out of bounds. He knew these things didn't matter unless you were doing them for Christ and then they mattered like hell. When he had taken up his position against the resting ruckman, who was fifteen stone of geniality, he had prayed, *Dear Christ, let me at least kick one goal, or rather let me kick at least one goal.* Pleased at the punctilious syntax of his prayer, he made a supreme spiritual effort to rise above the earth. As he remained earthbound, he knew he was making another mistake. Brother Kiernane, who was playing at full-forward and who really could take a mark, was making the same mistake. Brother Hopkins, the ruck-man, came through with fifteen stone of desire for the ball.

Michael Hannigan felt dumped into another, hellish world. Pain cried down his back and into his legs. Father Smythe, the seminary's canon lawyer and moral theologian, rushed up, blew his whistle and stuck it into the pocket of the cricketing creams he always wore when umpiring football. Faced with a moral decision, and wishing to preserve the spirit of fierce charity that characterised inter-seminary football matches, he looked with paternal disappointment at Brother Hopkins.

The ruckman looked down at his victims. 'Sorry, mates, came through a bit hard there.' He laughed to show that he was forgiven and trundled off to pick up the ball.

'That's all right then,' said Father Smythe. 'Let's ball it up then, shall we? No hard feelings.'

Hannigan managed a kneeling position, while Kiernane sat up suddenly as if eager for prayer. 'I'm fine, Father,' he said looking up at the sky, 'it's all in the game, it's a man's game.'

'Would you like a free kick, perhaps?' asked Father Smythe. 'Think that would be OK, Brother Hopkins?'

Brother Kiernane took the ball confidently and prepared to kick it in the wrong direction. Michael Hannigan remained kneeling. Father Smythe dispensed with the last five minutes of the game.

While they drank orange cordial and ate lamingtons, they all agreed, as they always did, that it was one of the best games they had ever played. The Marianites and the Missionaries of the Sacred Heart found common cause in discussing games they had played against the Jesuits. In all charity, one had to admit that they were a bit up themselves, the Jesuits, both on and off the field. They didn't set the laity much of an example of humility, but if you came from posh schools like Riverview and Xavier you probably couldn't help it. Not that winning mattered but it would be nice to beat them at something.

'We'll beat them at theology,' said Brother Kiernane, who was famous for his humility.

'Bet you a rosary we can't,' challenged Brother Forsyth who was famous for being the only Marianite seminarian to understand the Jesuit theologians Karl Rahner and Bernard Lonergan.

Brother Kiernane, who frowned on betting rosaries, turned back to Brother Hopkins, who was threatening to escape to a conversation on football. Dressed in the Marianite religious habit of black soutane, with blue sash and the letters MOM, Missionary Order of Mary, monogrammed over the heart, Brother Kiernane looked thinner than ever standing against Brother Hopkins, who was radically wearing jeans and a white shirt with a grubby collar and strained buttons.

Brother Kiernane was explaining an article he had written in the seminarians' magazine, which Brother Hopkins had rashly admitted not reading. Brother Hopkins wanted to talk football, but he was a gentle man off the field and was prepared to listen. He even threw in an idea: 'I mean to say, I don't know much about this, you know, but don't you think the ideas about unbaptised infants are a bit rough?'

'Ah, but, canon 1239, section 1, is quite clear.' Brother Kiernane waved his glass of orange, spilling some on Brother Hopkins' shirt, and continuing to explain as he mopped up with a dark white handkerchief. His voice took on the wobbling earnestness of an Irish folk singer. 'It is quite clear: an infant who is unbaptised may not be given ecclesiastical burial. Of course, I do agree with you' – and Brother Hopkins looked pleased that he was contributing he knew not what – 'that if such a burial has been given, it neither violates the cemetery nor does it incur the penalty of canon 2339.'

'There you are then,' and Brother Hopkins chewed on his lamington and looked around again for escape. Michael Hannigan sat, vaguely guilty, in one of the few comfortable chairs in the recreation room, and looked at Gerry Hopkins' fat and plainly uncomfortable back with as much pleasure as the pain in his own back would allow. He wondered if it would be giving in to the flesh too much if he were to ask the infirmarian for a Veganin, and in his indecision just sat and listened.

'Pure poetry, a Fraser drop-kick,' Gerry Hopkins was saying. 'A dying art.'

'Like the Latin mass,' said Brother Forsyth from another group who were discussing the seminarians' next meeting, a day's conference of CROSTA, the Combined Religious Orders Seminary Theological Association and Melbourne's response to Vatican II. The conference's theme was 'Mary, Mother of Christ, Co-Redemptrix or Co-Mediator?'. Forsyth was explaining that he had submitted an abstract titled 'Woman and Salvation' for approval by his superiors. Father Finnegan had said that 'Woman and Salvation' sounded a bit like a contradiction in terms and then announced a joke, declaring that he loved Mary as much as the next man and more than some he could name. Father Smythe thought that, in the spirit of Vatican II, Brother Forsyth should be allowed to explore ideas, as long as they were the right ideas explored correctly. Father Brown, a retired missionary, couldn't see what the fuss was about. 'Can't see anything wrong with women, as long as you know how to handle them. Never gave me any trouble in the Solomon Islands. Taught them netball, I did. Keeps their minds occupied, strengthens the womb.'

Brother Forsyth was happily worrying about the CROSTA meeting. 'Could be a pretty rough day, when we meet at the Carmelites,' he told Gerry Hopkins longingly. 'They get pretty possessive about Mary. They think they invented her, don't you reckon?'

Brother Hopkins clearly felt inter-Order conflict should be confined to the football field. 'The Carms are OK, if you handle them right. They're very good at basketball. About your conference paper: has it got anything to do with Pius XII's proclamation of the Assumption?' he asked not very hopefully.

'I must confess, I do get a bit confused about this mediatrix business and Mary's role in our salvation. Is there anything else to eat apart from lamingtons? We always put on sausage rolls ourselves.'

Brother Forsyth took up his missionary position, both arms outstretched, his rimless glasses dangling dangerously in his left hand. Sitting close yet distant, Michael Hannigan could see a theological passion coming on.

'Look, Gerry,' (Brother Forsyth was notoriously casual about addressing his fellow religious with the title of 'Brother' but, then, Brother Hopkins was not dressed like a religious) 'you've just reminded me of what Karl Rahner wrote about how long one should stay in prayer after receiving the Body of Christ in the Sacred Host – I'm sorry, there's only lamingtons, though there are some pink ones over there – but it's fascinating, isn't it?' He offered the ruckman a choice of brown or pink lamingtons. Hopkins picked a brown one and held it at a distance as if it were a bad thought. Forsyth who had once played rugby was now up and running with the ball. 'You see, both Rahner and Galot query what should be the length of thanksgiving after receiving the Body of Christ at mass. Amazing stuff, have you ever thought it through?'

'Actually, I was thinking about getting a bit more cordial – you know, all this footy and theology – be back in a minute.' But it didn't work. Forsyth was right there with him, pouring cordial and ideas.

'...they in actual fact query the idea that we should stay in thoughtful thanksgiving, in prayerful thanksgiving, as long as the Eucharistic Christ is sitting in our stomachs.'

Michael watched Hopkins stare at his lamington thankless-ly. 'You see, compare the size of the host with that lamington. Can I borrow it for a minute?' Hopkins surrendered his lamington to Forsyth and himself to working off time in Purgatory. Hopkins had, in a moment of on-field intimacy, confessed to Michael Hannigan that he was repeating second-year theology and hating it, apart from two weeks on the theology of sport. Michael felt disembodied from his pain and remote from the world, eavesdropping randomly on theological debates and a discussion of rovers from Lou Richards and Billy Hutchinson to Bob Skilton and Darrel Baldock.

Hopkins couldn't resist the temptation to stand up for the truth. 'Baldock's not a rover. What the hell are you talking about?' but then apologised quickly for his intrusion and his language. Forsyth was not going to lapse into sport. 'You think about this: in a way, it touches on the whole problem of God becoming flesh. The small host – you know, the people's host, not the big one the priest uses – it remains in the stomach – bet you didn't know this – for not less than half an hour.' Michael Hannigan didn't know that either.

Forsyth took Hopkins' blank look as one of query. 'It's true, I checked it out with my cousin's second husband who's a gastroenterologist. That's a hell of a long time for thanksgiving. By that time most people are filling their bellies with Vita Brits, mixing that mush up with the Body of Christ.'

'Father Superior has just introduced Weat Harts? Do you have Weat Harts?'

'No, just porridge and Weet Bix.' Forsyth, who could discuss wordly topics like the Labor Party and Marilyn Monroe and had heard of Barbra Streisand, was not to be distracted this time.

'Weet Bix, that's Sanitarium, the Seventh Day Adventists. Didn't you know that?' The opposing ruckman had got the ball at last.

Forsyth grabbed it and drop-kicked it out of sight. 'Of course, Christ doesn't mind getting mixed up with the Seventh Day Adventists. The stomach's very ecumenical. Ironic isn't it? The mystery of transubstantiation. Not to mention the Incarnation,' preparing to mention it as he handed back the lamington, forgetting he had taken a bite out of it.

Hopkins licked some coconut from his lips. 'Where did you say the toilet was again?'

Hannigan felt like crying with the pain route-marching down his back and foraging spasmodically down his legs. The seminarian talk chanted round him like a litany whose meaning he had once known and now lost. He shivered. He was in pain. But he would not give into the flesh and get a Veganin, or his thick green cardigan with the hole in the left sleeve. The flesh was all around him, in the talk, and in his head. Forsyth was trying to explain to Hopkins the poetry of the Incarnation, God becoming flesh, becoming man; the poetry of transubstantiation, the bread becoming the flesh of God, while the ruckman was eavesdropping on the fleshly achievements of famous rovers. At least all around him were young men of almost perfect flesh, some a bit overweight, some clumsy, but the Church was insistent that only those perfect in the flesh could become priests. Christ could cure the halt, the lame, the blind and the cripples but he could not, well, would not, ordain them his priests.

Hannigan realised from a long distance that Forsyth was saying that Rome had all the answers to the flesh: Sophia Loren, Claudia Cardinale, Gina Lollobrigida. Women were flesh, not people. He was into his twenties and had not had a conversation with a woman, outside his family – unless it was a nun.

As a fourteen-year-old junior seminarian, Michael Hannigan had carried, with guilt, pictures of film stars in a wallet that was a birthday present from his six sisters. They would have been shocked to find out that it was to become the hiding place of Jean Simmons, Audrey Hepburn and Elizabeth Taylor, looking as though she was still fresh from *National Velvet*. He had had fantasies about kissing them and had taken his bad thoughts to confession, even then worried about the status of his fantasies. Had he given full consent to such thoughts? Had they skulked unbidden into his imagination? And once they were in there, cajoling, had he worked hard enough to get rid of them, by thinking of French homework and cold showers? He had once kissed the picture of Jean Simmons. That was definitely a sin. And full on the lips. That was definitely a mortal sin. He had sought refuge in other fantasies: himself as Audie Murphy playing Billy the Kid, with Gale Storm looking on in pure love as he shot down those who misunderstood him. Now, in his mature twenties, he had to fight off Marilyn Monroe from *The River of No Return* and Bella Darvi as she stood naked over her garden pool from *The Egyptian*.

One day he would get to talk to a woman about magpies swooping in spring, about this Vietnam business, about the poetry of Gerard Manley Hopkins, about being lonely, about whether she was scared of men, about sunsets and God and birds settling down the night, about Saint Clare and Saint Francis of Assisi, about Saint Teresa of Avila and Saint John of the Cross, about friendship. Maybe one day he would talk properly with his sisters. Or even with his mother. One day when he was a mature and holy priest, he would ask his mature woman friend if women were as scared of dying as he knew men were.

Some day, when the oils of ordination had brought the fire of his lust for Marilyn Monroe to a conflagration that reduced it to harmless cinders. Some day, when he learnt to love, beyond the skirts of the old men in Rome, the Church as his Mother. Right now, Brother Hannigan loved the Church both for the precision and the tolerant probability of her love, even as his back and legs clamoured with pain.

Brother Kiernane was being intense about this precision. He was quoting with a canon lawyer's neat passion for the niceties of the law of love: '*An unborn and unbaptised foetus of a Catholic mother may be buried with the mother, and even an infant already born of a Catholic mother, if he dies with her, may probably be treated in the same way although he did not receive baptism.* That's in Bouscaren and Ellis, quoting Arregui. With them Mahoney and Cummins, quoting Jorio.'

Hannigan almost expected a page reference.

'See canons 746 and following,' said Brother Kiernane to Brother Hopkins who was trying to break into a conversation about Ron Barassi and Bob Skilton. But Kiernane lolloped on like the Hound of Heaven. 'It's all right, don't you see,' pouring some more cordial, 'the priest can explain that the original prohibition is not a punishment. The prohibition is logical, from the fact that the child has no right to a Catholic burial because he was unbaptised.'

'What if it's a girl?' Forsyth interrupted himself talking about the Incarnation, and scratched his left armpit.

'Yeah, what if it's a girl?' Hopkins thought for a moment that he had found a saviour, but Forsyth went back to fussing through the mysteries of God and flesh.

But Brother Kiernane was not going to be put off his coded stride by the intrusions of woman. He brushed at his red hair that stood defiant in its monastery crewcut. 'It's all right, but. The priest – the Church is very kind about these things, don't you think? – he may accompany the funeral to the graveside – and that's helpful to the mother, don't you think, if she hasn't died too – and he can say some prayers there.'

'I always say the sorrowful mysteries. I barrack for St Kilda,' said Gerry Hopkins sorrowfully.

'No, not the sorrowful mysteries,' said Brother Kiernane, barracking for God. 'Don't you see, it's really a *joyful* occasion for the family. The baby – well, OK, the foetus – well, I mean it's gone to Limbo. It's happy, damn it all. Sorry. Of course, I know what you're going to say: no Beatific Vision. I grant you that. But happiness, hell, it's got happiness. What else can you ask from death?' He concluded with the air of a man who had been there, or at least to the Gold Coast.

'Actually, I'm dying for a piss,' the suffering Hopkins confessed.

Michael, remote from the world and further than ever from God, watched as the ruckman scuttled off, still holding his glass, to the urinals next to the recreation room. 'Twyfords Doulton' – he wondered if that was the same as 'Royal Doulton'. One of his monastic jobs was making toilet bowls pure.

He heard Brother Forsyth working into an un-Marylike joke to amuse one of the visitors, Brother Pearsall-Smith. 'Why is semen white and piss yellow?'

The visitor stood, chilly with politeness.

'So an Irishman can know whether he is coming or going.'

Brother Pearsall-Smith went. Hannigan gave a chuckle, charitable and reproving. He was always shocked by Irish jokes, even when he didn't understand them.

Next to Hannigan's chair was the radiogram, a gift from Brother Milton's mother. Brother Koenig was putting on a Peter Paul and Mary record, a gift from Brother Milton's father.

Brother Koenig stopped to talk, 'Blowin' in the Wind' sighing in the background. 'Old Brother Kiernane's got the papal bull by the horns today.'

'Yeah, he's milking it for all it's worth and not noticing he's making a balls-up.'

Hannigan remembered his own study of canon law, a boring but necessary measure of God's love. He sometimes found comfort in cutting down the immeasurable to the size of 2414 canons.

Brother Koenig realised that his confrere's mind was busy elsewhere. 'Well, I'll leave you in peace then. If you want some Veganin, give me a yell.'

Tim Koenig, a slight intense man, who always looked as if he was about to worry a smile into surprised existence, was the monastery infirmarian. He handed out cough mixture and cold-sore cream, as well as lumps of sulphur for seminarians afflicted with dandruff. Hannigan heard him start up an awed conversation.

'You know these blokes from other Orders get round a lot more than us. One of them has actually read *Lolita*. I read about that book in the *Advocate*. A parish priest had been told by his cousin in America that it was filth. You know, I thought Lolita herself sounded a bit like Saint Maria Goretti, another sexually abused teenager.'

'She couldn't be canonised as she wasn't baptised a Catholic,' said Brother Kiernane.

'Lolita doesn't exist,' said Brother Koenig, who disliked novels because they weren't true.

'She exists all right,' said Brother Williams, who loved novels and hated football and had spent the afternoon reading Graham Greene, which was forbidden. 'She exists all right. She exists to be raped, and then the popes can make a saint of her, and we can pray to her and forgive ourselves. The Church doesn't need women, but it needs virgin martyrs.' Tony Williams was a bit weird.

'I think that shows a lack of understanding of the idea of Incarnation,' said Forsyth.

'Who do you barrack for?' Hopkins asked Hannigan, who he was pleased to see was contributing nothing theological.

'Puff the Magic Dragon,' said Michael, who had tuned in to Peter Paul and Mary.

They left him alone, and he thought about Incarnation and Veganin. He rejected the Veganin. Asking for pain-killers was like wearing two jumpers in winter. It meant that your spiritual life was becoming tepid.

Also alone, seated in the opposite corner, was Brother Lynch, who was reading TS Eliot's *Murder in the Cathedral*. A big man, and a fine footballer, he preferred poetry to sport. It was sometimes suspected that he preferred poetry to people and often accused himself in the Chapter of Faults of being unsociable towards his brothers in Christ. A rather unrepentant accusation, Hannigan had often thought admiringly. He also knew that Father Superior, in his random sampling of seminarians' letters, had been shocked by two letters to nuns in which Lynch had earthily discussed with nuns their marriage to Christ.

Hannigan realised that conversation had passed from football to Vatican II.

'Two thousand bishops, and they've been meeting in the Vatican for two years. They've talked a lot, but they haven't said much.' Brother Hannigan worried sometimes about the irreverence of Brother Williams.

'That's because they're talking in Latin. Australian bishops can't understand themselves even when they're talking in English.' Brother Forsyth wasn't very good at reverence either.

'Steady on, Brothers. They're intelligent and dedicated men,' said Brother Kiernane, who often mentioned that he wouldn't mind being a bishop if God demanded it, so he could serve the people.

'But, Brothers, seriously, the times they are achanging.'

'Gosh, did you think that up? Can I quote it?'

Brother Williams inclined his balding head to the small visiting seminarian, Brother Pearsall-Smith, who had made this intervention.

Pearsall-Smith thought for a moment. 'What I was saying was that I believe in progress, in keeping up with...'

'Like you kept up with play this afternoon?' Brother Kiernane was known occasionally to lapse in charity. Pearsall-Smith had spent the afternoon as boundary umpire, puffing round the oval, plump and unconcerned and well behind the play. He was chief organiser and founding president of the Seminarians' Theological Association. He also umpired cricket matches, knew all the right signals and presented them with a dignity that would have been appropriate either at high mass or at Lords.

'Look, I believe in bishops.' Pearsall-Smith looked at the pink lamington in one hand, the brown in the other, as if wondering whether to eat them or multiply them.

'That's because you rather fancy yourself as one, Ian.'

Brother Williams was also known to lapse in charity. Ambition was a sin. Talking about it was bad taste. In the euphoria of footy and theology and orange cordial, the Brother rule was slipping away, along with fraternal charity.

'Look, Brothers,' said Brother Kiernane, 'Let's put on "My Fair Lady" and have a singalong.'

Tony Williams and Ian Pearsall-Smith faced each other, the tall and the short, each holding a lamington. Brendan Forsyth stood alongside them, like a referee encouraging clean violence.

'Look Tony, I don't want to defend myself. I want to defend the bishops.'

'Same thing.'

'OK, I admit they didn't move very fast in the first session of the Council, but they did have to make some pretty stiff decisions. And you must, you just have to admit that they made some good hard decisions, what with concelebration, and the vernacular mass, and the laity allowed to drink from the chalice, I mean that's hard and radical stuff, and what I want to say ...'

'Bullshit!' Tony Williams often had to accuse himself at the Chapter of Faults of interrupting his brothers and using language unbecoming to a religious. 'Don't be so bloody stupid. They're a lot of slack pricks, ninety per cent of them. The only thing hard about them is their pectoral crosses and their hearts.'

'Come on, Tony,' Pearsall-Smith tried to pacify, 'their hearts are in the right place.'

'Yeah, and their minds have yet to be located. Come on yourself, Ian. Those bastards Menzies and Johnson will be sending soldiers to die in Vietnam. I mean, Jesus, what did the bishops say about that?'

'They're waiting for Bob Santamaria to tell them,' said Brendan Forsyth, who was suspected of not voting for the DLP.

'Give it a break, Brendan,' Pearsall-Smith tried again. 'This is a serious discussion.'

'You're damn right it is.' Williams swayed tall in his anger. 'Take South Africa – what the hell do they say about that? Thousands of people dying, just like in Vietnam...'

'Not to mention the Vietnamese.' Forsyth liked facts.

'Yes, mention the Vietnamese. And Nelson Mandela. Sentenced for life, because he wants a bit of bloody justice.'

'I've never heard such language in my life.' Brother Kiernane was probably speaking the truth.

Beyond the pain in his back, Hannigan wondered if Mandela belonged to some missionary Order. He wondered too, at such a rage of uncharity, the like of which he had never heard in all his seminary days. He longed to speed up the years to his ordination, so that he could stop devoting himself to becoming a saint and start devoting himself to the people of God.

'Well, be that as it may.' Perhaps Pearsall-Smith hadn't heard of Nelson Mandela either. 'But take *Sacrosanctum Concilium*, the constitution on the liturgy. That really says something. It even acknowledges the laity...'

'Big deal. The Indians get a mention.' Williams snorted.

Brother Hopkins was not to be left out. 'Gee, does it really mention the Indians. I didn't know that. That's great, isn't it?' he beamed.

'The point is, and remember this,' Pearsall-Smith was not going to lapse into metaphor, 'there were 2,162 for and only a few against.'

'Forty-six actually,' said Brother Kiernane, who liked the sacrament of voting.

'Well, OK, OK, OK. But that's really something. You've got to admit it. That means...well, it means something.'

'It probably means that most bishops can't count and don't understand Latin.' Williams waved a lamington at his enemy brother-in-Christ. 'You know what, Ian, I reckon Dawn Fraser and Betty Cuthbert had a better year this year than the Australian bishops.'

'Well, anyway,' Pearsall-Smith looked at his watch and waved his lamington hand to summon the troops of God from the ping-pong and billiard tables, 'you're probably right, well, in a lot of it. Come on, you lot, the bus'll be waiting. Thanks for a great afternoon. See you at the CROSTA.'

On his way out he turned back to Williams. 'By the way, those women you mentioned, were they the ones complaining about not enough female representation on the council?'

'Jesus!' said Brother Williams, and Brother Hannigan bowed his head automatically at the mention of the holy name.

That evening, after a tea of Irish stew, they sat in the recreation room, among the dandruff of lamingtons, and talked of a special day when the outside world came among them. Hannigan's back was still aching; his head seemed bustling yet peaceful; so, unusually, he sat and just listened. Besides, he had been nineteenth man to Brother Williams' public conflict with a visitor and conflict was the smirking face of sin.

'Father Smythe has written a paper approving a pill for contraception.' Brother Williams was enjoying shocking Brother Milton.

'He hasn't really! That's shocking.'

'I don't know, there are plenty of others. Dr John Rock in *The Time has Come*, Dr Anne Biezanek in *All Things New*. She's...'

'She's a woman, that's what she is, and she's started a birth control clinic, that's what. Those books are worse than *Lolita*...'

'Have you read any of them?'

'No, I wouldn't read filth. Besides she's a feminist.'

'So was Teresa of Avila.'

'She was not, she was a saint and a Father of the Church.'

Williams gave up on Milton and turned his attention to Brother Kiernane who was still explaining that the burial of an unbaptised infant did not deconsecrate a cemetery.

'I'm all for baptism in the womb.' Williams could fire canon for canon with Kiernane, and no one ever quite knew if it was with love or with laughter. He brushed back his already receding sandy hair, and stood tall and intense. 'Fury says that if the mother is dead, or about to die, the doctor has to rush through a caesarean, so the baby can be baptised on the spot. It's important to give him...'

'Or her.' Brother Forsyth sometimes accused himself of feminisation – or whatever they called it.

'Yes, it's important even for her to be baptised on the spot...'

'On the head, you mean.'

'But Saint Thomas and Saint Alphonsus both warn that you can't go round killing the mother just to make sure that the baby is baptised. That's why Genicot is so keen on baptism in the womb, done with a syringe, preferably sterile – very careful man, our Gen – and preferably by a doctor, good Catholic of course...'

'Not like those Biezanek and Rock characters. Come on, Tony,' Brother Milton was shocked into breaking the Brother rule, 'the difference between Limbo and Heaven is a serious matter. I for one would hate to miss out on the Beatific Vision forever, just because someone didn't take enough trouble to baptise me.'

'Kevin, you're just made for the Beatific Vision.'

Hannigan could see what Tony Williams meant. For all his fasting, Kevin Milton looked a little like a seedy cherub. Tony often maintained that Kevin would never die of lust but probably of disappointment.

'It's a serious pastoral matter.' Brother Kiernane was standing up for God and everyone else who needed his help. 'Lemkuhl says that every aborted foetus should be baptised. Limbo's no laughing matter.'

'Ah, but it is. It's supposed to be great fun, except that you don't get to see God and Brother Milton.' Williams scratched some dandruff from his thick eyebrows.

'Of course,' Kiernane pressed on, 'Saint Thomas taught that the soul wasn't infused until the second month for boys, and the third month for girls...'

'Does that mean girls have smaller souls than boys, or is the month for the penis?' Brother Forsyth interrupted.

'No, but it makes the whole bit about both abortion and baptism a bit tricky, doesn't it. Look, Genicot says the baby...'

'The foetus.'

'...the foetus, or whatever – it ought to be baptised again conditionally once it's out in the open, just in case the doctor missed with the syringe, or only baptised a foot.'

'One foot in the door of Heaven.'

'You know it's not valid unless it's on the head.'

Brother Forsyth was wiping his rimless glasses. 'You know, Karl Rahner questions the whole idea of Limbo. And of hellfire.'

'Bloody Jesuits, always questioning.'

'Come on, Brother Kiernane, we are allowed to ask questions.'

'Only when the Church has the answers.'

The bell rang, giving them five minutes to assemble in chapel for night prayers, when silence would settle on the monastery until after breakfast the following morning. Brother Hannigan loved the Greater Silence. It brought peace, or at least its promise. He realised that he was the last left in the recreation room, listening to Julie Andrews sing 'Wouldn't It Be Luverly' and dreaming of Marilyn Monroe. As he rushed to the chapel, BA Santamaria, the monastery beagle, chased him, barking along the cloisters.

The monastery settled into the peace of plain chant, and the litany of Our Lady, and thoughtful prayers for unbelievers. Brother Hannigan tried to think of the special intention that Father Superior had asked them to pray for. His mind had to climb over Marilyn Monroe to find it. Brother Milton's teeth, that was it. Brother Milton had his fifth appointment with the dentist tomorrow, and the dentist was talking about oral surgery. *Lord, fill Brother Milton's teeth with peace and his soul with grace.*

Then came the sweet stillness of the examination of conscience. He loved those five minutes of the quietly breathing chapel. It was quite different from the ten minutes Particular Examen that preceded the midday meal. Then you rushed in from a lecture or study and tried to contemplate the particular fault that kept you back from God and sainthood. Five years ago Father Master of Novices had decided that Brother Hannigan was holding himself back from union with God by his tendency to unkind thoughts and rash judgements. Personally, he thought it was mostly lust and sometimes ambition, but he knew he would never become a saint if he questioned Father Master's judgement. All these years later the midday examination was still hard work, and Hannigan practised thinking kind thoughts about Brother Milton.

At the evening examination, you paused on all your sins, on all your faults. An arithmetic of sin gave meaning to the kindness of God. For the moment, however, God seemed kindly settled over the waters, and sin, though as universal and voracious as ever, seemed to be sleeping. Now, as he knelt and his mind fidgetted for grace, his back ached, but he would not be seen giving into the flesh by sitting up. He longed for bed, but he loved God and saw that all things were good and wondered about the problems of the Essendon full-forward who had to wear glasses when he played.

He felt seized by God and peace. He knelt, feeling above himself, looking down on a world waiting, wanting to be saved. Uplifted from his pain, he felt already free of his body, saved, and eager to save others. *God bless Brother Milton and Brother Milton's teeth.* Holiness is the art of the possible, cold showers, avoiding women, not having seconds of dessert on feast days, loving people. *God bless Brother Hopkins, another bully at footy.* But sin was the art of the probable, as Father Superior often reminded him. Sin was all around him and all through him, like his prayer for Brother Milton being pushed aside now by Marilyn Monroe, in her red dress, black stockings and high heels from *The River of No Return*.

At other times, when Hannigan looked around him, people he knew well (which sometimes included his own parents) were rather disappointingly incompetent and unambitious about sinning. Forgiving sins was easy. He had already forgotten about Brother Milton hogging today's dessert and Brother Williams almost talking about sex. God *was* active in the world, but when he thought of himself ordained as God's messenger, 'according to the Order of Melchisedech', priest of the Old Testament, he lost faith in himself, and wondered if God bothered at all. It was hard to find attractive evidence, unless you concentrated on Father Superior. Being good enough and bad enough to attract God's attention was hard work, even though Father Superior could prove that sinking a ten-yard putt was an act of worship.

Hannigan felt himself hovering with the Holy Ghost above the bent world. They forgave Brother Hopkins for being a bully at footy. They forgave Brother Williams for his silliness, which would have been heresy if it was not so silly. Heresy was always serious, if not sensible. A joke couldn't be heresy. And it must be a joke to say that God becoming flesh was so shocking that the Church could be forgiven for not actually believing it.

Hannigan felt taken up by a storm of stillness, taken up by God. He felt sick with a holy sickness. It was all a bit of a mess. He knew that man was such a miserable, crawly creature that he needed salvation and lots of it. In his own case, sin was easy to believe in and he wondered at times if his guilt was fully comprehended by Father Brown in the confessional. He was a pretty innocent old bloke. Suddenly his mind exploded in a dark peace and he felt, from a long distance away, his head banging down on the top of the seat in front of him.

It seemed no time later. He was lying on the floor of the sacristy. Tim Koenig was folding a chasuble beneath his head. He wanted to sit up and protest at the irreverence, but when he tried to say something he found the brass spoon used to place incense in the thurible jammed between his teeth. He let the spoon fall to the floor and lay back into his strange peace. Perhaps this was what Juliana of Norwich or Teresa of Avila meant when they wrote about their bodies dying of love after their mystical embrace with Christ?

From the chapel came the chant that ended night prayers: *Parce, Domine, Spare us O Lord.* The chant hesitated and he was vaguely aware of Brothers Forsyth and Kiernane carrying the bulk of Brother Milton into the sacristy and dumping him on the floor. Their voices drifted around him.

'Not the same thing? God, who's going to be next? The Devil's on overtime.'

'No, silly bugger's just fainted. Too much fasting, though you'd never guess by the look of him.'

Hannigan eased back into a serenity that he felt somehow he had earned.

But later, some time later, he knew that something disrespectful had burrowed into the Greater Silence, when his body protested awake in pain on the parquet floor of his bedroom. There had been a roaring somewhere. *The Devil goes about like a roaring lion seeking whom he can devour.* Voices were breaking the Silence, so something important was wrong. His head ached, and he could feel a slide of blood out of the corner of his mouth.

Father Superior and Doctor Ryan were standing kindly over him. Brother Koenig stood respectfully at the door in his pyjamas with the fly drooping open. There were instructions and important bustling. Words hurried above him: 'Second time...paraldehyde.' Then he slipped into his own peace again, into peace far away, into God is love, into a soft, enfolding darkness.

Hannigan was puzzled to find next time he woke that he was in Saint Vincent's Hospital and that the day was well into its busyness.

'I'm Nurse Counahan. How do you feel?'

'Well,' and he sat up. 'I'm fine, I guess. Perhaps a bit sore, just a bit.'

Her blues eyes looked disbelieving and her full lips smiled in concern. His muscles yelled, his mouth seemed lacerated. He lay back.

'I feel just fine,' he lied, wondering whether he was carrying out his resolution never to complain or trying to impress her.

'Now you just lie back.' He enjoyed her closeness as she bustled with pillows. Seminarians blessed themselves, nurses rearranged pillows.

'Got a bit of a knock at footy.' He heard himself sounding manly, at the same time surprised at how many muscles had stiffened after a knock at football. 'Back is a bit sore, I guess. Don't know how I came to be here.'

'You're fine. You have had a bit of a knock. Might need a few days rest and some tests.'

She was good at smiling. He tried not to keep looking at the belt with a monogrammed buckle that held her waist in tight.

They took obs and a case history, and Nurse Counahan ('Call me Moira, when Sister Xavier's not around') told him to ring the bell any time he wanted anything. Doctor Bloom, who introduced herself as Doctor Conmee's registrar, examined him from head to toe, calmly feeling even his testicles. She wrote down lots of things, then put aside her clipboard, took off her steel-rimmed glasses and kept brushing back her short black hair that hardly dared fall forward.

It seemed like he was being given permission to speak. He explained about his back, feeling this was really an explanation and not a complaint. He joked about his surprisingly lacerated tongue, mentioning that he had read somewhere, probably in Rodriguez – you know, the *Practice of Perfection and Christian Virtues*, well probably not many people had read it, not recently anyway – that God split the tongue that was doing the work of the Devil. Well, it was nice that she was still friends with the nuns at Mandeville Hall. When their talk wandered surprised into nuns, he stopped babbling and fell asleep.

When he awoke, Doctor Bloom was still there or back again. Nurse Counahan was taking his pulse and hovering with a thermometer as if to wave it in blessing. He felt comforted by women in a way that brought him back to winter nights before he entered the junior seminary, when his mother would close the windows against the rain and put on another blanket. He stayed off the thermometer long enough to announce again that his back was quite OK and he needed to get back home to the monastery as he had to give a paper to CROSTA on *The Song of Songs* as a love song. Pretty radical stuff, but Doctor Bloom wasn't interested. Sister Xavier Herbert, standing nunly official in the doorway, her religious habit gleaming white, didn't seem very interested either. She had a drug round for Nurse Counahan as soon as she had finished there. Perhaps *The Song of Songs* was rather strong meat for convent tastes.

Doctor Bloom wasn't very interested in his back or the pain in his leg.

'You see, I had a cartilage operation when I was a kid, and it got mucked up. Here in Saint Vincent's actually, but nobody's perfect,' showing he still had a sense of humour.

She didn't smile, and she wasn't interested in his diagnosis. Again she went through her routine of scratching the soles of his feet and getting him to follow the movement of her upraised finger with his eyes.

She commanded him to stare at a point on the ceiling, while shining her clever torch into his eyes, the window of his soul.

Then she replaced her implements into the crowded pockets of her white coat, sat on the end of the bed and took off her glasses. She looked about to pronounce. Instead of pronouncement, he was tossed an irrelevant question. 'How's the head feel?'

'The head, hell – sorry – there's nothing wrong with my head. It's very restful, for a change.' He was surprised at how true this was. 'Back's a bit sore, though, must admit that.'

But, about his back, Doctor Bloom was as deft in dodging questions as Father Hartigan had been when asked about the Virgin Birth in scripture class.

'We'll run a few tests, an EEG, just routine you know. You just have a rest, that's what you need.' She pinched his toes through the pink counterpane and stood up to leave. 'About the back' – and he felt pleased for the sake of his neglected back – 'I'll get the orthopaedic boys to have a look-see. And don't worry, I'll order something for the pain.'

Nurse – Moira – Counahan brought him a medicine glass with a pink mixture in it. 'M and A – morphia and aspirin – settle you down,' she explained as she disciplined his pillows.

'Finished now, nurse?' Sister Xavier was standing at the doorway, holding out a bunch of snapdragons as if she were passing on the Olympic torch. 'Just put these in a vase for me, there's a dear. Mrs Boylan won't be needing them where she's gone. Then there's the pan room. Then there's Mrs Harrison's drip: it's going too fast or too slow. And Herbie's done it again in his pyjamas. Lovely to have you, Brother. I'm sure you know I'm Sister Xavier Herbert. I'm sure you'll want communion in the morning, I'll fix it up. We usually keep Saint Margaret of Cortona's ward for priests and seminarians, though occasionally we've had a nun in this room, of course never at the same time, they usually go to Saint Aloysius. God bless you, Brother.'

When she left, the only ones with their mouths closed were the snapdragons.

As she arranged the flowers, Moira – Nurse – Counahan explained that in the afternoon they would take him up to neurology for some tests.

'But it's just a knock on the back. Or do they think I'm a neurotic?'

She smiled quickly. He knew it was a quick, warm smile, but it stayed with him as his mind slowed and his world stilled. Moira was still smiling to him as his body gathered up its energies, first in a twitch, then in a jerking, lunging chaos, as he was pulled downwards into a pit far deeper than that momentary threat of happiness.

He woke up, permeated with a terrible stillness. He woke up tossed, confused, into calm.

He woke up and stank. Doctor Bloom was standing at the end of the bed scanning his charts. He was surprised his body was still with him, that he was back among the snapdragons, that the world hadn't died. Some time ago – minutes, hours – he'd had an intimation of immortality, as though his body was going to break free, escape the limitations of the soul and live forever. Now he was lying in bed and smelling awful.

'Brother, this is Doctor Conmee.'

Coming into focus for the first time was a tall man, his hair doctor-grey, his suit doctor-dark. He had ascended beyond white coats and pockets bulging with medical bric-a-brac.

'You'll have to take it easy old chap, you've had a bit of a turn...'

'Well, I feel a bit sore. My back...'

'Your back is a cross you'll have to bear. Actually, you've probably had a bit of a knock on the head. We've just given you a shot of something.'

'Actually, stuff called paraldehyde.' Doctor Bloom spoke as if she had broken the official secrets act.

'Yes.' Doctor Conmee smiled at his protégé as if at a well-performing child. 'Yes. It settles things down a bit. Has a way of coming out through the pores with a funny smell. Well, really not that funny.' Doctor Conmee looked as though he had heard of bad smells but had never been actually introduced. 'Just a few tests, old chap, and a break from all that study...' and he firmly tweaked his patient's toes with the authority of a senior doctor.

He was alone again with Nurse Counahan. *Solus cum sola.*

'An EEG, that's what they've got you down for. Just to make sure the old brain's in one piece. It obviously is: you show great judgement about leaving hospital food,' and she looked with distaste at some congealed gravy that had died half way across the piece of fatted lamb. 'Of course, no one ever gets food poisoning: the germs round here are too fussy and too well-bred to touch the stuff.'

Moira Counahan worked at cheerfulness. She kept taking her nurse's cap off to pin back her blond hair, as Sister Xavier was fussy about neatness; and about the nurses spending too much time in the room with the seminarian.

'A Franciscan's coming in tomorrow. For a minor operation. You'll be pleased to have company. You don't looked pleased.'

That afternoon they took him upstairs. He felt pleasant after saying the joyful mysteries of the rosary and a dose of M and A.

A woman with grey hair and a young face glued electrodes to his head, assured him that it was nothing painful and told him to lie quite still. 'Give us a look at how your head is working.'

'Slowly, but serenely.'

The machine whirred. 'Still now.' He tried to think calm, pure thoughts, but Nurse Counahan's image kept intruding. A sheet of paper streamed from the machine, bearing cryptic witness to his brain's exertions. He thought of the Virgin Mary and Greer Garson, probably the only two women thoroughly approved of by Father Superior.

The kind woman used cotton-wool soaked in spirit to remove the glue that held the electrodes. 'Doesn't do much for your hairstyle, but then it's nice to see short hair. My son Benedict wants to look like those poor Beatle boys. Nine-day wonders, won't last as long as Bing Crosby. Lennon, McCartney – they must be Catholics with names like that. And they can't even spell, let alone sing.'

He had heard of the Beatles, but never heard them, just as he had heard of the world.

He asked, 'Well, did I pass?'

'I'm sure you did, but it's all Latin mass to me. Doctor Conmee will explain it all, such a clever man. God looks after his own. God bless you, Brother.'

In the monastery cold of the basement, he lay on a trolley next to a woman who told him about her whiplash, her neck brace, her horseriding-broken pelvis, her hockey-broken ankle, her skiing-broken leg. He didn't learn what her present x-ray was for, but he apologised for his shamefully intact limbs and congratulated her on her life of action.

'More breaks than Jack Purtell. Good Catholic, damn good jockey,' and then she pointed complacently to an envelope of x-rays sitting on her stomach.

Just then an orderly wheeled her away for another photo opportunity, saying, 'Your turn, Sister James.'

The Brother lay back and practised humility.

Even down here in the catacombs of the hospital, they were interested in his head. Standing behind a barrier, a young man in a lead-plated green apron intoned, 'Big breath in, still now,' and Brother said a quiet prayer that all the equipment hovering above him was securely bolted to the roof. His head was photographed from all angles, and then, as an afterthought, they took one x-ray of his back. He felt it was like giving him a Fantale to shut him up.

When he was wheeled back to the room, he was surprised to find Brother Pearsall-Smith sitting up in the other bed reading a book called *Inside the Council*.

'Hello, Mike, they told me you were here.'

Hannigan longed to lie down alone, but Pearsall-Smith had plenty to talk about.

'Have you read Lonergan and Rahner? They're a must. I'm organising papers on them for the conference after the one on Mary, Co-Redemptrix.'

'No. I tried "The Concept of the *Verbum* in the writings of Saint Thomas" but it beat me.' (Though he had impressed a few by weeks of poring intently over Lonergan as he enjoyed the monastery's best meal, wheat porridge, at breakfast.) Lonergan and Rahner were the Marx and Engels of modern Catholic theology. 'Explain Lonergan to me, Ian.'

'Well, I haven't actually read them either. Yet. I've been too busy reading up on Vatican II. Concelebrated masses, dialogue masses, that's the way the twentieth century is going...'

'Are they going to say something on Vietnam?' Hannigan asked, suspecting that this was an issue he ought to know something about.

'Of course they won't interfere in politics, but I bet they'll be in favour of peace. And this year the Pope's going to proclaim Mary Mother of the Church. Trust Vatican II.'

Pearsall-Smith balanced his big weight over the side of the bed and picked up a guitar that was leaning against his locker. 'Like to hear a new folk mass I've composed? I don't suppose you've heard of Pete Seeger and Joan Baez and Bob Dylan?' he asked, clearly having lost faith. Brother Pearsall-Smith didn't exactly name-drop, but he did like to juggle three or four important names in front of you before returning them to the humility of his dressing-gown pockets. Brother Hannigan had never seen a silk dressing-gown before.

As Ian strummed, Michael lay back and thought how old-fashioned he was; how self-centredly he went about becoming a priest, trying to catch fire from Aquinas while quelling the furnace of masturbation. There was a world out there waiting for a priest with a guitar and a good voice. At least Ian had a guitar. Brother Hannigan repeated to himself a prayer that he knew was worth two hundred days indulgence: *O good Jesus, grant that I may become a priest after Thine own heart.*

Every good priest knew that the world was clearly divided into good and evil. Pope John (God rest his soul), Bob Santamaria, Daniel Mannix, Jean Simmons, Bing Crosby, Bob Menzies versus Nikita Krushchev, Marilyn Monroe, Arthur Calwell, Brigitte Bardot, Vladimir Nabokov, Mao Tse Tung, Frank Sinatra, DH Lawrence…an eternal list, with God giving the other team a ten-goal start. But it could be confusing, like barracking for Essendon, the Masons' team, against Collingwood, a team that loved Catholic battlers. So he lay back and prayed for Arthur Calwell, papal knight, for Elizabeth Taylor – Father Superior had given him permission to pray for her when she was going to die from pneumonia and he presumed the permission still held – and for Brother Pearsall-Smith who was now swearing.

'Shit, my arse! Christ, it hurts!' Ian Pearsall-Smith had dumped his guitar and lay on his belly. Brother Hannigan gave up praying and pressed the buzzer for help. Nurse Counahan arrived and Hannigan worried at his resentment that she declared herself 'Moira' to Pearsall-Smith too, at his resentment that she was so soothing to such noisy suffering. When she had gone, Ian wallowed round onto his back. 'Sorry, mate. Got haemorrhoids, you know.' He persisted in explaining the mysteries of piles and constipation and suppositories and the anaemia that could be caused by bleeding.

That evening Father Superior visited on his way to a progressive dinner organised by the monastery auxiliary. He joked about nurses, gave Brother Pearsall-Smith a list of bishops who had haemorrhoids and left Brother Hannigan a pile of books to read: Philip Hughes' history of the councils of the Church, biographies of successful Catholics such as Chesterton, Belloc, Waugh, Crosby, Shakespeare, and for recreation, a funny novel with a serious mind, *Murder in a Nunnery.*

To establish his claim that the Marianites were a bit medieval in their reading, Pearsall-Smith made his bow-legged way across the room and dumped another pile of books on Hannigan's bed, declaring he'd borrowed a few from the Jesuits. There were novels by Greene and Mauriac, Mary McCarthy's *The Group*, a clearly unread copy of Lonergan's *Insight* and what was obviously for Brother Pearsall-Smith a joyful mystery of a book, *Lolita*. This had been smuggled in from America by a priest returning from a conference on Mary, Mother of the Church.

Partly in hope of buying some silence, Hannigan borrowed *The Group*. He was starting to enjoy it when Sister Xavier came in to replace the snapdragons.

'Good to see you reading, Brother. My goodness, God help us, where did that filth come from? You must lie back, you shouldn't be straining yourself.'

And his erection subsided before such authoritative virginity. Brother Pearsall-Smith had become engrossed in reading *Insight*.

'Mostly good news, old chap.' Doctor Conmee announced himself by tweaking Brother Hannigan's toes. 'Head's nearly perfectly OK, nothing much in the way of damage there. But a bit active, so we'll keep you around, say a few days, give you a few tablets, that sort of thing.'

Dismissing the patient from his presence, Doctor Conmee conferred with Doctor Bloom. 'I've discussed the EEG with Martin. Very interesting, didn't you think. Did you notice the unusual configuration and distribution of the spike-hump discharges? Tonic, clonic, with a touch of myoclonus? At this stage it looks idiopathic, though given the circumstances, I thought the aetiology might have been different. What say we start with phenytoin and carbamazepine? Two hundred milligrams and four hundred? What say we get some blood levels in a week? Have you back to the books in no time, won't we old chap?'

Pearsall-Smith had been pretending to read *The Power and the Glory*, but now he was ready to talk. 'Not that I was listening, but you're lucky with Doctor Conmee, he's a Knight of the Southern Cross, collects butterflies, very cultured man...'

Hannigan wondered briefly whether the missing Franciscan patient would have talked less than Pearsall-Smith, and what it might have been like sharing a room with a Cistercian who had taken a vow of perpetual silence.

'...and she was one of the best tennis players ever to come out of Mandeville Hall. Could have done anything, Mary Bloom. Accountant, skier, nun. Very gifted for a woman...'

But already Hannigan was high on serenity, already tunnelling into the visible darkness, while his body lunged away from him and he fell again into that night bereft of pity. He came into the darkness and the darkness knew him not, and laughed at him. And he felt afraid, and then annihilated, and then he did not care.

A long, stolen time afterwards, back to a world reeking of paraldehyde, he crept embarrassed. He lay in the quiet that he had borrowed. He made a perfunctory grab at consciousness and then allowed himself to dwindle into a foreign sleep.

When he awoke, Moira Counahan was standing next to the bed with some tablets and a glass of water in her hand.

'Here, you'll feel better soon.'

'I feel fine. Strangely rested. My muscles feel achey though.'

'Your body will soon get used to it.'

'Get used to what?'

She reorganised the snapdragons and his pillows and the pink bedcover. As he sat up, he noticed that Brother Pearsall-Smith's bed was empty.

'Has Ian gone for his op?'

'Well, no actually. They thought you'd be better if you were, well, sort of left quiet, you know.'

He swallowed two tablets and one capsule.

'Get used to what?' he asked after a while. 'Why am I blacking out like this? Have I got something wrong with the head?'

Nurse Counahan was scrubbing down the other bed with an intensity that absolved her from answering. Hannigan thought of the pleasure he had when she washed his hair after the EEG. Her soaping hands had been soft, firm, sensual with no hint of sin. Now, as she made the bed with the hospital tuck, he saw her as kind and blue-eyed and beautiful.

'Get used to what?' he asked again.

'Well, it's hard to say...' But he wasn't hearing. He kept sliding back into a stillness that was somehow a demand of his body and quite different from the peace he had experienced as a novice and younger seminarian. Then, when he had finished a retreat, catalogued his sinfulness, written up his resolutions, he had felt he was on his way to God, that he and God were both pretty pleased with themselves. That peace was fragile and murky, like ice on puddles. This peace was not earned but claimed by his body. Now it was his body that dreamed, and he felt he understood a little more of that wearied passivity that Teresa of Avila claimed after a vision of God. Perhaps it was like post-coital sadness. *Post coitum, omne animal triste est.* Aristotle had said that in Greek. After sex, every animal is sad. Sanctity could be sealed up and tagged in Latin. Brother Hannigan loved Latin and was pleased that, until the Vatican Council, God had preferred it too. It made holiness succinct and achievable, like a football score.

'Get used to what?' He wanted to hear her talk. She had a laugh in her voice that he envied, not a giggle, but a memory of happiness. She liked nursing seminarians, she claimed, as it made her feel like Florence Nightingale, nursing men from the nineteenth century. How could priests forgive sin, she teased, when they didn't know how to commit it. She was as innocent as Father Brown.

'You probably think sin is urinating in the shower,' and he

didn't dare say that this was indeed an external fault that had been mentioned in the Chapter of Faults.

She liked to throw names at him: John Profumo, Christine Keeler, Mavis Bramston, and chuckled at his bewilderment. And tried to teach him a little. For the four days he had been in hospital, Brother Hannigan had been so glad that Nurse Counahan was assigned to nurse him on the day shift. At the mid-afternoon changeover, Nurse MacDowell took over, a thin rigid girl with a limp. She was the boast of Saint Margaret of Cortona's, for she proved that the handicapped could do the work of God with relentless efficiency.

But now Nurse Counahan was on duty and, for once, she didn't want to talk to him. She was nursily busy. 'Doctor Bloom will be back soon,' she said in determinedly professional tones. Sister Xavier Herbert hurried in, looking as always fresh-from-God. 'Nurse, when you're finished here, could you please see to Herbie. He's wet again. I'm glad to see you're feeling better, Brother Michael. And Nurse, Mr Gallagher is asking for a bottle.'

Nurse Counahan stopped wiping out the drawer of Brother Pearsall-Smith's locker, a cloth in one hand and a packet of Fantales and a pair of rosary beads in the other. 'Sister, is Doctor Bloom still on the ward?'

'I'm not sure that is your business, Nurse, but Doctor Bloom has gone up to neurology and she will visit Saint Margaret's on the rounds in the morning. I've arranged for communion in the morning, Brother. I'm sure you will be pleased. It's ten minutes to the drug trolley, Nurse, I'm sure you're almost finished here. Don't forget to change Herbie's pyjamas. God bless you, Brother. I noticed you're not wearing a scapular, I'll bring you one tomorrow. I'm sure Our Lady wants you to have one. And, Nurse, don't forget Mr Gallagher's bottle. Perhaps I could also get you a Saint Philomena cord. Terribly good for chastity, so our chaplain, Father Hawke, tells me. I've got to get off to chapel now. God can't be kept waiting, can He, Brother?'

Nurse Counahan was standing next to his bed. She was talking now. 'Bastards! Bitches!' She threw the Fantales and the rosary beads across the room. The beads, Irish horn, scattered across the floor with the Fantales. As she bent to pick them up, Hannigan gathered up the five beads and the one Fantale that had landed on his bed. He was already sucking through the chocolate and reading 'Marilyn Monroe (Norma Jean Baker)...' off the wrapper, when he realised he ought to be shocked.

Nurse Counahan stood next to the bed, holding up rosary beads with a few mysteries missing. He knew then that he loved God and all the world and that one day he would sort them all out.

'I'm not supposed to say anything. "Get used to what?" They'll come and make a speech to you about it in due course.' She touched his cheek lightly, 'But it's all right, honestly it is, they control it these days. Honestly they do, truly.'

She turned away and was fierce with the snapdragons. 'You've – damn it, you are bloody dumb – you've got...I'm sorry...you've got – bugger it – epilepsy,' she told the flowers. 'They can control it, these days, really they can.'

She turned and smiled, 'Besides, I've read the reports. I'm not supposed to tell you anything, of course,' and she bent down and picked up some more beads and Fantales, 'but I think that Doctor Conmee suspects it's probably only temporary.' She waved a dead snapdragon at him. 'Your brain's in perfect working order, given its natural limitations of course.'

When she stroked his cheek again, it was easy to lie hard into his peace, and say *Thy will be done*.

'I've got to go and change Herbie's pyjamas again.' She stood at the door, holding it open, as if waiting for the right words to come in. 'It'll be all right, you know. OK?' she said sadly.

When she had gone, he lay back and felt OK, a bit like God owning the universe on a night anxious with stars. *The world is charged with the grandeur of God,* and he wondered about the Word being made flesh and God having to piss, God having fits. Epilepsy sounded important and interesting. His back ached and he thought of ringing the bell for some more M and A, which tasted horrible but felt nice afterwards. He was too serene, however, and offered up his little pain for the suffering souls in Purgatory, for Marilyn Monroe, and for an Essendon premiership, on which he had rashly bet five rosaries. And for once he could think quietly of his past, so he offered up his backache for Roy McDougall and Brother Bernard.

'Trial and error, then we get it right. We're just a bit slower than the Pope.' Doctor Bloom was doing the next-day talking, while Doctor Conmee hovered behind like the Holy Ghost. She was reassuring Hannigan, but he already felt good, even though he knew that sometimes his body was going to grab him and throw him into a half-world of lightning and darkness.

Hannigan felt like reassuring her that all things would be well, but Doctor Conmee was talking. 'Ethosuximide. Certainly *petit* as well. Write it up, will you, there's a good girl. Have it sorted out in a few days, old chap. How about we give him two fifty daily as a start. No pain, old man? We'll get you out of here in no time.' He stood at the door, passing on information impartially to both beds. 'You just have to adjust a little, you know. Plenty of brilliant people with it.' He had not mentioned the word 'epilepsy'. 'Handel, Byron, Julius Caesar, Agatha Christie, Dostoyevsky...know their work? And probably Saint Paul. Bet you've read him at least. Every road leads to Damascus, eh?' And trailing Doctor Bloom, he hurried off his pin-striped wisdom to answer other needs.

Of course, they were right. Nothing to worry about. It wasn't painful, except for some glimmer of horror as his eyes heaved up. He was aware in the after almost-sleep that his head had been plunging back as if to follow his rolling eyes, aware in the spent muscles of his face of a now-dwindled contorting energy, aware that some time in the past his limbs had been jerking, struggling to be free.

I see now through a glass darkly. Now, he knew what Saint Paul meant. He wanted to tell them of plunging light and darkness and of the world greying into stillness. But they didn't stop to listen, they only stopped to talk. Sometimes when they visited him, he would be returning from some oblivious meditation, realising he had been sitting up in bed, Buddha-like, with a nowhere look in his eyes, while they had been trying to talk him back into their world. These sudden horizons of almost-peace were *petit mal* fits, which he recognised from others' embarrassed attempts to re-thread conversations. And the *grand mal* fits came at him like the Virgin in a vision, like the Devil in a dream. He kept telling himself to get out of the way, but he would not. And he knew that he had overwhelmed himself again when he came back to visit the world and found Sister Xavier or Nurse Counahan or the night sister standing quietly over him. Words had been made flesh and they had no words to answer it. He came to recognise *grand mal*, the big evil, because he began to sense its coming and feel its going. When he came back to visit his body, the room had been cleared of visitors, for others must not be made to suffer the body raging against itself. He knew that every muscle had been flinging itself into a spasm of escape, and that his body was now smiling itself back into a repose that he could never explain.

He liked it best when Moira Counahan was his waking world. She cheerfully changed his pyjamas when he wet himself. She made sure his M and A came every four hours, even though his back pain was gradually receding, like the temptation to sin, into the past. 'Your religion,' she'd say, 'the opiate of the masses,' and laugh when he didn't know what she was talking about. She warned him that if he didn't get a bit of action in his bowels he would have to deal with suppositories, enemas even.

Nurse Counahan cheerfully accepted the reading he organised for her: *A Letter to a Young Woman*, by Father Andrew Greeley, and a book on marriage by Gustave Thibon, who was French and enthusiastic about the joys of the flesh as blessed by God and the Pope. Brother Hannigan explained the theology of sex, he explained the theology of celibacy. He became eloquent about the theology of marriage. She listened, she laughed and she argued. Then she became serious. 'Brother Michael, I want you as a friend, and I want to see you as a priest. Please leave me out of your theology of marriage.' And she touched her hand to his cheek. That night he wept in self-pity and loneliness and love. And thereafter was careful not to scare off the first woman he had ever talked to.

One day she told him 'I'm going out tonight with a resident from Gynie. He's got a bit of a reputation, you know – I'm not sure I like that idea, but I do like the bloke.' He told her the next morning that he had said a rosary for her, well, you know, just in case. She had smiled, kindly, but he had wondered whether it was in gratitude or in reminiscence and found that he didn't want to know.

'You know, I quite like nursing you,' she had silenced him with a thermometer. 'Bugger it, this blood-pressure machine's on the blink again. You're doing much better, you know.' He didn't mind not talking; he liked just watching her move.

Brother Hannigan found that he now enjoyed even the visits of Sister Xavier Herbert. 'We'll make a great priest of you yet,' Sister Xavier had told the vase of camellias. He was wearing with pious pride her gifts: over his shoulders the brown scapular of Our Lady, and tightly knotted round his belly the red and white cord of Saint Philomena. He could not explain to her that these were the colours of his second-favourite team, South Melbourne, but he did discuss with her the thoughts of Father Rodriguez, SJ, on chastity, as expressed in volume three of *Practice of Perfection and Christian Virtues*. He liked being able to explain to her *Castitas dicitur a castigatione:* the word chastity comes from the word punishment. She was pleased.

She took to turning up with her own well-thumbed copy of Rodriguez to read to him, standing at a proper distance from the bed. '*Of Saint Hugh, Bishop of Grenoble, Surius relates that he was so extremely cautious in this matter of looking at women that, though he was bishop for more than fifty years, and confessor to many women, and had a great deal of business to transact with ladies of high rank whom the fame of his sanctity attracted not from his diocese alone, but from all quarters, yet he never knew any woman by sight, since he never looked them in the face so as to know them, except one ugly old crone that was a servant in his house.* Isn't that beautiful?' said Sister Xavier Herbert, looking him hard in the eye.

As they swapped holiness, he couldn't explain to her, and was too reticent to explain to God, that he felt a new tranquillity. Sister Xavier, fierce with flowers, was soft about priests. They had both read an article by Father Lécuyer on the priesthood. She was putting in a new harvest of camellias and with each flower she announced another title for the priest: 'the Second Christ', 'the Mediator of the New Covenant', 'the President of the Assembly', 'the Consecrator', 'the Man chosen by Christ to bind and loose the sins of the world'. It scared the hell out of Brother Hannigan.

He wondered a little and with some surprise if Father Master had got it wrong about his particular fault: rash judgement of one's brothers (and sisters?). Perhaps, just perhaps, his particular fault was (forgive me, Father Master) that he wanted to be the most famous humble priest in the world. He wanted to do great good with his powers, even if he was not so good himself. Sister Xavier Herbert was a better person than he was, but maybe his particular fault was that, despite knowing this, he rejoiced in the fact that God chose men only to be priests, and that he would have more Godly powers than she. Or perhaps his fault was that he didn't believe strongly enough that this God-given fact made sense.

So he gave up reading Fantale wrappers and *The Group* and went back to reading Saint John, who was almost as confident about love as Sister Xavier. *Beloved, let us love one another, for love is from God. And everyone who loves is born of God and knows God. He who does not love does not know God; for God is love.* He lay back and loved God and knew that he had something to tell the world, humbly and importantly. If only he could find the words. *In the beginning was the Word, and the Word was God...and the Word was made flesh and came to dwell among us.* Epilepsy was the flesh talking. Moira Counahan was the flesh, God love and forgive her. He had a fit.

In the days that followed, visitors came as if to a shrine, two by two, except for the priests, who were ordained to the privilege of aloneness. Sister Margaret, his almost-friend from the neighbouring convent, visited him in the company of Sister John. She brought a rose and three Charlie Brown books. She kissed him on the cheek and quoted her favourite saying, Christ to Juliana of Norwich: '*All manner of things shall be well, and thou shalt see for thyself that all manner of things shall be well.*'

Father Brown, smelling of cough lollies and old-manness, blessed him with a relic of the Little Flower, Saint Thérèse of Lisieux, and then laughed about his visit to the basilica at Lisieux, where they had on show the saint's arm. 'In "perfect state" – can't remember whether it was left or right – but God, if that was its perfect state, she must have been a poor shrivelled darling. Actually she was quite a big girl. When she got to heaven she was going to send down a shower of roses.' He sniffed at Sister Margaret's rose. 'You lucky devil, you've been visited. I've brought you some reading. God moves in mysterious ways. I've left you something spiritual in the drawer.' The reading was a new edition, unexpurgated, of the autobiography of the Little Flower, *The Story of a Soul*; Agatha Christie's *The Body in the Library*; PG Wodehouse's *Doctor Sally* and *Ice in the Bedroom*. The spiritual gift was a half bottle of Remy Martin brandy.

Nurse Counahan decided it was medicinal and ostentatiously checked that Sister Xavier had gone to chapel and that Doctor Bloom was up in neurology.

Hannigan confessed 'I've never had a drink. We're not supposed to.'

'What about saying mass? We'll call this a practice mass.'

He was a bit shocked. But when they drank from the same medicine glass a couple of times, it did seem like a form of communion. They then shared a packet of musks to cover up their spirits.

And so they came, two at a time, his seminarian brothers, talking about football and Vatican II and the move for concelebrated masses and the attempts to persuade Father Provincial to allow the seminarians to wear shorts on their holidays at Cape Schanck. The conversation flowed round him, always with a brother on each side of the bed.

'Collegiality of the bishops, it's coming,' said Brother Kiernane.

'So are shorts for Schancks. The revolution is on the way.' Brother Forsyth was being irreverent, enigmatic but also serious. 'I've been reading up on epilepsy in canon law...'

'Canon 984,' said Brother Kiernane, defending his territory.

'...and the Church's got the same problem with epilepsy as with unbaptised foetuses. It's a problem of understanding the Incarnation. God made flesh. God became flesh. But the Church doesn't want to accept all the messiness that is involved in the flesh.'

'That's stupid – sorry, Brother – that doesn't make sense. The Church is Christ on earth. Of course She understands Herself.'

'Holy Mother Church. Doesn't it worry you, Brother Kiernane, that the Church is a woman?'

'Just an analogy. Christ was a man.'

'And the Church is the Bride of Christ. Another virgin, do you think?'

Forsyth then abandoned the game, assured Hannigan that Essendon would one day be premiers if he prayed hard enough, and gave him Father Smythe's surprising document, for private circulation only, which argued that the Church should, and would, approve the contraceptive pill.

Kiernane urged Hannigan to have faith in the forthcoming Vatican II decree on priestly formation.

Walking stiffly, Brother Pearsall-Smith also visited him. He had used the back of Father Smythe's paper on contraception to draw a picture of an anus with a large, cross-hatched haemorrhoid.

'Aren't haemorrhoids like seminarians and rosary beads? Don't they always come in plurals?'

But Brother Pearsall-Smith was meditating on anaemia, cancer of the rectum and the bishops at that very moment seated in council at the Vatican. 'Put your faith in Vatican II, Mike. We live in great and privileged times.'

'Yes, we could soon be over in Vietnam, getting shot.'

Pearsall-Smith looked shocked. 'There's only one V worth worrying about, and that's V II, the Big V, that's where the action is.' He held up two fingers like Winston Churchill.

Brother Hannigan could forgive him easily, because he was serious and because he was kind. In his kindness, he left Xavier Rynne's book on Vatican II, the latest issue of *News Weekly* and Graham Greene's *The End of the Affair*.

Hannigan read the Greene with an energetic depression, then passed it on to Moira Counahan. A few minutes after she had gone, he pressed his buzzer and summoned her back to tell her that he didn't think it was really suitable reading for her.

'Thanks, that's very kind of you,' and she touched his cheek, after an over-the-shoulder glance against the coming of Sister Xavier, 'but I think I'll be able to manage for myself.'

Now that his back felt better, he was encouraged to be mobile. He took to wandering round the main part of Saint Margaret's, which he found to his surprise was an orthopaedic ward. He talked a lot to Noel, who had been four months in hospital and who would race past in his wheelchair in flashes of plaster-cast and tattoos and who still longed for his Honda 750, which he had ridden into a timber jinker. Noel was intrigued by Brother Hannigan, what he was doing in hospital, what he did out of hospital. Answers on both fronts left Noel more puzzled, but Brother Hannigan felt he was learning about the world as well as about motorbikes.

Whenever a nurse appeared, Noel would yell, 'Over here, dear, and off with your gear.'

'Go to hell, Noel, you're permanently plastered.'

'I might be stiff, love but by Christ I'm stiff where it'd give you the thrill of your little life.'

Though he was used to living a half-life on monastery double entendres, Brother Hannigan was still shocked by this irreverence to Christ, and even more by the irreverence to women.

The seminarian also enjoyed talking to Herbie, a diabetic who alcoholically neglected the rules handed down for his good health. Herbie loudly blamed Henry Bolte – fucking Liberal parasite – for the broken leg that was the result of falling down a flight of stairs in a block of Housing Commission flats in Carlton. Having just come back from buying his heart starter for the day – a flask of whisky – Herbie had been standing on the stairs trying to find a last drop from a flask that was surprisingly empty after only nine floors.

'Fucking flats, on the ninth floor and the lifts out of order. What's fucking Henry ever done for the working man? Been a battler all my life, Brother, excuse the fucking French. So you're going to be a priest. Still, could be worse, don't worry, but I'm buggered if I can think how.'

Herbie was also a wheelchair danger to the public, though he curbed his wheelies and his tongue when Sister Xavier was on the ward. He often left pools of piss on the floor of the ward. 'Sister, Sister,' he would yell with the indignation of the concerned citizen, 'Albert's going to light a cigarette and there's petrol all over the floor. Don't know what hospitals are coming to. My old man always warned me against Catholics.' He looked with horror at his own pool of piss. 'You stupid Catholic prick, Albert, don't you know never to light a match next to petrol. That's the trouble with Catholics, they're so fired up with the DLP, they can't tell piss from petrol. God bless you, Sister.'

Waking to a stroke on the cheek from Nurse Counahan, Brother Hannigan realised that he had embarrassed the ward by plunging into a *grand mal* while discussing that afternoon's match between Essendon and Collingwood. He loved the camaraderie of the men's ward and was just beginning to feel less clerical, less mysterious to them. Now, as Nurse Counahan sponged his cheek, he realised that the blood on the lino tiles was his, that his insolent body, jerking its own assertion, had truly set him apart. Yet he was pleased to be apart, and felt, once again, that strange and unlikely peace, not with God but with himself. He felt a disordered and demanding tranquillity which disowned the world and refused it a focus. For the first time in his life, he felt distinguished, not as a future mediator, other Christ, shriver of the sins of the world, but because his body yelled to the world and he was important and he was not to blame.

He had been looking forward to listening to a football match, for the first time in years, on a wonderful little radio, a transistor, that Nurse Counahan had lent him. She was soothing him now, pretending to be interested in the fate of Essendon, when Father Superior walked in. Brother Hannigan felt he had been caught in *flagrante delicto*, but Father Finnegan was warm and friendly and in charge of the world.

Father Superior discovered that he knew Nurse Counahan's uncle, who was a well-known – you probably wouldn't realise this, Brother – Catholic lawyer, who had been very helpful to a number of priests – nothing serious, of course – you don't mind if I call you Moira, I've known Sean so long, he's got a handicap of six and is a mean putter.

Then Father Finnegan became serious. Even though dressed in civvies, because he was off to play a round with the Vicar General – good contact for the Marianites – he remained convincingly a priest who carried the kindness of God about with him. 'I've had a long chat to Doctor Conmee – his sister is a Dominican, by the way, fine man – and he's sure he'll have this thing under control in a few more days. God is present in the miracles of modern medicine. Used to be a bit of a problem but this is the sixties and Vatican II. Well hardly any problems. You're just like your mother, young Moira. Remind Sean he owes me a game and a bottle of . . . well, no matter, he owes me a game. I've left you something to read, Brother, God bless, lovely to see you looking so fit, God bless you both.'

As if in response to this almost-nuptial blessing, Brother Hannigan's body became his manic master once again, dragging him away into the valley of shadow and wild light, into the valley of mocking voices and listening silences.

When he came back to the world, Brother Koenig and Brother Williams were standing round the transistor on the locker as if at an altar. Jack Dyer was talking about the sort of Courage you need in this Game of Football. Hannigan sat up. His brothers noticed him, felt guilty for enjoying themselves and switched off the radio.

'Great theology conference. I read your paper on the Song of Songs. The Carmelites got really mad. They thought you didn't give enough to Mary. They think they own the Mother of God, when we do.' Williams, looking older and balder, had obviously enjoyed baiting the sons of Mary.

Koenig was keen to fill in the details of monastery life. 'Things have been happening. Things have been really happening. BA Santamaria has had pups.'

'But he couldn't have. He's...' Hannigan suddenly took an interest in the mysteries of life.

Koenig, slight, dark, intense, clearly felt that BA's pregnancy indicated his own failure as monastery infirmarian. 'Well, Father Superior named him, and once Father Superior named him, no one ever looked. You know how it is.'

Both his brothers were holding their clerical hats in front of them, as if concealing something. Accustomed to their free-flowing religious habits, unused to wearing hats, unused to wearing clerical suits, they were uncomfortable about being marked out publicly as 'other Christs'.

Brother Williams was staring at the Salvation Army Citadel. 'You know,' he said to the fortress of God, 'epilepsy' – and Hannigan was grateful for the word, he had been prac-tising it – 'epilepsy worries them because the Incarnation does. God becoming flesh seems like bad taste. They prefer the angel to the animal.' He thoughtfully scratched some dandruff from his balding scalp. 'They think any flesh is a mistake by God and flesh out of control is the work of the Devil. All clerics are heretics at heart.' He turned to Brother Hannigan. 'It's funny, isn't it, the Greeks and the Egyptians talked about epilepsy in terms of possession by God; it took Christians to talk about it as possession by the Devil and what that says about us is...'

'I must tell you about Brother Milton,' interrupted Brother Koenig, anxious to get back to more down-to-earth facts.

'I've been worrying about him, keeping him in my prayers,' said Hannigan, partly telling the truth.

'Well, you had better keep praying for him. He's shot through.' Koenig was pleased to be announcing such an important, non-theological truth. 'You see, Father Superior was so worried about Brother Milton's teeth that he rang the dentist. Brother Milton hadn't been near him for months. God knows what he had been doing on all those pretend visits. Next day, Brother Milton had disappeared. He shot through on Augustus. You remember Augustus, the second best monastery bike?'

'A bike so old,' said Williams, 'that it got its name from AA Calwell, when the bishops still let us like him.'

'Hell,' said Hannigan, 'who'd believe it of Kevin Milton? I've been with him for ten years, and he was always so holy.'

'Pious, I would have thought,' said Williams. 'I'll miss Augustus more.'

Tim Koenig gave Hannigan some books sent by Father Brown, among them PG Wodehouse's *The Mating Season* and his own copy of Gury's *Theologia Moralis*. 'I'm not sure what that's about, but Father Brown was insistent. Anyway, we've got to get going. It's open day for the monastery auxiliary, and you know how keen Father Superior is for us to mix with lay people.'

That night, Hannigan used the miracle of the transistor to listen to the news. He had not listened to the news since the time when all the seminarians had gathered round the wireless to hear the ABC declare Pope Pius XII officially dead. They had felt bereaved, for he had been Pope for all their lifetimes and had seemed eternal. Tonight, there seemed to be a lot of worry about that war in Vietnam. Nurse Counahan came in and Hannigan lost all interest in world affairs. Though she was off-duty, she was still wearing her uniform, and Brother Hannigan had a brief, chaste fantasy of seeing her in more defining clothes. Moira – he now had Father Superior's implicit permission to call her that – insisted on cutting his toenails. He had protested, embarrassed by his carelessness about personal hygiene. She had laughed and gone ahead, declaring that the clippings would make rare relics when he became a saint, and then threw them in the rubbish bin.

Now she sat in the visitors' chair, never used by his brothers, and offered him her blue-eyed friendliness. *Beloved, let us love one another* and he loved her purely. She sat with three books, left by Father Superior, hesitant in her hands. The top one was his recently published biography of the Order's founder, *Giovanni Buongiorno, Virgin Soldier*. The second book was the tiny, dense code of canon law. The last book, which she handed to him with puzzled reluctance, was Hannigan's own copy of volume two of their moral theology text book, complete with his own doodlings of women in capes. In this book, *Institutiones Theologiae Moralis* by Eduardus Genicot, SJ, Father Superior had left a note between pages 324 and 325, written on monastery note-paper with the Order's insignia, the merging hearts of Jesus and Mary with the letters MOM beneath them.

Dear Brother,

This is all a bit old hat, but I thought you'd better read it. I've spoken to Father Provincial and to Doctor Conmee. Both assure me there are no problems really. But we'll have to make special application. The Auxiliary are praying for you. God works in mysterious ways.

At present there is a working party down at the Schancks holiday house. We've decided, we took a vote on it, to do up the chapel before installing the septic tanks. Still some discussion on whether to build a handball court or a swimming pool, back home here at Saint Patrick's. Looks like the dialogue Mass in English will be coming soon. Good idea, I suppose, but I worry about losing the universal language of Mater Ecclesia and Saint Thomas, not to mention Cicero. I still like the idea of saying Mass in Sydney or Saigon and being understood. Brother Joseph has a wonderful crop of turnips. We have twenty chickens ready for the table. Pity you'll miss out on all that plucking. What a wonderful example for us all the laybrothers are. They teach us humility.

Father Provincial and Doctor Conmee have assured me that it will be all right, what with Vatican II and the miracles of modern medicine. Thought you might like to know the old-style starting point about this matter — though not very relevant to the sixties. God bless. I'll ring your parents and let them know everything is perfectly OK. Keep me in your prayers, Brother. Sincerely in the heart of Mary,

PJ Finnegan, MOM

PS I forgot to mention that your mother rang me to say that Bernadette had a miscarriage. God works in mysterious ways.
PPS We beat the Jesuits by three goals.
PPPS I forgot to mention that this stuff is all very old-fashioned, but it's still the law.
PPPPS Perhaps you could write to Bernadette and mention Limbo.

In Christ, PJF MOM

It was a warm and human letter, redolent of the kindness of God, and written in black ink and a beautiful, printed script. Father Superior had kindly underlined the relevant passages in Genicot, which discussed 'the irregulars', those ineligible for ordination: *Epileptici, vel amentes, vel a daemone possessi...* – the epileptics, the demented, those possessed by the Devil, formerly or presently. Genicot noted that a dispensation from Rome was required, and only when the illness was perfectly cured. This was an unlikely possibility, but then Genicot wrote before the coming of modern medicine and Vatican II.

Taking up Father Brown's even older book, Gury's *Theologia Moralis*, annotated with Father Brown's energetic comments and questions ('Godswallop!!' 'Silly buggers!?'), Brother Hannigan discovered that women were *by divine institution totally excluded from any form of ordination*. The Fathers, the

Doctors, and perpetual practice of the Church had said so. For example, Saint Paul had insisted: *Let women keep silence in the churches, for it is not permitted for them to speak, but let them be submissive* ... and again, *Let a woman learn in silence with all submission. For I do not allow a woman to teach, or to exercise authority over men; but she is to keep quiet.* 'Silly old bastard!' Father Brown had written. Finally he found the passage on irregular men. They were *the perpetually demented, lunatics, the uncontrollable epileptics* ... Taking up the code, with its fine, small pages reminding him of cigarette paper, he found that canon 984 repeated this law of God. In the code, Father Superior had slipped another note. 'This was before the wonders of modern medicine. Not to worry. I've already written to Rome. God bless.'

'Find anything exciting?'

He returned to Moira's voice as though coming back from a *petit mal.*

She had placed her nurse's cap on her knees and was pinning back her hair.

'Yes. We've got a hell of a lot in common. Neither of us would make a good priest.'

'You mean you've been elevated to the status of a woman?'

'Well at least you get a paragraph for yourself. I'm landed with the demented and the possessed.'

'Well, that means I've got two paragraphs.'

'But you're commended to be submissive.'

'I am, I always am. I'm a nurse, after all. Here take these tablets and stop reading that crap. Just because it's old and by old men and in Latin doesn't make it wise.'

God so loved the world and he felt the quietness sneaking up on him and a surprised erection. *Virgin Mother of God, keep my body pure and my mind holy.* He would try to be a good religious and a good priest, and he loved the world and God and the kindness of Vatican II. And he also tried to love Moira in a spiritual way, as she straightened his pillows, ran her finger across his cheek, and then stiffened to attention as Sister Xavier stood at the door, sweetly demanding. 'Nurse, go and change Herbie's pyjamas, there's a good girl. Brother, you get some rest.'

God was love, and the seminarian hoped that Doctor Conmee would take a long time to stabilise him, and that Nurse Counahan would continue to bring him the sacrament of his tablets and his M and A. He knew that another fit of light and darkness was coming, that his body was going to become himself again, in lunge and spasm about the bed. He knew that God had created the world and saw that it was good and that God was mostly right. And that Moira was coming back and that one day he would be able to offer a mass in love for her.

'I've got a lovely surprise for you, Brother.' Sister Xavier was standing at the door, bestowing gifts. 'They're bringing your Brother Kiernane up here. Seems he hurt his back last week playing football. I don't know why you men bother. But you'll have a lovely time talking theology together. God bless you, Brother.'

And Elizabeth Taylor, and Brother Milton, and Essendon and Bernadette and her stillborn child and Marilyn Monroe and Arthur Calwell, and BA Santamaria, both of them, and...he was going to pray for himself, but the darkness came.

1965

five

*M*adeleine

*I*N AFTER YEARS, he often masturbated in her honour, guilty to God and guilty to her. Madeleine, if that was her name.

The seminarian had been allowed out to a Young Christian Workers' meeting to discuss food for a mission in Kashmir. The chaplain, newly ordained and eager in his black Vatican II polo neck, was eloquent and moving on the joy of hearing confessions in a soap factory in Braybrook. But, for the present, Kashmir would have to survive on spiritual food, and the meeting ended early. They had abandoned Kashmir for the needs of Braybrook.

The seminarian lost track when the meeting became dishevelled in a democratic sort of way. The chaplain talked movingly about how much joy he had got out of Light Fingers winning the Cup. Then they discussed finding factory chaplains for Braybrook. A fat man, who vied with the priest for spiritual authority and whose voice quivered towards tears when he spoke of Our Lady, knew an Italian priest who said 'mate' and 'bugger me dead'. They set up a working party to find a Greek, a Maltese and a Turkish priest. Someone suggested that the Turkish priest would be a rare specimen with lots of time on his hands, and there was some suspicion that this was a racist statement. To clear the air, the fat man started to strum a guitar and they sang 'We Shall Overcome'.

The seminarian was tone deaf and didn't know the words. He mumbled his excuses, talking vaguely of monastery curfews. Yes, Brother could find his own way home. He had the monastery car, not telling them that this was a break-through in the Church of Vatican II and he was the first seminarian his Order had allowed 'out on the town', as Father Superior had joked. He would find his own way home, eventually.

At one a.m. he was still finding his way. The wind was swirling-up the tatters of the night street, Gertrude Street, not yet dead. The late-night pubs had locked in their own darkness and the street lights fumbled away the night uncertainly. At the age of twenty-three, he was having his first night out, not entirely as Father Superior had intended. He had been impressed by the Young Christian Workers, and somewhat overawed by the ease with which they chatted to and about God when they had never chanted the Holy Office in their lives. Their enthusiasm was impressive, even if a bit splashy, as though they too could walk, unordained, on the waters of Lake Galilee.

Now he stood lonely and spuriously free in Gertrude Street. Till midnight he had been drinking at the late-licence Champion. Now he stood a short distance away – say the length of the monastery path to Our Lady's Shrine – from the VD clinic, which looked like a reformed bank, which it was, still anxious to warn and punish.

The Champion had been his first real visit to a real pub, discounting lunch in the dining rooms of some country pubs before he entered the junior seminary at the age of twelve. He had stood at the bar entrance, frightened that 'someone' would see him sightseeing. He had thought with a shudder of defiance of his mother, of Father Superior, and fleetingly of God. Inside the door, people plunged and lurched past him, and he soon gave up wondering if anyone would know him.

The blacks were standing or sitting in the far corner near the juke-box. The newer Australians were along the bar and around the snooker table. The newest Australians, Greeks – or were they Jugoslavs? – sat at tables at the far end. Here and there were the loners talking to their half empty pots. Through the crowd moved a man selling watches whose prices had fallen from trucks, and another in a blue boiler-suit selling chocolate pieces in cellophane bags, three for ten bob. Also selling were the women whose night had already come. In the black corner, the juke-box yelled at itself, unnoticed, until the record returned to bed, then someone produced another two bob.

At the bar, two men, pinstriped, as conspicuous as nuns in old-fashioned habits, ordered double whiskies, Johnny Walker, well whatever, and do you have a good Genders McLaren Park Vintage Port? The seminarian, another voyeur, running out of mother-sent money that should have been surrendered to Father Bursar, leant against the bar and the noise. Carefully nonchalant, he studied the used band-aid floating in the drip tray, and waited for service.

'Want a good time love, give you a really good time?' She had a good square face, with a black left eye.

'I've been fucked by experts, like to become one?' A rival bid, she was forty, fifty, sixty, random in rouge and lipstick and blond hair, her eye-shadow eroded by sweat or tears. She wore a yellow pants-suit and grey, flat-heeled boots.

He felt a virgin guilty joy. Then he thought of how much of his thirteen quid he had left, and of Doctor Deighton's talk on VD to the seminarians. And, finally, of his vow of chastity. She smiled at him and he liked the smile. He liked her, as he disliked himself. Last night Father Superior had quoted Cardinal Agaginian to the seminarians: *May Christ with the help of the sweet Queen of Virgins sow in the souls of this house lilies and roses. Sweet Queen of Virgins keep my heart pure and my mind holy.*

'How about a fuck, love?'

Gently, like real talk of love.

Burn our thoughts and affections, Lord, in the fire of the Holy Spirit, so that our bodies may be chaste and our hearts clean to serve Thee.

He turned back to the bar, happily confused, and drank his first beer in his first pub, with what he hoped was a sexually confident air. He realised that the pinstriped visitors from outer space were now standing next to him.

'Geez, this has got to be seen to be believed. How do they live like this?'

'And not a decent fuck in the whole place.'

He moved away from them, suddenly feeling conspicuous in his new blue shirt and his new baggy, out-of-date trousers, Our Lady's colours.

The woman in yellow picked up a slick, brown briefcase from between the two men, and held it up. 'Hey Curly,' she yelled to a bald man with holes in his sandshoes, 'it must have been a hard day on the Stock Exchange, you left your port-folios on the floor.'

'Get fucked, Rita,' he said cheerfully to his empty glass.

'I'm trying, love, I'm trying.'

Two young policemen, with an unconvincing controlling look in their eyes and twin moustaches, stood over her.

'Ah, constable, your play lunch,' bowing to the confused boy with the blond moustache and a missing front tooth.

The seminarian moved further away, uncomfortably aware that God was everywhere. He stared at a woman seated at a laminex table by the window. Red hair, red dress, white high-heeled boots, she stared at her full glass and ignored the world around her.

He wanted to talk to her. He'd rarely talked to a woman on his own, except his mother, and then he'd listened. He studied the upended bottle of spirits, beneath which were the bar-maid's off-white high-heel shoes, resting while her greyish thongs were now on duty. Voices fought for space and occasionally sentences floated across.

'But Menzies thinks his shit doesn't smell.'

'I didn't take the rent money, you bastard. You took it to Flemington, prick.'

'Real shit, aren't you. Bumped me when I had the red lined up.'

The woman in yellow was persistent. He was embarrassed and excited. Her brown eyes were the challenge of experience, eyes that he was sure could recognise a virgin desperate to be cured.

'Good time for you, love, my place. Only five quid. Whatever turns you on. Mind you, I have standards, I mean, I'm clean.' The rival bid came again from the woman with the black eye, with another motherly, sensuous look.

Where were all the young sirens, swaying erotic on high heels, that he had been warned about by the Christian Brothers before he knew what an erection was? They danced nightly in his head, but not in the bar of the Champion. The woman in yellow had her hand on his shoulder, staking her claim, and he liked it, though looking around to see how many were watching. None.

'I'll buy you a beer. Both of you, I mean,' he added quickly.

A black man with a distinguished beard threw a five-pound note on the wet bar. 'Four pots for me and my brothers.'

The Brothers shall live in community, said the constitutions of his Order. *The Brothers shall never be alone with a person of the opposite sex, except where necessary for pastoral care. Each monastery shall have a parlour for visitors that can be seen into from without.*

The blond woman moved in and gave him an accurate, sluicy kiss. Another first. He looked around, still worried that 'someone' would see him. But everyone was watching a redheaded man in PMG overalls hitting his mate over the head with a billiard cue, while Maria from *West Side Story* was singing 'I Feel Pretty'.

Across the bar, the woman in red removed the pinstriped arm, now impelled by enough whisky to join what it thought of as action. She winked at the seminarian. 'Fuck off,' she said with the dignity he thought would have belonged to Mary Magdalene.

'Piss off,' the blonde said to her dark rival. 'I got him first, didn't I, love?'

Martha and Mary at work. She covered his pause for a reply with another kiss, quick, promising and welcome to his penis.

'I need a piss.' He was getting into the vernacular. 'Mind this, will you, love,' he said, passing over their beers and pointing to his own. 'Whoever,' waving grandly and wondering if he was already drunk.

'Get me a sandwich, love,' ordered the black-eyed woman.

He had decided that this dark woman, who looked like a lifetime of listening, was Mary. She was now asserting herself. He looked at the warped corned-beef sandwiches, lying in funeral slabs next to the high-heeled shoes.

'I need a piss.' It was sounding like a response to the endless litany of the saints.

He moved towards the toilets at the back of the building. From across the room, the woman in red, still alone, gave him a careful wink, and then looked disowning into the distance. Coming out, he pondered the graffiti wanting the Pope off the moon, wondered if Lena really sucked cocks, if those phone numbers were genuine, what on earth crabs were. *Mother Mary, Virgin Queen, keep my mind holy and my body pure*, as he sidled with an attempt at purpose through the bar crowd, bumping a pot of beer in a woman's hand.

'Sorry.'

'Mind where you're going, prick.'

He muttered his apologetic way across the floor, but she was still hissing. 'Did you see that creep? Got a good mind to give him a swift one in the balls. Hey, you, shithead!'

Next to the juke-box, a black girl was swaying gracefully to 'Love Me Do'. 'Don't worry, mate, she has a fight every week. She's never won one yet.' And to the balder of the pinstriped, swaying gracelessly, as if to the wavering rhythm of his glass: 'Fuck off, mate, you're way out of your league.' Kindly.

The seminarian had given the Champion his best, and left,

walking up Gertrude Street against the wind, with a vision of his two women at the bar, one of them drinking his beer, the other eating a corned-beef sandwich. Jesus, Mary and Joseph, nothing wrong, he had just wanted to see what it all felt like. After all, the Brothers shall always live in community.

Somewhere up the street someone lit a match to see if the night was still there and the wind took away the light.

It was time to go home. He wandered the street. He looked up, and saw stars that occasionally dodged the home-hurrying clouds. He thought of his favourite poet, Father Hopkins, SJ.

> Look at the stars! look, look up at the skies!
> O look at all the fire-folk sitting in the air!
> ...This piece-bright paling shuts the spouse
> Christ home, Christ and his mother and all his hallows.

He felt comforted. Further up, on the opposite footpath, the street light shone on a shop window that seemed to be full of religious statues. It was a plumbing supplier and the statues were toilet bowls and hand basins, artistically arranged.

It was one o'clock in the morning. He would be too tired even to have to fight off masturbation. But first he would have a cappuccino; he had always wanted to try one. The only cafe open was a short tunnel of laminex tables, red plastic chairs, and tomato-shaped plastic sauce containers that reminded him of the Sacred Heart. There were six tables, with all the seats taken, except for the table at the far end, near the trays of mummified dim sims and greased chips. Here sat the red woman from the Champion, alone, staring at the remnants of foam in her cappuccino cup. He stared at the roaring, disbelieving red of her hair. He stared, remembering that Father Superior had recently reminded them that Saint Aloysius Gonzaga had practised such modesty of the eyes that he never looked even his mother in the face. *Look only on what Christ would look on.* That included Saint Mary Magdalene.

He would go home and say vespers from *The Little Office of Our Lady*. The other Lady sat attentively ignoring the four men bunched at the next table, while they talked in an Irish whisper that could be heard in London.

The Champion men had dropped in on their way home. A man with strands of hair smeared across his baldness thumped a matey fist of challenge into the shoulder of the redheaded man in PMG overalls.

'You fancy her, don't ya?' himself staring his lust.

She sat spooning up bits of cappuccino fluff, carefully oblivious of four men and a staring seminarian.

'Never know where she's been, mate,' said the PMG man.

A tall man with a suspicion of a blond moustache stood hovering over her. 'How would you like a lift home, love?'

The other three half-stood to hear the answer. It didn't come.

'What do you say then, love?' The tall man, whose moustache seemed to make his jaw cringe, spoke more loudly. 'We could give you a great ride.'

'We could take you where you have never been.' They were gloating in the wit of their metaphors.

'How about a fuck?'

The man from the PMG was glared at for his crudity. 'Shut up, Morrie. You're a prick without any class.' The fourth man with a baseball cap and a red face looked righteous and blew his nose on a paper napkin.

'What he means is...' It was one of the pinstriped men from the Champion, now looking dishevelled, his belly bisected by a disappearing belt. 'What he means is,' putting the crust of his ham sandwich in her ashtray, 'what he means is, perhaps we, all of us...' He looked at the seminarian, leaning alien against the 'Hot Do Not Touch' sign of the cold food counter, and qualified, 'Well, most of us,' intruding on the four and looking matey at their surprise, 'perhaps we could go off somewhere and have a drink somewhere, you know.' He tried to find his belt for a pants-hitch and smiled at her.

He abandoned camaraderie and recharged his smile. 'Come on, be a sport.' His hand on her shoulder became firmer as she did not resist, and therefore invited. 'My car's outside, new Fairlane, honest. Well, just you and me,' as though he had startled himself into this better idea.

'What he means is,' the man from the PMG, whose red ears were the wrong toning for his red hair, was drunkenly and kindly explanatory, 'what he means is, love, How about a fuck?'

She lifted up her cup and looked with patient surprise at its emptiness.

'What I mean is,' the man of business was trying to rearrange himself by fiddling with the knot of his club tie with his free hand, 'there's places nicer than this I could take you to, got a few contacts. Don't let them upset you. You know what men are like,' removing his hand from her shoulder, standing roundly erect, dissociating himself and making claims. He ran his fingers through his hair as if to emphasise that he had more hair than any of the others and a better haircut.

The seminarian stood irrelevant as a dim sim, thinking of the scroll on Father Superior's wall which read, *When God shuts a door, Mary opens a window.* The scroll, in fairy-floss Gothic, embarrassed most of its seminarian viewers, as their Superior's friendly, manly talk of sin and sex would have embarrassed the artist, Father Superior's mum. They had seen her once, a tiny woman wearing a black dress and lots of energy, who had come from Perth to enjoy the kingdom of her son. They all said she was simply amazing, but what else would you expect from the mother of a great Superior. They had seen her scroll and now her; it was all a bit of a revelation. They were reminded, a bit surprised, that Father Superior had once slithered, wet body and dry squeal, into the world. But, no doubt, cleanly and cleverly. Like his friend Christ, born graciously of a woman.

The woman in red didn't look up until the man in the spat-
tered white apron, oblivious and controlling, brought her
another cappuccino. They smiled the smile of friends swapping love in a horde of strangers.

'Thanks Bruno, you're a gem,' and the seminarian was
jealous of her smile.

Bruno, noticing only her, picked up the ashtray, held up the
crust as if holding a dead mouse by the tail, and said to her,
'Some people must live like pigs in their own homes'. Then
he walked away, disowning. 'Sorry mate,' as he rubbed
shoulders with the seminarian.

She silted her coffee from the pour-in jar of sugar. Then she
looked up, as if discovering for the first time that she had
company.

The silence was hers and she smiled at them.

Leaning against the counter, the seminarian saw the five
men shuffle to an almost-reverent almost-attention. She took
a sip of her coffee. She looked them over with a smile. She put
down her cup. 'Fuck off, the lot of you. Right now.' Then she
ignored them.

The seminarian had never heard such dignity of swearing.

The silence was still hers. She raised her head as if surprised
to find them still wearying her presence.

The man in the suit collapsed into talking. 'Look, come on,
sweetie, we're just men, just blokes,' and she looked at him,
appraising, thighs, belly, shoulders – well, that's news. 'We're
professional men, sort of,' grabbing authority by pointing to
the PMG logo. 'Hell, we're all only having fun. Be a hell of
a world if a man couldn't have some fun, wouldn't it? Shit,
excuse the French, obvious isn't it, love?' He was asking for
absolution, smiling, his bottom lip hanging loosely.

He looked around at the backs of his almost-mates, who had
moved off to become imperious about their take-aways.

She looked up at him, her cup poised, with the kindness of
interested contempt.

'No harm meant, love, you know that.' Battling alone, manfully.

Absolution had not yet come. 'Compliment, really,' wheedling. 'You have to say that – four, five men, blokes really, not young, I do realise that,' putting his arm on her shoulder again, 'but not really, not really over the hill...choosy we are, well I am. Got a nice little business in surgical appliances.'

She smiled at him. He straightened his tie and tried to reorganise his leer into a smile.

'Must be lovely when you want a new truss.' She kept smiling, kindly.

'Bit below the belt, eh, love?' He laughed away her gibe and became low-voiced confidential, so that the seminarian could hardly hear him. 'Some real sluts around here, I don't mind telling you. Ever noticed that? Well you wouldn't, would you? Not your scene is it? Certainly not mine.'

His mates were busy in talk-contemplation of a calendar showing a blonde in a red bikini whispering to a Michelin tyre, made at-home by a collage of fly spots and a fragment of egg.

'Jeez, I could tire her quick smart,' boasted the man from the PMG.

'God, I could give her a ride,' bragged the tall man with the moustache, running his tongue through his little whiskers.

Somewhere, from Vatican II seminary culture, TS Eliot floated up uncertainly, erotically. *Grishkin is nice... Uncorseted, her friendly bust gives promise of pneumatic bliss. Grishkin has a maisonette.*

'Got a nice little flat in East Brunswick,' crowed the businessman. The tie, his umbilical to his better world, was being straightened yet again. He was enjoying the Coke mirror. Coke people live younger, better...'Just a drink, love, nothing serious, bit of fun, you know, joking aside.'

She looked up at him, as if waking, puzzled and new, to the sudden world. 'O hello, you still here?' Solicitous. 'Could

I take you home to your wife in Brunswick? It was East Brunswick, wasn't it? We could tell her all about your successes at the Champion, the Cary Grant of Gertrude Street.'

On his dim-sim, outer edge, the seminarian realised that her flow of red hair was real, that her smile was real. Remember, Brothers, that God was born of woman, and for that reason all women deserve the respect of every priest, who is after all another Christ.

'Well, what I want to say to you, love...' The suited arm now hovered fatherly above her shoulder, as she tidied her table. 'What I really want to say to you, love, is...' He paused as if to track down an important thought and she looked up at him expectantly as she lit an Alpine. 'Well, I mean... Jesus Christ. Ah, fuck it,' and he muttered his way towards Gertrude Street.

His almost-mates were now paying, now grabbing their hamburgers.

The seminarian was more shocked by the obscenity than by the blasphemy. *Fuck.* The Oxford did not support Father Superior's etymology of 'Found-guilty, Unlawful Carnal Knowledge'. Connection with German *Fiken* could not be demonstrated, but it sounded possible.

She sat in her own silence, looking at nowhere

Virgin mother of Christ, keep my body pure and my mind holy. His own absent mother was always present, busy protecting him from sin and loving his priesthood-to-be.

Near the doorway the four mates were becoming loud and confident, while the businessman hovered uncertainly, holding the door open.

'I fucking told the wog I hate lettuce and tomato sauce.' The balding man was becoming assertive and reorganising his countable strands of hair. 'Can't a man get anything he wants around this place?'

'Horsemeat and horseshit,' the tall man was holding up a pie but looking at the woman.

'I'd love to go for a ride in her bush,' said Morrie, pointing a hamburger at Our Lady of Michelin, but looking at the woman.

Graze on my lips, and if those hills be dry,
Stray lower, where the pleasant fountains lie.

He had meditated, masturbated, mortally sinfully, on these lines from Shakespeare.

Still at the doorway, the four men cramped themselves back into a routine, turning back for a moment from Gertrude Street and a night of death clouds and the wind prying along the street, into a sort of life. The businessman let the door close, as if hoping for a late invitation to join the team. But the other men talked inward.

'Best you could get, Morrie, old son, is a dose of clap.'

'Or the crabs.'

'Or give one.'

The seminarian had been robbed of his virgin ignorance by the *Encyclopaedia Britannica*, under 'Syphilis'; by a nudge-nudge talk from Doctor Deighton; by a copy of *From Here to Eternity*, smuggled by a newly ordained priest from the Fathers' library, where all the interesting books were kept under glass. He had been left despoiled of ignorance and totally confused. 'Well, we all know, don't we, it doesn't come from toilet seats,' said Doctor Deighton, good Catholic father of six, who took time off from his vocation at Saint Vincent's to give the seminarians the facts and fictions of life. The seminarians, most of whom didn't know what he was talking about, had shifted on their hard chairs in unison, confirmed in their vow of chastity. Brother Williams, who always wrinkled his eyebrows and forehead when he had a bad thought, relaxed for a moment and smiled, then relapsed into his permanent frown.

As the seminarian meditated the distinction between *clap* and *crabs* – he felt that he had *clap* sorted out and didn't contemplate pimples on his penis with such agony anymore, but *crabs*? – the men were in conference at the door.

The man in the red face and baseball cap was being matey to the man in pinstripes. 'Look Albert – it is Albert? – no? well look, Alec, Morrie here – ' thumping his mate from the PMG, 'Morrie's having a few of us around for a barbecue tomorrow. Like to come?'

Morrie was less than welcoming. 'You don't have to come, you know. You'd have to bring some chops and some grog.'

'I'd love to come, mate. I'll bring some steaks'. Then, offering more gifts, 'Mind if I bring a couple of girls.'

'Jesus, then come early...'

From the edge of their universe the seminarian automatically bowed his head at the Holy Name and was mortified by an errant pubic hair.

'...and fuck the steaks.' Morrie looked around at his world and saw that he was good.

'Christ, you fancied her, didn't you, Morrie?' Alec was now a friend, and he looked down at the woman with pitying amazement. They went matey into their night. 'Don't be a stupid cunt,' came Morrie's affectionate quip from Gertrude Street.

As the door closed, the seminarian heard the voices of the two remaining customers, who sat at the table nearest the door.

'To hell with poverty. Give the cat another canary,' from a man wearing a broad Scots accent and an Essendon football jumper.

'I really loved my mum, I really did,' from an old man with a misdirected nose and a Harvard University windcheater, chatting to his toasted ham sandwich.

The seminarian walked past her table, his body pure, above all this. He stood in Gertrude Street as the night wind fossicked along the street. He still hadn't had a cappuccino; it would have been a nice change from monastery tea. He stood in front of the greasy cafe window, feeling cold and alone and thought about Sister Margaret. She had written him, with her

Mother Superior's approval, embarrassingly earthy letters that discussed their mutual passion of a life in love with Christ. She consistently referred to him as a virgin soldier of Christ. He stood in Gertrude Street thinking of a cappuccino and Sister Margaret's spiritual problem with the teapot. She loved her tea strong and black, but the convent habit was to pour the milk into the large convent teapot. In the spirit of the sixties, some nuns had drawn the attention of their superiors to this violation of the teapot and the matter was going to be discussed at the next General Chapter of the Order in Rome in two years time. Through the steamy window he could see Bruno at the juke-box, a grubby tea-towel over his shoulder. Elvis Presley burst into 'Walk Like an Angel'. Sister Margaret had said, 'I know I don't look as good as Audrey Hepburn in *The Nun's Story*, but I can bloody well nun better than her.' Her nunning seemed so chirpy and peaceful, his monking so impatient and restless. Home is where the heart is and he went back into the cafe.

'Celtic forever, and bugger the Prots,' said the man in the Essendon football jumper. 'I'm an orphan you know,' said the old man to anyone who would listen. The seminarian walked back past the woman, slowing at her legs. When he came home to the dim sims and the chips, he didn't feel hungry any more, though hunger was the perpetual state of his monastery stomach. Bruno was exploring his left ear with a match. He threw the match on the floor and attended to the seminarian by twisting a knob on the baroque tabernacle of his coffee machine.

'Buy me a coffee, there's a good love.'

The seminarian looked back at her, allowed to notice her properly for the first time, and gave her a look of you-don't-mean-me-please-mean-me.

'There's a good love, buy me a cup of coffee.' Sweet command. She still had a bubble of cappuccino on her bottom lip.

As he paid for the two coffees with his undeclared monastery money, he thought of her alone and drunk and proud in the bar. Later, freed from the cigarette ethos of the Champion, he had paused in the doorway of a shoeshop to light his secret and forbidden pipe, a birthday gift from his rebel sister, Bernadette. As he had glanced up from the window display of thongs and sandals, he had seen the woman being cuddled in the cabin of an unloaded Carlton & United truck, and felt vaguely jealous of the truck driver. She had broken away, slamming the door of the truck and shaking the liquid amber of her autumn hair. The seminarian had thought yet again of an often-meditated picture in his sister's scrapbook of a film star, halter-necked in red, her red lips pursed, inviting, her hair flowing red beneath her. *Woman's crowning glory*, Saint Paul had said, as if he had an eye for Rita Hayworth, without noticing her breasts.

Now the woman was talking to him. 'Join me, if you're not doing anything.' She sat back with an air of home into the moulded red plastic of her chair.

He joined her quickly, frightened she would change her mind. They sat stirring their coffees in communion. At the next table there were now four Italian men, scrubbed, silent, intent on the best of all possible cards.

A man leant against the juke-box that was old and frilled with curves and loved by flies. 'Christ,' he told the world, 'I press Eartha Kitt and bloody "Love Me Do" comes fucking up.' He thumped the machine. 'Piss off back to Liverpool, white boys.' The back of his aggressively white T-shirt had a message: *Menzies is a prick that never stands up for anything*. As he turned from collecting a hot-dog from Bruno, his chest showed another message: *We own this bloody country still*.

'Poor bastards, they got a shit deal, didn't they?' She finished her coffee with grace. 'They shouldn't worry, they'll get worse yet, won't they. See you. Thanks,' she waved at Bruno. 'You coming?' she added to the seminarian, as a don't-care question. She stood up, smiling, plumply and finely sensual, her brown eyes shining with kindness and fragile aggression. 'Please yourself, it doesn't mean a bloody thing to me.'

She walked towards the door, her legs graceful in black stockings above white boots. He felt absurdly that he had let escape one of those opportunities of Grace that Father Superior was always warning them about. He sat sad, and gulped his coffee.

She came back slowly, partly absent, picked up her white shoulder-bag from the chair, gave him a nod, and a cool smile worthy of a statue of Our Lady. 'See you. Or are you coming?' And she walked away.

Near the door a young man was collecting his hot-dog. His hair was dyed blond, tightly cut. He smiled at her, burbled at her with his hips, then pushed his hot-dog against her belly. 'This is only sample size, you should see the real thing but.'

The seminarian knew he was again irrelevant, replaced. As he looked at the crotch of the boy's tight white jeans, the four card-players looked at the same spot in a unison of contempt, nodded solemnly at each other and picked up their newly dealt cards.

She tapped the boy on the shoulder. 'Funny thing these days. All this arse-over-tit enthusiasm for a fuck. I've noticed it too, haven't you?' Smiling as though eager to share an answer. 'Not you of course,' she said into the boy's blush, 'you're a gentleman, and you're too young to be a man, you lucky little thing. And besides,' as if to stroke his hot-dog, 'samples are being made bigger than the real thing.' She pinched his cheek and walked out the door.

The boy tried to recover for a punch line, but, turning quickly, sprawled on the off-white lino tiles, patched with chewing gum, a black thong dangling from his big toe.

The seminarian stepped, 'Excuse me', over him.

Outside the cafe they stood, she busy in balancing, a wobble of sensuality and fading drunkenness.

'Like to take me, home I mean?' It was a statement bundled into a question. Surprised at her own loudness, she stared at the wan radiance of the high-rise flats. Gertrude Street was as empty as the monastery tracks that cut their luxurious quietness through their swathe of bushland living in the suburbs. Through the week of the annual retreat the seminarian had paced the tracks, asking God if he existed.

But here God was, watching, sleepless and anxious.

The woman looked through the sleeping street. 'You can't get near me, you shitheads.' She spoke quietly.

Then she turned to the seminarian. 'Got a car, have you?'

He was staring at the top floor of the Housing Commission flats, dimly lit, as if day was hesitating on the edge of their private-public night. Gerard Manley Hopkins, remote and agonised Jesuit, slipped unlikely into his mind. *The world is charged with the grandeur of God. Oh, morning, at the brown brink eastward, springs – because the Holy Ghost over the bent world broods with warm breast and with ah! bright wings.* Hello God, hello Father Hopkins, a good spot for both of you to celebrate your nervous breakdowns. He looked at the Commission flats, knowing that you can't give blasphemous cheek to a God who doesn't exist.

But she existed, and she turned to him as though interrupting her own thoughts rather than his. 'You got wheels?'

She presumed his answer and wandered into the friendship of facts. 'See that belted-in biscuit tin, the one with the clothes-hanger aerial, that little shit of a VW, more rattles than a millionaire's baby? Anyhow, the fact of the matter is,' smiling around her relief of words, 'I have to dump the thing at their place, good friends of mine really, in South Yarra, you know. Maybe you can follow me if you like. Only if you want to, maybe you don't want to, that's fine by me, I'm not … well, hell.'

She looked at him as if she really cared about his answer.

But he escaped an answer by looking down the street to where the late-night pub was dumping its inmates into the night. Waking to the half-darkness, the crowd, with its parenthesis of blacks, was hailing taxis, looking for AWOL cars,

looking suspiciously at their keys, looking sideways at themselves as they prepared to head south and east to the gods of
their respectable hearths. Or across the street and up towards
God in the high-rise flats.

'You follow me. The night's only a pup. Then maybe we
could spend a bit of time together.'

To the east his monastery rested oblivious and free from this
sort of decision, while the Holy Ghost was brooding over the
bent world with warm breast and with ah! bright wings.

She looked at him: her experienced, sensual eyes feared and
demanded. Her red hair flowed strident and touchable.

He put his hand on her shoulder, and then his tentative arm
wandered around her. 'Look, well, what's your name? Mine's
Michael, by the way.' His voice fought through the husk of
his excitement.

'Madeleine. Classy, aren't it, eh?'

He snuggled manly into her warmth on the pretext of
keeping her steady, her perfume wonderfully unsteadying.
'I mean, do you really think you should be driving?' He knew
from arguments with the Mormons and studies of water-into-
wine at Cana, that Christ approved of grog. But Christ was
always modest in his eating, in his drinking. That wasn't in
the Gospels, but Saint Bonaventure had told his novice master
in Latin, and the seminarian's Latin had got as far as food
and drink.

A tall man was suddenly next to them, leaning against the
wall of the Saint Vincent de Paul Op Shop, oiled hair dripping
over his ears and back into the fifties and Brylcream and Keith
Miller and young Elvis. The seminarian jerked back, as if
Father Superior had caught him in sin and Keith Miller had
caught him in slips. His arm suddenly became free, as if ready
to bless any part of the world that would put up with it.

'Madeleine! Haven't seen you – must be a week.' The man's
face was a jigsaw of stubble, red blotches, purple blotches, and
a grubby on-the-chin band-aid.

As he rose from the gutter he had stumbled back into, the seminarian removed a Violet Crumble wrapper from his bum and prepared to surrender to Father Superior, to God and to his mother.

'Had a few, eh, china? Looking for a bit, eh?' The man was friendly, accusing.

'On my way home actually,' claimed the seminarian, kicking aside a bottle. And rising further to life, 'And how about you,' strongly, 'mate?'

'Good for you, mate.' The tall man leant more firmly against the window of Saint Vincent de Paul to straighten up the world. 'Nice night, in't?' challenging the stars and the lights in the Commission flats. 'Madeleine, I'll take you home, no obligations, but I could do you a real good service. Take you home to Ralph, I mean, of course.'

The seminarian announced he was abandoning the field of sin by jangling loudly the keys of the monastery car.

'Could do you a bit of good on the way home, eh Madeleine? Though got to save something for the old woman.'

'She'd die of surprise, poor Alma, if she got any of the little bit you've saved up, Ray.'

'Not nice, not nice, Madeleine,' playing schoolmaster, but uncertain which finger to wag, and smiling, 'but, always nice to see you love, must've been a week.'

'Lovely to see you too, Raymond, love,' patting his shoulder gently. 'I don't come here very often these days.'

'Business better down at Fitzroy Street, eh?', sweetening malice with a smile. 'You and the missus, fuck off, both of you.' He smiled into his private comedy and slid practised down the wall and sat on the footpath.

'Home and sleep it off, Ray. I'll get you a taxi.'

Raymond regrouped his body and sat at attention. 'You women, the lot of yer, you only want one thing.'

'And what's that, Ray, love?' She seemed to want an answer, and the seminarian, fondling the Saint Christopher medal on the keys of the monastery car, was also interested in the answer.

'There you go again. Women all over, never give a man time to think.' Then Raymond fell asleep.

'Let him be,' she turned to the seminarian, and fondled his face and gave him a quick kiss. 'Poor silly bastard.' Then, 'It's Ronnie's car, see,' pointing to the red VW, as if that explained all. 'Got to get it back tonight, see, love,' again taking his face in her slim and startling hands. 'Otherwise it's the elephant shit hitting the fan, know what I mean. You follow me, I'll get you there safe, don't you worry.' She slapdashed a kindness of kisses.

'God bless you both,' said Raymond to the world. Then, focusing on the seminarian, 'God bless you, china. Be like me. I'm dyin by degrees, takin my time. And one of these days, I'm gonna start fuckin enjoying it. Ni ni.'

Madeleine wafted him another kiss as she rock-n-rolled the car along the tramlines. She bustled the car across the Victoria Parade intersection, and even as he struggled to keep pace with her, she gave him the impression that she'd leave the old VW behind if it didn't make a better effort to keep up with her. He pushed the monastery car through two sets of red lights to catch her at the top of Punt Road hill. She paused almost absentmindedly at the traffic lights and then slalomed down the other side of the hill to Toorak Road. Keeping up with her was now easy, keeping away from her was more difficult.

As she surged down Punt Road, the lights at Toorak Road were abruptly red. As he braked, she rushed across the lights in a burst of indecision. The police car came out of Toorak Road in a joyful flash of blue. They herded her against the kerb, eventually. The VW came to a stop, brakes slewing, bumper playing tiggy-touch with the police Falcon.

The seminarian was scared for her, terrified for himself, as he sat parked behind the VW, conspicuous to the empty night.

One cop was suddenly leaning down on him, and he hurried the window down and looked up, abjectly cooperative. The cop was young, tall trying tough. 'You with her? Madeleine?'

'Well, yes, sort of. Helping her, you know.'

He was looked over and found guilty. He knew that now was the time to produce his licence, Brother Michael Hannigan, Saint Patrick's Seminary, Balwyn. He was going to shock a Catholic cop.

'Well you'd better look after her, hear me, know what I mean?' The cop folded his tallness down so that he was almost kneeling on the street. 'Make sure you do, see, or I'll come after you, see. She's a friend of a friend of mine, see. Got that, brother?'

The seminarian hadn't got it at all, but he knew the answer. 'Yes. Yes. Yes.'

The policeman tightened his face into a tough silence, but his acne-remembering skin and the cold-sore on his bottom lip placed him many scowls away from Marlon Brando.

He stood up and started to walk away. He turned back. 'Get the picture?' Then he walked tall back to Madeleine's car. 'You'll be right, love. I've taken care of it. Regards to Ralph. See you in jail.'

The police bipped their horn and drove off gentle into their good night.

He walked to the VW when the police had gone, feeling conspicuous, praying that Punt Road was empty of homing members of the monastery auxiliary and hard-nighting parish priests. The window was down and she pulled his face to her in a sloshy kiss with a flash of tongue. 'Follow me and we can dump this car,' with a smile of unkempt invitation, with a smile of friendship ghosting behind it.

They dumped the Volks outside what Madeleine thought was close enough to her friend's house. 'Hard to tell these bloody houses at night. Right street though, so let's go.'

She had taken possession of the monastery car, pushed her lips hard against his neck.

Behind the rampart of St Kilda beach, she smiled at him and gave him a muddled kiss. 'Not very expert are you,' she said kindly.

'I like talking to you.'

She stroked his penis. She looked out to sea.

He struggled to get his penis free.

'I hate the sea. I dunno, but it always seems to be saying goodbye.'

She moved her hand. 'Don't get too excited. Not here. Let's go where we can talk. Got any motel bread?'

He added up his monastery money, and tried to remember how much his parents paid at the motel on their three-monthly visits. He drove to a motel off Fitzroy Street, knowing vaguely that St Kilda was famous for being broad-minded. *Mother Mary, keep my body pure,* but it was hell not knowing.

Madeleine sang quietly 'On the Street Where You Live'. He drove, nervous excited, expecting a police car to pounce on his sin before it was more than a bad thought and an almost-passionate kissing.

'Go on, love, get us a room.'

Licence, did he have to produce his licence – Saint Patrick's Monastery, Balwyn Road?

But the man at the desk showed the friendliness of the late-night lonely. 'Goodday, mate, been cold. Just been reading about the Bogle-Chandler case. Must be a couple of years now, and no joy. I think it was the Russians, myself.' He held up a copy of the *Truth*. 'Probably the same with that President Kennedy. Bloody Catholics. Christ would have had to risen on the first day – like set his alarm clock early – to keep up with them bastards. Want a room?'

The old man patted his bald head, bustled the large ginger cat from his lap and looked at the seminarian with eyes that knew. 'Single, double, twin? Fill in the card.'

The seminarian didn't know the registration of the monastery car, so he made one up, JMJ007. For an address, he gave the street of an uncle who lived in Tumbarumba. Then he panicked, thinking the old man would study the licence plate and know it should be yellow, because he also had an uncle in Tumbarumba. But the old man showed no interest in the registration. 'These dentures'll be the death of me.' Then he looked up, and the seminarian knew some finding-out question was coming. 'You got dentures? No, half your bloody luck. You going to fart-arse round all night?'

After a long pause, the seminarian realised that the last question went to the cat, who was slopping milk over the sides of a sardine can.

'Yes, I've got all my own teeth,' he said, running with the conversation.

'Eight quid'll be the damage, mate. Bet you don't even know what sciatica is?' The old man's nose was red and wide and seemed to stare more than his eyes. 'You can pay in the morning if you want.'

'No, now. I mean, if you don't mind, now. We'll be leaving early.'

The seminarian took his two pounds change and his breakfast menu as the old man settled back to his *Truth* and his cat.

'Enjoy yourself. Room twenty-one. Just thump the telly if it mucks you round.'

Inside the unit, he offered an almost-prayer of thanks that the four loud youths who passed them as he fought the key were not recognisable Young Christian Workers. All night he had expected to turn a corner of his sinning and be confronted with half the Catholics he knew in Melbourne, on the march against evil. He had lost his vision of the Holy Ghost hovering with bright wings and felt he could explain himself better to God than to the president of the monastery auxiliary.

Madeleine put her large white bag in front of the mirror, took out a brush and a half-bottle of Remy Martin brandy. The smell of it reminded him of Moira and their hospital brandy.

'Nice, isn't it, love. Make yourself at home.'

As he sat on the bed, lost for the next rubric, she brushed her red hair and redeemed her lipstick.

He placed his hands on her shoulders.

'You really fancy me, don't you, er, Michael – Mike OK?'

He hated it, but anything was OK, except plump red loveliness.

'It's nice being fancied by a nice boy.'

He kissed the back of her neck and she turned and pecked his cheek.

'Do something for me, Mike.'

The rites had begun.

'Turn on the TV, there's a good love.' She examined the bathroom fittings, delighted that the toilet had been sanitised and the box of Kleenex was new.

'Silly,' she said as she looked at the bright crackle of a deserted TV channel. She found the one channel still alive and sat down in the easy-chair to watch Doris Day wander around Rock Hudson's flat in her anti-erotic pyjamas.

The seminarian wandered twice round the unit, before he knelt down beside her and tried to kiss her breasts.

'Would you get me a brandy, please? Turn the heating on. I love old Rock. I should have got poor old Ray a taxi. Just had the shingles, poor bugger. Lay off, there's a good love,' pushing him away distractedly and picking up her packet of Alpine from the floor.

He tried his pipe. It wouldn't draw.

'Here have one of mine. Fix yourself a brandy.'

A novice at both, he gasped at both.

'Come on, we'll both sit on the bed and watch it together.' She plumped up a pillow for him, and while she watched Doris Day and Rock Hudson, he watched her legs, surprised at their long slimness.

'Lovely, aren't they? I love the way he grabs her and tells her she's silly and then kisses her.'

As Rock Hudson wandered out of his bathroom in a modesty of terry-towelling, the seminarian butted his half-smoked cigarette and said nonchalantly, 'Think I'll have a shower.' 'Good idea,' she said abstractedly, 'Cosy here, isn't it?'

It was one way of finding nakedness. He also found, in the hip pocket of his trousers, his monastery prayer book, *The Little Office of Our Lady*.

Scrubbed clean with motel mini-Palmolive, he came back to bed dressed in a towel. He was cold by the time Doris and Rock were moving slowly into a kiss that proclaimed pre-marital chastity. He knelt down on the bed, stroking her knees, wondering how long he needed to stay there before he could move with courtesy to touching her cunt.

'Lay off, there's a good boy. I'm not some St Kilda tart, you know.' She pushed him away gently. 'Get me another brandy, please.'

She hurried into the toilet, and then called out with a voice obviously seated, 'By the way, what do you do?'

'I study. Accountancy, sort of, I guess.'

'You worried about being called up for Vietnam?'

Too old, and living in a privileged profession, he had never worried about it.

'That bastard Menzies gives me the shits, he does. He'll send more and soon, betcha. Good old Arthur Calwell, one of the few honest bastards left. He doesn't want to send those poor bloody kids to Vietnam. Shit a brick, Menzies just wants to crawl up the arse of that prick Johnson. Jesus,' and the seminarian caught himself bowing again, 'these towels are lovely and soft.'

There was silence from the toilet. The seminarian rearranged his trousers over the chair, because he had noticed that *The Little Office of Our Lady* was pushing up from the hip pocket. From the TV came calls to Light up a Viscount, Brush up Bright with Colgate, Give Generously to Catholic Aid, Myer's Maxi Sale of Minis. Television, like the world, was another country to him. His erection subsided; Doris and Rock had retired to their separate beds.

Madeleine had tied herself into a motel towel, defeating his fantasy of slowly unzipping her red dress, which she now threw over his monastery underpants and hiding *The Little Office of Our Lady*. Her large breasts sat over the top of the towel and he longed to suck them. She sat down on the bed and lit a cigarette. He – six-sistered – was still disappointed out of seeing for the first time a naked woman.

Noel Coward and John Mills served stiff with patriotism and subdued heroism on the ships *In Which We Serve*.

'O good, another film. Isn't this nice, Mike?' She breathed contented smoke at John Mills.

He pulled again at his still-refusing pipe. *This night! what sights you, heart, saw, ways you went!* Father Hopkins, SJ, came discontented and uninvited to his mind. He threw his pipe on the floor and leant across and sucked a breast.

She leant upwards and shrank at the same time. 'Slowly, Mike. I love this film, lovely, silly men being silly about war. I wonder if silly old Ray got home. I'll give Alma a ring tomorrow.' She gave him a peck on the cheek. 'Just a minute, I like this bit. Christ, you are keen. That's nice but I like seeing what happened to Richard Attenborough.'

Into their silence he said, 'You know, when you were just talking about him, I remembered he was made a papal knight no so long ago.'

'Go on, Richard Attenborough?'

'No. Of course not.'

'Not Noel Coward?'

'No. I meant Arthur Calwell.'

'God, are you some sort of religious nut? You're a bloody Catholic, aren't you.'

'Me. No. Well, used to be.'

'Well you still should be. You blokes, well you young blokes, you think you're too clever for the Church. I never miss mass on Sunday. I don't suppose you know any priests, but I've got a special friend called Father Finnegan.'

He was silent for some time.

'You poor bugger, get frightened by religion, do you? You shouldn't be scared of God. I can handle him right. He knows about the flesh. Mary, can't take much of her myself.' Madeleine lay back with her brandy and her cigarette. 'You know what I think, Mike, Mary was born of priests' wanting to fuck. The buggers can forgive themselves for wanting to fuck her. But they can't forgive her for their lust, poor pathetic bastards. Oh hell, they're all right, some of them. Like Father Finnegan I told you about.'

The seminarian listened to a speech by John Mills, whose men listened respectfully. Father Superior didn't listen very much, but his silences loudly gave others almost equal time. Perhaps Madeleine listened.

'The flesh ...' But he couldn't match the loudness of his erection, or formulate his worry.

'God went into a lot of mucking about to become flesh,' she said, stroking his penis and looking at John Mills.

The seminarian's worry was that the Word hadn't become flesh at all. Perhaps the Word had just become words.

'But what I often wonder ...' And then his lust for faith became simply lust.

She looked kindly at him, pulled off his towel, poured some brandy on his penis, licked it off, slid under the blankets and returned to the TV. He hurried into bed with her.

'Get me another drink, there's a good love.'

He brought the drink to bed, spilling it on her belly as he pulled back the sheets.

She dragged the covers back over her. When he grabbed them back and licked her belly, with its soft, small flows of lovely fat and a horizontal scar, he realised that she was rigid as she tried to pull the sheets back over her.

Once safe again beneath the sheets, she offered him her brandy. It scalded again.

'Let's watch some more TV, eh? It's cosy. And tell me about yourself. I love to talk and listen.' She hunched her shoulder as he tried to kiss it but even so smiled at him, wanting him in some other way. 'I'm not a St Kilda whore you know. You know that, don't you?'

'I know. I know that. I wouldn't want you if you were.' His tenderness came out off-key, like most lies.

'Let's have a watch and have a talk.'

He pulled the sheet back, grabbed at her breast, made a quick fumble at her thigh and fucked her.

She heaved up her body and shuddered.

'Was I good? I was good, wasn't I?' She still held the glass of brandy in her hand and a frightened look in her eyes.

'Terrific. You were great, great really.' He pecked her cheek and crept out of bed.

He was already zipped into his trousers when she became aware that the worst was over. 'I was good, wasn't I? You did like me, was I the best?' To his head in his shirt: 'You're not going? You're not, not now.'

'Of course not, don't be silly. You wanted something to eat. We can have something together.'

'That'd be lovely, Mike. We can eat in bed and sit and talk.'

'I'll see if I can find some hamburgers. You're hungry.' He gave her another peck on the cheek and lit an Alpine for her.

She was suddenly confident again and forgiving. She held up her brandy to him. 'That would be cosy, nice.' She looked friendly at him. 'Then we could talk a bit and have a bit of a cuddle and you could tell me about yourself and we could have a drink and watch "Dangerman". I always think he's sexy.'

I want to lick your cunt and have you lick my prick, but words died against the thought.

'Then we could do it again, maybe,' and she smiled at him again.

Though her brown eyes still looked as if they were waiting to be filled with tears, she looked contented as she sat, with her brandy, beneath the motel chocolate-box print, an anywhere autumn countryside. He picked up his wallet from the round tray of teabags and dwarf cornflakes and counted his money, pausing for a moment over his card: *I am a Catholic. In case of accident please call a priest.*

'I was good, wasn't I?' careless now of the answer. 'Better than you've ever had?'

'You were great, you know, really fantastic. Want sauce on your hamburger? You were absolutely terrific. Do you like lettuce? Best ever. Stay warm. You look terrific.'

He leant over and kissed her lips with soft propriety and feeling the joy of her perfume and her body. She hugged her smile into herself. As she snuggled into the pillows and raised her shoulders, her breasts rose above the sheet. He felt sheepish at his shudder of desire.

'Well, I'll be off then. Won't be long. Dim sims OK, or pizza, if I can't manage hamburgers?'

He went to the toilet, pissed, and splashed his face against the sound of a pious voice declaring that 'Every woman needs it ... the confidence of Cool Charm.'

'Won't be long. See what I can get.'

'Lovely, love. It'll be nice eating with you.' She smiled as though she liked him for the first time. She smiled at their setting up house, and she smiled at Dangerman. 'Lovely ... whatever ... you know. My belly's bubbly empty. And some Smith's chips. They're the best. I'll be better next time. Before you go, could you grab me a Kleenex. You will hurry, won't you.'

At the door, he turned back to her. She was now relaxed. Domestic, he walked back and took her red dress and put it on a coathanger in the wardrobe. He tidied, fondlingly, her black bra and panties over the chair. She smiled sideways at him, as though now comfortable about having done her duty to some absent god. Her face had borrowed an uncertain sensuous peace. He wanted to talk to her with a certain sort of love; and then stroke and kiss her breasts and belly, kiss her cunt and fuck her again. He wanted this time to see and know the body he had just fucked, he wanted to make love.

'Dim sims. Pizza. Whatever.' And she was really smiling at him and looking not at all at Dangerman.

He drove to Fitzroy Street, thinking inconsequently of a Hopkins poem, 'The Blessed Virgin compared to the Air we Breathe'. After counting his money, he went to a laminex cafe. He waited patiently as the Italian proprietor waited patiently in front of two take-away hamburgers. The buyers were two prostitutes who were arguing about territorial rights in Robe Street. The blond woman wearing a fur cape, jeans and thongs seemed to be winning. They took their hamburgers and their argument into Fitzroy Street. The seminarian subdued his lust for both of them when he recounted his money. He bought seven dim sims and a packet of Alpine for Madeleine.

Seated alongside seven dim sims and a packet of cigarettes, he drove up Punt Road and then into Victoria Street. Next to a park in Barkers Road, he found a rubbish bin, in which he dumped the cigarettes and the three dim sims that remained from what he had eaten. Already the prayer was coming, sudden yet expected, like a milepost surprised out of the darkness. *O my God, I am heartily sorry,* to the God who was always there. And sorry to Madeleine, watching 'Dangerman', waiting for her hamburgers, wondering why he was so long getting them, with the night alone before her. In the monastery driveway, he cut the motor and let the car roll home. He crept up to his room with his shoes in his hand and went to sleep without having said vespers from *The Little Office of Our Lady*. Instead, he made a few ejaculations: *O most excellent Virgin, obtain forgiveness of all my sins, and the grace of fear and the love of thee.*

O my God, I am heartily sorry. Moira, I am heartily sorry.

However, God was easy to love. But hard to forgive.

1966

T*he Insiders*

*B*ILLY HANNIGAN was another liar. He had been the pride of Slight Street, Elwood, during the Vietnam war because of a photo of him returning to action after, as he wrote, 'having a high time in the low dives of Tokyo'. Though puzzled that the letter bore an Australian stamp, his mother had accepted Billy's explanation about Viet Cong infiltration of the Japanese postal service. She faithfully tattered the photo round the neighbourhood, until Nellie Withers proved that Billy, battled in full dress, was actually leaning against a wall in a lane in Brisbane. Mrs Withers cousin Neville travelled for Rawleighs in Townsville. But he had been to Brisbane, and actually knew the lane. So did the police and many commercial travellers. In fact, if you looked at Billy's wall carefully, with a magnifying glass, it read *Witch's Soap. No Rub. Boil Only.* His mother decided that Billy's 'interpreter', suprisingly blond for Tokyo, was a brazen hussy. Bold as brass, all of them, making it hard for our boys, these Brisbane girls.

Billy still had nightmares about his Vietnam war. He *had* thought it was a stupid war and he *was* scared. His mates at the meatworks thought it might be fun, so he had ducked being a draft-dodger to prove he wasn't a coward. Then AWOL, military police, military prison, pack rape just to show what they thought of pricks who ran away when their mates were getting their arses shot off. He had been quite happy for them to go on killing each other without his help. Billy didn't have a good war and his family no longer trusted him.

Except for his niece Margaret, who was six years old.

'Of course you can't go swimming. Don't be a stupid girl, you know how you are.' Her grandmother, still in her pink chenille dressing-gown, was wiping down the pink laminex bench, floating toast crumbs and molten cornflakes and onion peels into a Safeway bag. 'No swimming. I won't have it,' she said to the Safeway bag. 'Not for you. Besides, the weather,' and she waved her blue Chux cloth towards the clouds shouldering their way across the sky beyond the one-armed apricot tree that stood against the kitchen window.

On the other side of the room, Maureen, Margaret's mother, was slicing tomatoes on the bench beneath the picture of the Sacred Heart. Next to her, Billy made another cross on the *Sun* form guide.

'I'll take her to Luna Park,' said Billy at the racing guide. Where his niece was concerned, it was even money on whether his sister or his mother gave the orders. The Saturday morning lapsed into the kitchened sounds of summer salad-making.

Mrs Hannigan took her corned beef off the stove. 'An hour for every pound and an hour extra, that should do it.' She handed another tomato to Maureen, then returned to slicing another onion on the bread board.

'Margaret!' Mrs Hannigan waved her best knife at her granddaughter, and the auburn head came up from using a piece of stras to mop up some tomato sauce on the bench.

'Look, do take her out, Billy, to Luna Park. But none of this big dipper stuff. You know what she's like.'

'Like me, that's what she's like,' said Billy, transferring his pencil to the unused side of his mouth.

'Then God help her.'

Margaret's mother didn't say a word, but lined up her slices of tomato as if thinking of offering them to the Sacred Heart. But when Billy said 'Luna Park, sure thing,' she did look happier.

As the Elwood tram ground its way along St Kilda Road, with the Saturday afternoon passengers bare of newspapers and work-weariness, Billy and Margaret watched a father and grown-up son sitting on the other side of the aisle, mixed and matched in yellow rain capes, Safeway bags, white sandshoes and other-place eyes. Their bodies were stiff, and they talked ahead, never looking at each other.

'Don't stare,' said Billy when he had finished, and was unrolling the form guide.

'I like them. They're different. Trams are better than the big dipper. Dippers are full of the same people. I tore Tony's picture this morning.'

'Well I scribbled on a few of your mother's in my day. Mind you, she was a lousy drawer. Why did you tear Tony's?'

'Because I was miserable.'

'Well I hope you said you were sorry.'

'Well, Tony said if I wasn't too miserable to tear it, I wasn't too miserable to say sorry. So I gave him my purple icypole, only had a few licks taken out of it.'

Behind them, an old man was talking affectionately and articulately to himself. 'A preponderance of pseudo-intellectual pseudo-socialist peaceniks, but you've got them fucked old chap,' and he chuckled.

'He's speaking French, I think. How long till Luna Park?'

'A few minutes,' as Billy replaced a cigarette, unlit, himself burnt by the connie's stare and the thought that Luna Park was smiling a mile behind them.

'It was minutes to go hours ago.' Margaret stood up on the seat and looked out the window. On the oval of Wesley College, an Italian-looking man was throwing a boomerang. As she stared back at the wheeling boomerang, Margaret swallowed her chewing gum. Billy wasn't having a good day with the form guide.

'Does it really wrap round your lungs? The chewy I mean.'

'Of course not. Goes out through your gut.'

'Into the dunny?'

A woman with a scatter of blue through her hair lowered her *Age* Saturday supplement to glare at this indecency.

At Flinders Street the two men in yellow got off, precision-marching towards the station, both balanced by a shopping bag in each hand, both of them still staring and talking at the middle distance. In profile, the older man's face was an exact promise of the younger man's in twenty years time.

Margaret watched them. 'Pity, I liked them. It's going to be a happen day.'

'Happy?'

'No, silly. Good things happening.'

The tram passed a woman wheeling a pram, her shoes tied to its handle. Families trailing children and children dragging families. A man in heavy army boots was buying flowers outside the town hall.

'Doesn't he look funny?'

And Billy didn't know whether 'he' was the flower-buyer or the man next to him selling biros under the supervision of his guide dog.

Margaret started singing quietly, ignoring the stares and nudges of four boys, happy in their drink and tight jeans.

> *Everybody knows*
> *that daddy picks his nose,*
> *rubs it in the dirt*
> *and eats it for dessert.*

Without pause.

> *Firecracker firecracker*
> *boom boom boom,*
> *firecracker firecracker*
> *boom boom boom.*
> *The boys have the muscles,*
> *the teachers have the brains,*
> *the girls have the sexy legs,*
> *so we win the game.*

Billy had given up his form guide and was studying the sign above him: *In the interests of fellow travellers, please refrain from spitting, which is prohibited by by-law 763a. Penalty £5.* A sign almost as old as the tram. He was softly embarrassed. Margaret sang on. Tuneless.

'What would you like to eat when we get there?'

'Fairy floss and chips.'

They got off at the Collins Street tram sort-out. The old man paused next to them, adjusting his cravat. 'Amicitia shall prevail against eros and the concupiscence of the prurient, eh, and fuck 'em all, eh,' he whispered to Billy.

'Sure thing, mate, every time.'

'I didn't know you could speak French.'

'One of the many things I picked up in Vietnam,' and Billy nudged his niece, who knew him.

In their new tram, Margaret asked again, 'How long till Luna Park now, Billy?' and then she started to sing again, as though she didn't expect an answer.

> *Yankle Doody*
> *stayed at home*
> *cooking for his pony.*
> *He stuck spaghetti in his pot*
> *and called it macaroni.*

Billy approved of singing in trams, but Melbourne didn't. Margaret was comfortable about being stared at and she liked to stare back. She looked with green eyes unblinking until the other passengers surrendered and showed a sudden interest in the window-shoppers lusting after the over-priced fashions in Georges' windows. They even stared at the name-plates of over-priced doctors. Always glancing back at the kid who kept looking them over. And at the bloke who kept returning to his form guide, as though he didn't know her. Enough of being stared at. He didn't want people to think she was a precocious brat, which she sometimes was. But not today, just alert and oblivious, believing that trams and the world were good places to be in.

They got off the tram.

As they walked towards Victoria Parade, Billy explained his idea of tipping streets up on end. They rearranged the city and

Margaret tumbled Saint Patrick's cathedral down into Collins Street to give people something else to look at as they went round it. She was then absorbed by the men in dark suits and scrubbed up, grown-up schoolboy faces, hurrying with their dapper brown bags towards the Masonic Temple.

'Are they catching a train? They look funny, sort of.'

'They're not funny, love, they're Masons.'

He was saved from his unhelpful explanation when they moved up to Victoria Parade.

'What's that?' and he pulled her back from the path of two fiercely bearded joggers as she pointed.

'That's Saint Vincent's Hospital, the big Catholic hospital.'

'Why don't I go there? I'm a Catholic. You're not a very good one though.'

'The Children's is your hospital. You like it there.'

'That old grey one, what's that?'

'That's the special part of Saint Vincent's. For rich sick Catholics … look we won't go to Luna Park just now, I want to drop in on a few friends of mine first.'

'Hello, Billy. Long time no see.' A tall young man in a clerical suit was coming out of the hospital for rich Catholics.

'Well, if it isn't our sainted cousin, Brother Michael? What are you doing in this part of the world? Visiting the poor?'

'Yes, actually. Visiting Father Superior. He's just had a hernia operation from playing golf. Who's this then? I'm Michael.'

He gave up studying Margaret. 'Is she yours?'

'No, she's Maureen's. You remember my little sister, Maureen?'

'I sure do. She gave me a hard time at school.'

'I've been meaning to visit you at that monastery of yours, Brother Michael. But you know how it is. Besides, monasteries and me don't quite fit, you know what I mean.'

'I understand, Billy. I heard you were just back from Vietnam. I hope you didn't have too bad a time of it.'

'Nobody has a good time in Vietnam, especially the Vietnamese.'

'Sorry, Billy, I only meant ... well, you know what I mean ...'

'Come on, Margaret, we've got to get going. Lovely to see you, Brother Michael. See you in jail.'

As they stood on the corner of Brunswick Street, Margaret turned to watch the clerical young man walk away. 'Who's that funny man?'

'That's our very special cousin. He's going to be a priest. He's the pride of the family. He's not an outsider like us.'

'I think I like us better.'

After lighting his first cigarette for the day, the giving-up delay providing even more pleasure than a breakfast cigarette, he hurried her down to Gertrude Street, home to his pub.

He could see her startled by the noise as they entered the Champion. It was still early afternoon, but the juke-box and the races were going. He found a laminex table near the lounge door and sat her down on the ply and tubular chair. She sat quietly singing.

> *My lover gave me an apple,*
> *My lover gave me a pear,*
> *My lover gave me fifty cents*
> *and took me to the fair.*
>
> *I gave him back his apple,*
> *I gave him back his pear,*
> *I gave him back his fifty cents*
> *and took his underwear.*

Billy stood in the small group round the bar, listening to the conversation and noticing the band-aid in the drip tray and the barmaid's Scholl's sandals next to the Johnny Walker. Both men and women, at home, talking.

'Me gran died last week. Jeez, she was a great one, that was. Loved us all, you know that? Bloody amazing.'

'Christ, she kept me going the whole weekend. Couldn't get enough of it.'

'Liar, shit, you're always lying through your teeth, you are.'

'Not me, mate, not me. Nothing like a bit of the old Collingwood for a good fuck. Black and white all through the night.'

Billy looked across at Margaret. Her green eyes were quick and enjoying. She was pushing her long hair back, trying to readjust the flat aqua hairclip that proudly matched her dress. She smiled at a woman in a red dress sitting at the table next to her. The woman smiled back and got up and fixed Margaret's clip. In the far corner, the juke-box followed 'Love Me Do' with 'We Shall Overcome'. Billy sighed peacefully at the usualness of it all. A man wearing Carlton football socks and jumper, shorts and sandshoes, stood at the doorway and stared with the same discovery that glowed every time Billy saw him. He was pushed aside by two young policemen, who strode confidently and disapprovingly through the bar, as though looking for whoever was responsible for all this mess in the living room they had just vacuumed. Into the silence came Bill Collins from Flemington announcing 'I reckon Higgins on the favourite has just got up to win', and Margaret from the table near the door,

> Yesterday,
> All my troubles seemed so far away,
> Now it looks as though they're here to stay,
> Oh, I believe in yesterday.

'Who's she belong to?' the tall policeman asked the barmaid. 'Me, Sergeant.' Billy tried to look resolute, and sweated.

'Constable. And get her out of here. It's a bad place for kids.'

And the two policemen walked off, lords of creation, watching wary over all their world like the good guys from 'Homicide'.

Billy carried back a pot and a Coke. The woman in the red dress was fixing Margaret's hairclip.

'You've got beautiful hair, love.'

'I know.' Looking up, appraising. 'So have you. I love red hair.' The woman smiled at Billy.

'See ya, love,' and went back to her table and her empty glass.

A fat bald man slid his beer onto their table and himself onto a chair. 'Hello, Billy, how's tricks? I've come to chat with your girl.'

'Hi, Curly. What've you been doing since you got out?'

'Keeping out of the way of those pricks who were just in here. This 'n' that. Nothing much. Cheers.'

A man in tight jeans walked past, fighting his zip up. Margaret watched, interested.

'What's new, then?' asked Billy, looking round as if he didn't care about the answer.

A fat woman held the door open and yelled, 'Anyone seen Donny? You can tell the black bastard he's done it this time. I'm really after the shit this time. Let him know from me, will ya.' She smiled, leant over, took a swig of Billy's beer and left.

Eddies of laughs, and shifted glasses and 'Sure thing, Doreen,' 'You get the cunt, Doreen'.

'I'll get you one, Curly,' and Billy went to the bar.

'And what's your name, love?' Curly was asking Margaret and waving to a woman at the cigarette machine.

When Billy came back, Margaret was at the next table, listening to the woman in red. As he went to sit down, he felt the elastic on his underpants die and felt the pants slide in slow motion over his backside.

'Lovely to see you again, Curly. Fact is, I've got a problem.'

'Who hasn't, mate, who hasn't?'

'Look, it's like this. Fact is ... I'll give it to ya straight,' and Billy paused for another cigarette and some inspiration.

At a table on the other side of the doorway, three women were arguing. All were different versions of blond and different versions of fifty.

'Look, Marge, I can look after my own man. He doesn't bloody need you to look after him.' As an afterthought she turned to a potbellied man in PMG overalls, who stood blinking and irrelevant near the door. 'You don't need her, do you, Morrie love?' she asked and didn't wait for an answer.

'Come on, Rita, you couldn't give a stuff if the bastard starved. Pies 'n' pasties is all he ever gets from you, and frickin cold ones at that.'

The woman between Rita and Marge drank her beer and smiled an empty toast at both her friends.

'Essendon forever,' shouted the man in the Carlton football jumper, who was again standing guard at the door next to the PMG man.

'Shut up, you two,' the PMG man said to the women. 'I'm trying to listen to that bloody race in Sydney.'

'And I'm trying to read,' yelled a small grey-haired woman, holding up a Zane Grey western, *Mad Dog Shoot-out*. 'It's the Adelaide race, you dumb bastard.'

'Well I was gonna bet on that too, wasn't I?'

Billy bought Curly another pot. 'Look, just until Wednesday, even Monday. Honest, I'll ...'

Margaret was listening to the woman in red. Five girls swayed at the juke-box, two white girls ungainly, looking over their shoulders, the other three oblivious, enjoying themselves.

Rita's face crumpled into surprised life as Marge thumped a backhander into her cheek, the rings drawing blood.

'Naughty, naughty,' said the man in the Carlton football jumper.

'Smash her one, Rita, she's an up-herself bitch.'

The PMG man whined, 'Just wanta listen to the races.'

At Margaret's table, her friend put her head on her slim hands, and slid gracefully into sleep. From behind the bar came the barman-bouncer, a ginger man, with a faint hope of a moustache and a glowering belly. He pushed Margaret's red-haired friend awake.

'You're trouble, you are, you bitch Maddie. And you're heading for it too, kid.'

He pulled the woman awake. He dragged her up. His foot on her backside, he pushed her into Gertrude Street and followed her.

'You slut, you crawling bitch!' Rita was now wiping a sliver of blood from her cheek. 'Come on outside, come on, I'm gonna do you,' she screeched at Marge.

'We're all friends here,' said her friend.

'I'm jest trying to read,' said the little woman, shaking her Zane Grey.

From the juke-box, the Rolling Stones frenzied into silence and Petula Clark was surprised into a downtown song.

Billy was explaining to Curly, who didn't trust him. Margaret was looking at the door for her friend.

The ginger bouncer was back picking up glasses randomly. 'Pack it in you two,' he said to Marge and Rita, kindly, and their friend put pots in front of them.

As Margaret looked towards Billy, her body grabbed itself rigid. Green eyes heaved up, her face more than ever a startle of freckles. She banged to the floor, her head thudding on the red cement, next to a crack with browny spit in it. The glass shattering beside her. Her head plunging back as if to follow the rolling eyes. Deep from her throat came a twisted cry. Her head pummelled the floor, her aqua hairclip spun away. Her arms jerked to escape. Her face rushing the muscles round in a twitching search for repose. Her breath lurched and her eyes were intent on something far away.

The world breathed silent. Billy could hear his cigarette burning. The three black girls who had been dancing knelt around Margaret, one of them stroking her face. A sigh of silence went through the bar. Then busy talk and busy thirst resumed, Bill Collins' race talk incongruous against a 'Whiter Shade of Pale'. A blond man rolled off the two chairs he had been sleeping on, but did not awake.

'Can't a man listen to the races in peace?' the PMG man complained.

A boy with tattooed ears pushed open the door. 'How's it goin', shagger?' he asked one of his mates.

'Essendon forever.'

Billy picked up his niece, amazed as always at the soft, sure aftersleep. Margaret's woman was standing at the doorway, her graceful legs uncertain on stiletto heels, a tear of blood sliding down the left side of her face. The youngest of the Aboriginal girls came up with Margaret's aqua hairclip. The redheaded woman deftly pinned back her hair. She stroked Margaret's cheek gently. To Billy's surprise, the girl opened her eyes.

'Hello, it's been lovely,' said Margaret.

'It sure has, love. We must do it again.'

'See ya, Madeleine. Thanks,' said Billy.

Sick of trams, Billy took a taxi back to Elwood, by-passing Luna Park.

seven

*M*argarita

*F*ATHER BROWN died screaming against God.

Brother Hannigan went to Sydney for the Latin teachers' conference feeling more guilty than usual. He came away feeling more guilty than ever.

It happened this wise, in a year when Giovanni Battista Montini was Pope in Rome, when Lyndon Johnson was pope in Washington, when Harold Holt was the new pope in Canberra and Arthur Augustus Calwell was the Anti-Christ, when John Coleman was coach of Essendon.

Before going on the annual retreat, Brother Hannigan had found Wittgenstein's *Tractatus Logico-Philosophicus* in the seminary library. From a Cambridge philosopher's introduction he had learnt *Don't ask the meaning, ask the use,* and *the meaning of a statement is the method of its verification.* He had become obsessed with the problem of knowledge; it was safer than the problem of sin. He had learnt that a mumbled confusion about whether we can really know gave one the status of seminary philosopher. Father Superior, as eagle-eyed as God, discovered him reading Wittgenstein and pointed out kindly that Wittgenstein was a forbidden book and must be returned to the Fathers' library immediately. But after twenty pages of bewilderment, Hannigan had learnt a method of organising guilt, which was a form of holiness. He had gone into the retreat with an epistemology of sin.

1.1   Why am I always having bad thoughts?
1.2   Why am I always having bad thoughts (the other sort)

[144]

about Brother Milton, who was more dedicated to Christ than I am – even if he did disappear on the monastery's second-best bike?

1.3   Who put the glass in Father Superior's football boots?

1.4   Why do I keep watching the blond, big-breasted girl walk in stiletto heels down the monastery drive on her short-cut to the station? (She always wears a mini skirt.)

1.5   Does God exist? No, why am I not more positive about what I know – don't I? – for a fact?

1.6   When I am walking down the monastery drive saying the rosary, why do I keep looking for the marks of stiletto heels?

1.7   Did Mary know that Christ was God? (I think Father Superior knows the answers – from studies in Rome – but won't tell us.) Perhaps that's my problem, asking the wrong questions.

1.8   Must read more. I was surprised at my ignorance (and must admit to embarrassment – not good, shows lack of humility) in discovering that Christ did not come out through the vagina, but just appeared.

1.9   Why do I keep touching myself?

1.10 Should I continue praying for Marilyn Monroe and Elizabeth Taylor?

1.11 Maybe Jean Simmons?

1.12 Who removed the coverings pasted over the Greek statues in Breasted's *Ancient Times*?

1.13 I will pray to find out who prowls our monastery at midnight. Not one of us, please God?

1.14 Should I pray more for Kevin Milton?

2.1   I realise that 1.3, 1.7 and 1.12 are really none of my business, but I think it is all right to pray about things that are none of my business.

2.2   I will keep the girl who has big breasts and stiletto heels in my prayers.

The retreat passed as usual, a week of silence and doubt, and the dutifully boring talks. But in the joyful, depressing hours walking the monastery path beside the woodheap, Hannigan discovered that God's goodness exceeded – as usual – his own badness, just. So he ended the retreat – as usual – with a rush of joy and resolution. The resolutions were typed out stutteringly on the Adler portable, with the pressing ones underlined in red.

I can't, O Christ, you must.

Now, I begin.

I will be devoted and prayerful at Mass and <u>enthusiastic</u> about <u>singing</u> and praying with my brothers.

I will look well ahead, especially on free days, when I am <u>having fun</u> (a tendency I will watch prayerfully) and make sure that I have time to say the Holy Office reverently and prayerfully, even if it means abandoning my Brothers in a game of Five hundred.

I will <u>listen</u> attentively, to God and others.

I will praise those not present. Especially Kevin Milton.

I will be most careful in matters of purity:

– What I read and talk about; would I do this if Christ were with me. His mother? My mother?

– Would a priest do this? Should a priest <u>be seen</u> doing this? Thinking this?

– I will be most careful, circumspect, cautious in <u>all</u> <u>matters of women</u>.

I will at all times observe modesty of the eyes, keeping my eyes downcast whenever practical (practicable?), <u>except</u> when walking down the avenue after seeing that blond girl with the stiletto heels. I will not think about her breasts ever ever again.

I will not ever again touch myself, let alone masturbate ever again.

I will return to the practice of making ejaculations

several times each hour, more often in times of crisis.
I will not criticise, ever, nor grumble, ever.
I will look hard for the good qualities in others,
imaginatively.
I will abandon my ambition to study in Rome, to
become a famous Catholic novelist. I will stop reading
Graham Greene on the quiet.
I will stop arguing for shorts for Schancks.
I will keep praying for Madeleine, but stop imagining her.

Brother Hannigan sat on the woodheap and read his
resolutions to God and BA Santamaria. BA had spent the
week being puzzled by the seminarians' refusal to play with
anyone but God. Brother Hannigan talked to BA: 'Christ is
all; the priest is another Christ, a man chosen from among
men to preach the gospel to the poor, to restore the broken-
hearted. Christ can do it, I can't. Humility is the key. We must
take on the mind and heart of Christ. We must be all things
to all men.' BA barked. The girl in stiletto heels walked past
them.

Measuring out his life in teaspoons of holiness, Brother
Hannigan felt his cup overflowing after the retreat. He kept
warning himself against enjoying the coming trip to Sydney,
which was a city famous for its worldliness. After chatting to
God and BA Santamaria about his resolutions for a better
world, he had gone up to his room and written to Father
Brown, who was in Saint Vincent's Hospital.

Father Brown, gentle confessor, the speedy rattle of rosary
beads from the back of the chapel, old in holiness and jokes
and rosaries. Father Brown, who was slightly deaf, and often
talked loudly in the confessional: 'Did you say you touched
yourself or someone else?' Father Brown, who was so
perceptive: 'You're not so worried about offending God,
Michael,' (he never bothered to call his sons 'Brother' and
didn't play anonymity in the confessional), 'you're worried

about offending yourself. You offend yourself by not being as perfect as you think you are. Join the club. Say a prayer for me. I remember you every day at mass. You're on fire all right, Michael, and that's good. But I'm not sure if you're burning with God or burning with yourself. I'll think of your fires when I say a mass for you.'

Hannigan longed with a sort of rage to be able to offer that blessing: 'I'll remember you in my mass.' He knew by faith that all masses were equal, but Father Brown's mass was exceptionally equal. Even though he sometimes turned to the seminarian assisting him at one of the side altars – Father Brown was considered too erratic for the main altar – and asked, 'Have I done the consecration yet, have I said the words?' Father Brown was casual about making God, whereas Father Smythe always got stage-fright. '*H-H-Hoc est enim c-c-c-c-orpus m-m-m-m-eum.*' Brother Hannigan wondered about translating Vatican II vernacular hesitations into English. '*For this is my body*' did not sound like transubstantiation when it was spoken in stuttered English. Father Brown's quick, easy Latin sounded like God on the job. Father Brown stayed with the old dispensation, searching through the holy biographies in his greasy breviary, groping with disjointed eyes for the latest on a saint who dies punctually every year.

Hannigan wrote to Father Brown.

Dear Father,

Just a quick note at the end of the retreat (I've got Father Superior's permission). I'm sure you'll soon be better and glad they didn't put you in the hospice. I remember you in my prayers every day, practically. I know you will do the same for me, thank you, Father. I hope the doctors and nurses are treating you well, especially the nurses.

You will be pleased to know that I have thought a lot about your advice (not wanting to become too saintly too soon).

I am now much happier in my vocation and am determined to give my life in the service of Christ and the Gospel.

You'll be pleased to hear that I am no longer touching myself (one of my retreat resolutions, there are many others).

Get better soon, if not earlier. I thought you might be interested in the latest poem I have written (I don't suppose you know the work of Father Gerard Manley Hopkins, SJ?). I know you are very devoted to Our Lady.

> O Mary, sister of sinners,
> Your sadness trembles into joy,
> Your home, your husband, friends,
> And any mother's wonder at her boy.
>
> Your nerves sing like a power saw,
> You worry at the mystery of your son,
> And even when you cannot pray,
> Wife and husband form a dauntless one.
>
> Mary, when your patience frays,
> And God escapes behind your household care,
> Joseph stands as a sign of God,
> And soothes your faltering prayer.
>
> Teach, Mary, kindness in your boredom,
> To love through family and every friend,
> To find our God in every man,
> As you did in the end.

I had thought to add 'every woman' in the second-last line, but 'woman' doesn't scan very well. I feel that this poem fits the spirit of Vatican II, with its discovery of the laity and women. After all, Saint Joseph was a layman, and Mary a woman. They do deserve, their proper place, don't they, Father, and it's our job as priests and religious to give them their due, in the spirit of Vatican II.

Get well, soon, Father. I pray for you every day, practically.

Yours sincerely,
Michael Hannigan, MOM.

PS I'm sure you haven't forgotten that it's Brother Alfonso's anniversary.
PPS Do you think I should send this poem to the Advocate. *I realise that publishing can be vanity, but also we must not hide our light under a bushel, must we, Father. PPPS Father Gerard Manley Hopkins had the same problem as me. I mean about publishing, not touching himself.*

Hannigan had in fact forgotten Brother Alfonso's anniversary until Brother Williams had broken the retreat silence to remind him.

Benito Alfonso, twenty-two years old, slim, bubbling Filipino, expert at basketball and laughter. Dead. Suddenly. A year ago.

A child of the slums of Manila, he had spent some of his first plane ride – the trip to Australia – eating a bowl of cornflakes one by one from his fingers and drinking the milk. His loves were open and therefore embarrassing.

He had died on them without Father Superior's permission. A year ago, Brother Hannigan had looked into the open coffin that stood before the altar. Six candles flicked their light onto the face of peace. He could not pray. Into death, as into life, the words would not come.

'I love Australia, you know, I love our Order, I love being here. Gee, I'm lucky, mate.' He had said that two weeks before he died, as they sat on the cliff below the holiday house at Cape Schanck. Then, as darkness brooded on the water, he added: 'But gee, Brother Michael, I miss my mum, don't you?' Then he had gone back to the house to be joyful at a game of Five hundred.

Hannigan too missed his mother, his father, his six sisters, but it seemed impolite to God to mention it. But then, leaving home at the age of twelve made forgetting to mention it a habit. So, in the reluctantly fading heat, he went and sat on Brother Alfonso's now settled grave.

Almost a year ago he had written to Brother Alfonso's mother, telling her how happy her son had been in the seminary, how much they had all admired him. He had written 'loved him' and then wrote another version, feeling 'admired' was safer. Now he sat in the silence of Benny's grave, with the magpies carolling in the gum trees around the monastery cemetery. I'm sorry, I'd forgotten. I'm sorry, I never told your mother how much you missed her. I never told her that we – I – loved you. But then I never told you either. And he prayed for Brother Bernard in the cemetery in Eden.

That night, he wrote to his mother and father and six sisters and told them how much he loved them. But then he decided not to place it in the pile of unsealed letters left outside Father Superior's room for reading before posting.

When he lay in bed that night, he went over the story of his life, trying to improve it. The real story never seemed as good as the story he wrote of himself in his carefully typed retreat notes.

Mosquitoes came. Sleep did not come. He slipped on shirt and trousers, and took a barefoot illegal walk down the avenue. It was a night of hot stars. *Look at the stars! look, look up at the skies! O look at all the fire-folk sitting in the air!* Father Superior approved of poetry in much the same way as he approved of sunsets and stars. They proved the existence of God, but in rather an extravagant way, apt to be misunderstood by lay people and Protestants. And Father Hopkins, being a Jesuit, was a bit racy in his imaginings, and used funny words.

Tonight the busy stars weren't talking about God. As he walked, Brother Hannigan longed for his ordination, when he could have a certainty of faith and hand it out, when he could walk the avenue on hot nights, legally and in thongs, so his feet would not be rasped by gravel. As he stood at the monastery gate, he thought of his thong-wearing cousins, who had visited on the day before the retreat. They had insisted on calling him 'Brother Michael', which he enjoyed and hated. He could not confess that he envied their growing up with Buddy Holly and the Crickets, with Elvis Presley; and now with the Beatles whose name he had seen misspelt on the beach at Cape Schanck.

In a rush of disobedience, he walked outside the monastery gates, thinking of a cousin's black-haired girl-friend. Thinking of Marilyn Monroe dancing to Robert Mitchum, of Bella Darvi disrobing for Edmund Purdom, in the last films he had seen before entering the novitiate. With permission from the local curate, who spent a great deal of time discussing vocations with pubescent girls. *Lord, burn our hearts with the fire of the Holy Spirit.*

Obedience of mind and heart, submission of will, that was the path to holiness, Hannigan told the unheeding stars, as he turned towards home. Father Superior was God right here on the ground, he told his disobedient erection. He started to march rather than stroll back to the monastery.

Two people walked whispering out of the night and almost knocked him over. Even in the moonlight, he recognised the girl with the stiletto heels. O God, the fast-disappearing back was – couldn't be – Jesus, was that Brother Koenig?

The somebody tall, with an almost-familiar back, was lost in the darkness. No, not Brother Koenig, as the back moved away, and, with it, a little bit of God. Hannigan removed the gravel from between his toes and frog-marched his mind to Our Lady, Refuge of sinners. Stuttering his way towards the monastery, he listed her unusual feasts: Our Lady of Health (Jan 1), Our Lady of the Pillar (Jan 2), Our Lady of Iron (July 6), Our Lady of the Hot Oven (Sexagesima Sunday), Our Lady of the Silver Feet (Sept 20); and, on reaching Our Lady's rose garden that led up to the chapel, he had also reached Brigitte Bardot in silver sandals, Maria Schell having her feet kissed in *The Brothers Karamazov*, John Donne starting love's mysterious progress from the toes.

He stood supervised by the statue of Saint Joseph. He thought of going up to his room and belting himself with the leather thongs of his discipline, but that was a Friday morning observance, and he would be going further against the spirit of holy obedience by hurting himself too often. Hearing more movement coming down the avenue, he dived behind the liquid amber that stood guard at Saint Joseph's back.

He stood troubled by sex and disobedience and God's absence. He tried Saint Jerome's method of driving away bad thoughts. But placing himself in the midst of the dances of the Roman ladies only conjured up Catullus and Lesbia. *Give me a thousand kisses.* A bustle of noise behind the cypress on the other side of the avenue brought more Roman ladies dancing into his mind. And body. He rustled up good thoughts from Saint Jerome: *Woman is the devil's gateway, the path of wickedness, the scorpion's dart, in sum a dangerous species.* Saint Joseph was looking down the rose garden to Our Lady who was guarding the other end. Would Saint Joseph, virgin father, have agreed with Tertullian that woman was *a temple built over a sewer*?

He sat down beneath the godless stars, beneath the worn toes of Saint Joseph, to wait out the rustle of sex in the nearby tree. Settling his bum comfortably on the grass, he thought more good thoughts. *God, having been a man, knows the minds and hearts of men, though he never suffered an evil thought. The brothers should always remember their own weakness. Therefore, always with the Mother of God in mind, let them avoid the company of women, abstain from all familiarity with them, however virtuous they might seem, keep their eyes from their bodies, however unattractive, guard against their useless visits and frivolous conversations …* The words of Giovanni Buongiorno, Father Founder, left Saint Joseph unimpressed, and the stars. And wandering God and Brother Hannigan, who now braved the soundless monastery grounds.

He hid behind Saint Joseph as headlights swept up the avenue. Hannigan had an impression of Father Superior sitting tall behind the wheel of the monastery car. When silence breathed again, Hannigan crept into the starlight. He stood, breathing in deep thoughts of the motherhood of Mary, but was overcome, surprised and frightened, by a flood of thoughts about the irrelevance of God and Father Superior. Temporarily. His mind zigged and zagged towards Saint Joseph and Our Lady outstaring each other through the night and through eternity.

As Hannigan scratched his left foot on the gravel he heard movement again from the cypress. This time he was going to outface the sexual violators of monastery grounds. Standing firm, he found himself nose to nose with Millicent, the second-best milker in the monastery herd.

He needed God, not cows. The stars had been fidgetty and useless. He knew God was in the chapel, the prisoner of the tabernacle craving visitors. As sacristan, he knew that one of the spare chapel keys was held by the statue of the Sacred Heart beneath the Judas tree in front of the chapel. The key was kept in Christ's right hand, the one that kept his exposed heart from falling into the bed of blood lilies. As he was probing for the key, BA Santamaria came sniffing through the darkness. Together they entered the chapel, and to hell with the rules.

Brother Hannigan sat in the front seat. BA sat before the altar, directly beneath the tabernacle. Peace seeped through the seminarian. He felt close to something, to everything. He felt a frightening, reassuring sense of the irrelevance of everything. As BA yawned and scratched himself, Hannigan felt the joy of waiting for God. The sanctuary lamp glowed its small, demanding light. He felt the wanting loneliness of porters at welcoming hotels. He heard someone moving at the back of the chapel, and knew that God or some other friend was wandering in. Light soaked into his body, as his soul watched, distant. Then darkness, God, mauled him unsurprised to the floor.

Coming back to the world, he was unsurprised at the throbbing of his head, at the world demanding he notice it again. BA, hovering above him, seemed the natural order of things. What was surprising was the now lighted chapel and Brother Williams smiling, anxious above him.

'You've had another fit. You've been praying too hard.'

'What the hell are you doing here?' Hannigan was surprised at his own aggressiveness.

'Nothing much. Just getting away. I often do.'

Hannigan wished for the solitude of sleep. 'Get away from what, for God's sake?'

'Hells bells, I don't know. From everything, I guess. Father Superior. BA, God. Myself, yeah, myself, I guess. Know what I mean?'

Hannigan was beginning to. He allowed Brother Williams to see him up to his room. On the landing, beneath the statue of the Little Flower, they heard steps behind them on the darkened stairs. The light went on. Father Superior was two-at-a-timing his way up. Tall and impeccable in his clerical suit, his dark red hair neatly in place, he looked morning fresh, as he always did. He was eternally in a dignified hurry, Father Superior, so it sometimes seemed as if he had sent his legs on ahead of him.

Now he turned and looked for a moment in stillness at two of his subjects caught in flagrant breach of monastery rules. Hannigan expected a blast. Then he realised, as often before, why this man, who counted God among his friends, who even sometimes hinted that God could be called mate, say when talking to laybrothers and women, was loved by all.

Father Superior smiled at them. He was very fierce in his preaching about smiling, at the same time pointing out the dangers of smiling at women and laybrothers. Smiling now, he stood close to them, breathing on them, steaming open their secrets. 'Out on the prowl, you two? Caught in the act.'

Behind the two seminarians Saint Thérèse seemed to be rustling her famous roses and about to let a few petals drop.

'I'll have to report you to Father Provincial when he comes over from Adelaide next week. And besides, you're nunquam duoing, so I might have to bring you back to earth by grounding you.'

Brother Hannigan could well cope with an afternoon spent reading instead of a sixty-mile ride on pre-Vatican II bikes, but a chat with Father Provincial was a matter of unholy fear. At worst, it could mean having your ordination postponed. Hannigan had already been waiting two years for Father Superior's friends in the Vatican to cast upon the waters their blessing on his epilepsy.

Father Superior was at the top of the stairs. He moved so quickly and so spiritually. He turned to them again. 'Come on, you two, get to bed. I was only joking. But, Brother Williams, don't forget you have to see me tomorrow about that other matter.'

Father Superior had a sense of humour. Or so the seminarians humbly believed, understanding his need to keep it for an audience that mattered.

'What other matter?' Hannigan asked Williams, when they stood alone again in the Greater Silence.

'You wouldn't understand, Mike. Old Joe's had a few.'

'You can't say that!'

'Of course I can, if it's true.'

'Well his second name might be Joseph, but you can't call him that till you're ordained.'

'No, I meant you could smell it … O hell, you're hopeless. Go to bed.'

Back in his room, Hannigan stood at the window, outstaring the stars, still hoping for God. He heard the door of the next room open and close. It was Brother Koenig's room. BA, locked in the chapel, issued a muffled bark.

Hannigan sat down at his desk in his pyjamas, mismatched with a striped red top and pale blue bottoms, slightly stained at the crotch. To strengthen his resolve, he had read again the thoughts of Father Founder and Father Superior's quotations about motherhood from Adolf Hitler, who had after all started life as a Catholic. To strengthen his faith, he read twenty pages of the letters of Simone Weil, mystical almost-Catholic Jew. He went to bed convinced that he would soon convince himself that holiness and therefore happiness were just a few more weeks of prayer away.

But the night had been too busy with surprises for sleep. He got up and did some disobedient reading. The Rule was God's more recent way of becoming flesh, and obedience was worship. He sat up and read disobedient books, with BA and God baying in the distance. Reading halfheartedly, he worried about Brother Koenig's soul, about BA locked in the chapel. When sleep finally came it was reluctantly, bumpy with demanding dreams.

He dreamt about a conversation he had overheard ten years ago. His mother was telling her cousin Merle how happy he was. Every letter home had said so. In his dream, he had walked in and tried to explain that it wasn't a question of happiness but of being called to fulfilment by God and enjoying the hundredfold in this life and next. Well, certainly in the next. As he explained about the dignity and status of the priesthood, as he eloquently expounded on the hundred-fold to be enjoyed in this life, the combined chorus of his eighty first cousins laughed joyously at him.

Waking, he took a few seconds to register the voice in the other room next to him. It was Brother Flynn, famous as the monastery sleeptalker. He was, as so often, carrying on a conversation with his sister Marcella. Flynn didn't mumble in his sleep, he declaimed. Sometimes he declared 'Bless me

Father, for I have sinned' and went on to announce some interesting sins. Since he was a light sleeper, Hannigan had been placed in the adjoining room and given the job of interrupting Flynn's potentially more dangerous revelations. Tonight he lay back and enjoyed them as part of the hundred-fold. 'Marcella, that's lovely, the MAM have reformed their religious dress. It's encouraging that our sister Order is following the lead of Vatican II and *Perfectae Caritatis*. And it's a very becoming little outfit you're wearing too, Marcella...hey, just wait a minute, you're not Marcella, you're a bloody Anglican nun...Jesus Christ!'

On Sunday morning, the retreat ended and there was an air of celebration as the seminarians, freed from talking only to God, chatted charitably to each other. Brother Hannigan sang cheerfully through the boredom of high mass, convincing himself that he was simply enjoying his new humility and not excited about leaving for Sydney that night.

After mass, Father Superior invited him for a stroll to talk over a few things. They sat on the trunk of a gum tree that had fallen across the basketball court. The tree had lain there for a month, but because basketball was a spiritual priority way behind football, tennis and handball – except for the Filipino students – no one had bothered to organise its removal. The Filipino students were loved and welcomed, but they never carried much weight.

Father Finnegan stopped picking his teeth and lit a cigarette; he was a Marlboro man. 'You won't tell anyone, if I have a little smoke while giving spiritual direction?' Father Superior sat on the tree trunk, blowing smoke rings at his knee, and revealing a section of hairless leg above black socks with purple diamonds. They both knew that eyes would be watching from the seminarians' rooms. The life of study and contemplation encouraged observation. Hannigan looked away, embarrassed as always by even a minor revelation of priestly fleshliness.

Across the peace of the cows and the gum trees, they could see two seminarians walking along the avenue, their arms waving in debate. Fathers Winton and McCarthy were recently ordained and therefore living on a higher plane. Perhaps they were discussing the seal of the confessional or the baptism of unbaptised infants, or the appropriateness of Father McCarthy opening the batting against the Franciscans, who were famous for wearing boxes when batting. Father Finnegan thought that boxes at cricked indicated sexual fantasies and a lack of faith. Hannigan wondered if the newly ordained priests ever noticed the girl who pitted the monastery driveway with her stiletto heels on her shortcut to the tram. He wondered if either of them would have been aroused by the advertising photographs that had followed an article in the *Women's Weekly* on the MOM leprosarium in the Kimberleys. The photos of gnarled cures had done little to distract him from the 'Breakthrough in Bras' or 'Perfection in Pantyhose'.

Father Superior pointed his cigarette towards the driveway. '*Numquam duo*. Never two. You know it never worried them much in Rome. Over there, they make the rules; over here, we keep them. Mostly.'

Brother Hannigan decided it was time to come clean. The vow of poverty was not yet much of a problem, though he had been tempted when his parents had offered to buy him an electric razor and a new style of coloured underpants. Cheerful obedience and unrestrained respect for superiors and officials of every rank was becoming harder, especially with Father Superior's passion for the killing and plucking of chooks. But becoming another Christ was starting to be less easy than it had once looked, and he was beginning to wonder if priestly holiness mightn't elude him forever.

He knew he would have problems in starting to talk about doubting the existence of God (Father Superior had added two more proofs to Saint Thomas' five), or wondering about the relevance of being a missionary of Mary (Father Superior had written an article in French and one in Latin on this very topic).

Sitting upright on the gum tree, Hannigan settled the skirts of his habit, reminding himself that this would be as good a place as any to start. Lately he had taken to kneeling down in sudden descents of prayer during the hour of meditation that preceded morning mass. This could be seen as an act of discipline and piety, but the reason was that, when he was kneeling, his flowing religious habit gave his erection a chance to subside unnoticed.

'Well, Father, what's been happening is . . .' and he turned to face the music like a man who didn't know what the tune was. If he bared his soul, opened up his heart, spilled his guts, he could kiss goodbye to Rome, city of saints, even to Sydney, city of sinners. Perhaps he would be sent, like other wayward seminarians before him, to one of the Order's far-flung schools, where he would work out his salvation by teaching schoolboys for a year.

But, as usual, Father Superior was answering questions with patience, always taking care to answer the question that should have been asked. 'I've been thinking about the last Chapter.'

The Chapter of Faults closed off the uplifting spiritual gloom of Friday, as the thwack of the discipline on a cold back opened it up. Each Friday night, each seminarian prayed the most devout prayer of the week: *Christ I hope it's not going to be my turn again.* Kneeling down and confessing one's external faults to one's Brothers-in-Christ was often not as painful as Father Superior's following commentary. Sometimes he would treble the list. Sometimes he would praise the humility of the list.

'You mentioned being inconsiderate to the needs of your brothers at table.'

Hannigan remembered last week's list. 'Punctuality'. A titter from his Brothers. 'Failing in. Failing in modesty of the eyes.

Being careless about the Brother rule. For these and any other external faults which I may have committed, Father, I humbly ask your pardon and a penance. Oh, yes, I forgot, swinging my sash.' The sash was that part of the religious habit that symbolised chastity. *Gird me, O Lord, with the girdle of purity* (here he kissed the sash) *and extinguish in my limbs the fires of lust, so that there may always remain in me the virtue of continence and chastity.* Then he tied the sash and was roped into virtue for another day.

'You still read *The Imitation of Christ*, of course.' Father swung up his right leg and revealed more flesh. He butted his cigarette, sucked on a gum leaf, and began to quote: *'Fight strongly for me and overcome these evil beasts — I mean these alluring concupiscences — that peace may be made in thy power and the abundance of praise in thy holy court — that is, in a clean conscience.'*

As he looked about the basketball court, Brother Hannigan thought about Thomas à Kempis, saintly because of his enduring and relentless book of spiritual thoughts, but regarded with four hundred years of suspicion because when they dug him up for canonisation they found that he had woken up in his coffin and tried to tear his way out. So he was presumed to have committed the sin of despair and was never canonised.

When as a first-former Hannigan had made his decision to go to Eden, he who was conspicuously second-rate at football and study had become suddenly important at the Christian Brothers, Wangaratta. Brother McDermott, who had always thought his name was Hanrahan, took him aside after he had been boundary umpire for an under-thirteens Possibles versus Probables, and said, 'Tell Mum and Dad we'll take care of *The Imitation of Christ*.' He thought this meant that the Christies were going to take over his parents' spiritual welfare, and was quite surprised the next day when he was called before the school assembly and handed a speech and a book. The only other occasion he had been called before the school was to receive six of the best from Brother McDermott ('this hurts me more than it hurts you').

Hannigan realised later that the decision for him to become a priest had been made then, at least partly, when he was waiting for an old man in a religious habit to belt him. He would escape to South India and return to his old school as an important missionary priest.

Father Superior was now chewing his gum leaf, but still managing to talk. 'I know it's a natural impulse. It's in all of us, you know.'

Now they were getting to the heart of the matter.

'I do notice these things, you know.'

Masturbation was a sin and therefore a matter for the privacy of the confessional and not the publicity of the Chapter of Faults. But as his spiritual director, Father Superior had access to all things between Heaven and Hell.

Father Superior replaced his gum leaf with a cigarette. 'We all have animal appetites to control. *Purity alone has power to look on what is unsullied.* Saint Augustine said that. Or did he say *sullied*?'

Father Superior was leading up to the end of the affair. BA came madly beagling across the basketball court and tried to snuffle his way under the skirts of Father Superior's habit.

'Piss off, bloody dog.'

The seminarians loved Father Superior's earthiness.

He aimed a kick at the dog's belly and missed.

Brother Hannigan tried to make it easier for Father Superior. 'Yes, Father, I just can't get it out of my mind, hardly.'

'Really? Then it's worse than I thought.' Father Superior sounded surprised at a failure at infallibility. But he turned to Brother Hannigan with the resolution of man grabbing large responsibility. 'Food. You've been becoming too interested in food. In fact, I've noticed it especially with porridge since we've introduced Weat Harts.'

Hannigan, who often accused himself of talking too much, died into a limbo of wordlessness.

'Porridge. That could be your path to chastity, if you ever have any problems with it.' Father jumped off the tree trunk and fired a few imaginary balls across the oval with an imaginary club. Brother Hannigan was sure he saw the cows duck.

'Golf, great discipline, you know.' Father picked up a stick and started putting. 'Remember that if they had organised sports two thousand years ago, Christ would have been a world champion. He was also just the man any father would want for his daughter. Remember that and you won't go wrong. And remember you will have to fight off women,' he looked carefully at his subject, 'not because of any attractions in yourself, but because of your priesthood. That's what they lust after, believe you me. The only way to fight with a woman is with your hat. Grab it and run. John Barrymore said that. Bit before your time. Of course, there are exceptions like Our Lady and Greer Garson.'

Fighting off BA, Father rode another putt with such conviction that Brother was surprised that he lost sight of the ball.

'You mentioned that there was something that you had forgotten to tell me about that woman with the red hair.' Father Superior had a photographic memory for the colour of women's hair. 'I know, of course. She tried to seduce you, didn't she, but you didn't notice until you got back home and started meditating. I bet she had an attractive body, too. These types always do. They want nothing more than the priesthood. Get lost, BA.'

Father Superior looked at Brother Hannigan with all the concentration he used in assessing a putt. 'You're certainly no oil painting, and you can thank God every day for that. You wouldn't understand what some of us have to go through. But you've got youth, I guess. And they're always trying to take away something from God.'

Father Superior blew wetly into his hanky. Hannigan wondered briefly why the handkerchiefs of Father Superior, who was a resolute and punctual nose-blower, were always an immaculate white, whereas seminarians' hankies were grey. But now he grabbed hold of the conversation, as the wind played with the leaves on the basketball court and BA chased the wind. 'Yes, Father. Well, it's something that I sort of mentioned before, only I haven't properly mentioned. And you're right, of course, in bringing up virginity.'

'Of course.' Father Superior had recovered his infallibility. It was just a matter of getting your swing right and your confidence back.

'You want to bring out the *Virgin*. You want to bring the *Virgin* back.'

Hannigan thought that Father was about to swing into his well-known speech, 'Every Woman was a Virgin Once', in which he spoke of virginity as a condition suspiciously peculiar to women only. But he was following a different inspiration. 'You want to carry on with *The Voice of the Virgin*.'

The Voice of the Virgin had been stilled recently on the orders of Father Provincial. It was the twice-yearly magazine in which, for sixty years, seminarians had offered their poems and articles to God (fiction was frivolous and too far from the truth).

The last issue had caused controversy. First of all, Brother Williams had submitted a short story. To make matters worse it was a story about a seminarian with unnatural habits. Father Superior had pointed out that stories were not permitted. Brother Williams had surprised Brother Hannigan by arguing the point. With Father Superior. Williams had claimed that the Gospels were stories. Then, taking a step up onto the cloister so that he was even taller than Father Superior, he had made an even more absurd claim, that fiction was the truth with the facts taken out. Father Superior had clinched his argument by saying that anyhow Father Provincial in Adelaide had forbidden stories. Hannigan had never seen anyone argue with a Superior before and the experience was frightening and a little thrilling. When Father Superior came back from the chapel where he had talked the matter through with God in a session of prayerful literary criticism, he said, 'Besides, Brother Williams, your story's just not credible. I can't believe in a seminarian who goes on to ordination with doubts about the existence of God.'

'Well, I guess I've got more faith than you have, Father.'

'I take it that your remark is a joke,' Father Superior had said, walking off unamused.

Then there was Brother Lynch's hymn to the Eucharist.

> *O Christ, locked sweet and cold and lone*
> *behind the tabernacle's dreaming door,*
> *you felt with love your Magdalene of bone*
> *and flesh; so manly enter through the door*
>
> *of my now hapless heart; and sweetly show*
> *that I do not need a woman's pulsing breast;*
> *not a woman's body, but you I want to know.*
> *Be it your bread I eat, and lay the flesh to rest.*
>
> *Sacramental, you live for us in breadly stuff.*
> *But dear, sweet Christ, make it seem enough.*

The hymn was generally much admired by the seminarians for its piety. Some few, who were considered of a more literary bent and who spent Sunday afternoons listening, with a spiritual look in their eyes, to records of Shakespeare's plays and to Richard Burton doing *Under Milk Wood*, thought it too sweetly devotional and metrically inept.

The priests thought the poem was obscene and were horrified. Except for Father Hartigan, who taught scripture, claimed to be the grandson of the poet 'John O'Brien', Monsignor Hartigan, and read James Joyce quite openly. Father Smythe was embarrassed: he had gone to see St Kilda beat Collingwood by a point in the grand final and had handed over his job of approving the seminarians' manuscripts to the editor, Brother Hannigan.

Hannigan's own article on the poetry of AD Hope had been charitably admired and in itself had caused no stir. But the article had mentioned, with approval and without quoting, two of Hope's poems: 'The Damnation of Byron' and 'Chorale', which Brother Kiernane promptly read. The poems of Lynch and Hope became the subjects of more passionate discussion than the new liturgy or the decree on the reform of religious life. Brother Kiernane took over the recreation room one Sunday afternoon and read with slow and delighted horror:

> *Vast Scandanavian divinities*
> *Superbly modelled, for all their cowlike air,*
> *The pale bread of their bellies' magnificent rise*
> *From the blond triangle of pubic hair...*

'Read that bit again. I don't understand.'

Brother Kiernane helpfully did as Brother Williams asked, and fulfilling various earnest requests, read the poem four and a half times. There was much quiet discussion of triangles of pubic hair, for while the seminarians were well up on vaginas and had read with interest the moral theologians' worry about whether the vagina was an internal or external organ, they were vague about female pubic hair which didn't figure much in the geometry of sin.

The Voice of the Virgin, having spoken out of turn, encouraged changes in the seminary rather different from those talked about at Vatican II. For his sin of omission, Father Smythe was deputed to remove all doubtful poetry books in 'the literature library', a tiny room, to be entered only on Sundays and holidays, and then only with Father Superior's permission. Rather than read through two shelves of poetry, Father Smythe contacted a literary friend of Father Superior's who lectured in marine biology at Melbourne University. This friend provided a list of Catholic poets, so that seminarians with a poetic warp were left with a choice of Joyce Kilmer, GK Chesterton, Hilaire Belloc, Alice Meynell, John O'Brien, Francis Thompson and John Donne. Brother Lynch pointed out that the marine biologist hadn't caught up with the news of Donne's conversion to Anglicanism and gave a reading from 'Love's Progresse'.

Gerard Manley Hopkins, difficult and dangerous Jesuit, was removed with many other authors to the safekeeping of the Fathers' library, which had glass-fronted bookshelves and keys. There he joined Graham Greene, Evelyn Waugh, Soren Kierkegaard and the *Catholic Worker*, which was known to be anti-Vietnam and not always hostile to Arthur Calwell. Since it was universally known, at least in the Balwyn seminary, that Shakespeare was a Catholic, his works were permitted to remain in the literature library, along with the novels of Cardinals Newman, Wiseman and Spellman, Monsignor Robert Hugh Benson, Father Owen Francis Dudley and even Father Francis Finn, SJ, who was a safer Jesuit and wrote books for boys.

So now, sitting on a tree on the basketball court, Brother Hannigan thought he would bring Father Superior back to earth by mentioning the temptations to pre-masturbatory reading still left in the library. There was Shakespeare's 'Venus and Adonis', for starters:

> *Feed on these lips, or if these hills prove dry,*
> *Stray lower where the pleasant pastures lie.*

He looked forward to the pleasure of checking this quotation to get it right. Father Superior had obviously never read the deep eroticism of PC Wren's *Beau Sabreur: They kissed until they could kiss no more.*

'Father, have you read PC Wren?'

'I can't recall him, but I probably have. Is he any relation to John Wren? Good Catholic man – awful the way that Hardy bloke attacked him. Communist of course. Anyway, we have decided that the *Voice of the Virgin* should come out again.

A good idea, don't you think, eh, Brother? But with a little more care and no poems from Brother Lynch.'

Dominic Lynch had already spent two years in a boarding school in the Adelaide hills, teaching and thinking over his vocation to the priesthood. It was rumoured that he might be in for another year teaching maths and science. He was clearly not to be trusted with poetry.

'So to keep your mind off your little problem' – and Brother Hannigan didn't know if this was a reference to his chastity, his porridge or his epilepsy – 'I've a list of suggested topics, which you will put in the next issue. We're going to make the voice of seminarians more theological and more topical.'

Father Superior reached deep into the pocket of his habit, looked surprised at a golf ball, reached in again and found a piece of paper. It was a long list, written in ornate print in black ink. Hannigan began to read it: 'Does Saint Matthew permit divorce? (No!)'; 'When bread ceases to be bread: the true theology of transubstantiation. Cupboard Protestants within the church.'; 'The burial of unbaptised infants'; 'Baptism within the womb'; 'The proper material for the sacrament of baptism (e.g. mud? saliva? soft drinks?)'; 'Sunday mass and Sunday work: how far do you have to go to avoid sin on Sunday?'; 'The Liturgy in English: bringing the Church into the twentieth century'; 'Celibacy and salvation'; 'Why Catholic women don't want the pill'; 'Abortion, the end of civilisation as we know it.'

BA stormed across the oval towards two disdainful magpies bargain-hunting for worms. Despite the list, somewhere, deep inside him, Brother Hannigan was relieved. The *Voice* would be heard again.

'I think you'll find some pretty relevant stuff in that list. You're interested in Teilhard de Chardin,' and Father Superior pointed to the last topic, underlined twice, 'Teilhard de Chardin: rebel and heretic'. Hannigan had been excited by de Chardin, his newness and vision and daring. So much for

Teilhard. So much, too, for his own article, often planned
during the hour of morning meditation, on the spiritual vision
of Patrick White; so much, too, for his half-written report on
revolutionary theology in Brazil and Argentina.

But Brother Hannigan also knew, as he walked in step
across the basketball court with Father Superior, that he was
walking into a different territory. He realised, for the first time,
that words are sacraments, dangerous sacraments. *That's* why
the Word became flesh. The unpriested seminarians would
have their own sacraments back again. Maybe he could even
get the laybrothers writing. And words had a way of
consecrating and forgiving that not even Father Superior could
control. After all, the Church had got itself started by daring
to make up the stories of the Gospels.

Father Superior thought that he had sorted out the *Voice* and
that he could now concentrate on the other burning
monastery questions: Who were the midnight monastery
prowlers? Who had removed the coverings pasted over
the Greek statues in Breasted's *Ancient Times*? And who put
the glass in his football boots?

Crossing the oval, Father Superior broke into a run and
threaded an imaginary drop-kick between the goal posts. BA
Santamaria barked his approval. BA and Father Superior still
believed in drop-kicks.

Somewhere, also deep inside him, Michael Hannigan understood a little more about the Word becoming flesh.

He was still looking for this thought, when Father Superior
became solemn on the steps of the cloister. 'Remember,
Brother, going to the Latin conference in Sydney is your first
big step into the world. Take your vows with you. It's the
sixties and we must keep up with the latest thinking about
the teaching of Latin.'

Then, as was his habit when communicating something
particularly spiritual, Father Superior joined his hands in front
of him and looked up to the sky. 'As a last thing, I want you

to come into the main lecture room with me and I will put certain questions to you.'

So, in an experience he had never even heard of before, Brother Hannigan found himself kneeling in front of the desk beneath the blackboard. Father Superior sat at the desk, on which was a copy of the Order's constitutions and a candle, honey-coloured and therefore with the proper percentage of beeswax for use at mass. After lighting the candle with matches from the Pink Pussycat Bistro – three were needed – Father Superior moved into the voice he reserved for the liturgy and important phone calls. 'Brother Hannigan, fully professed member of the Missionary Order of Mary, as your properly constituted Superior and as the representative of Christ, who was obedient unto death, I ask you, in virtue of your vow of holy obedience, if you are the midnight monastery prowler or if you placed glass in the football boots of me, your father in Christ.'

That afternoon, he caught the tram into the city. The afternoon was so hot that two Mormon missionaries were walking down Barkers Road with their jackets slung over their shoulders. In the small park at the beginning of Victoria Street a very Italian-looking man was teaching his two small daughters to throw a boomerang. Hannigan was pleased that Italians were keeping up Australian traditions.

At the old-world tram shelter at Brunswick Street, Brother Hannigan left the tram and crossed over to Saint Vincent's Hospital. Father Brown was sharing his old room in Saint Margaret's ward with an Irish Cistercian monk who was visiting the world for the first time in twenty years to have his appendix removed. Father Brown was sitting up in bed smiling baldly in his blue-striped hospital pyjamas. In his left hand he held his Irish horn rosary beads, in his right PG Wodehouse's *Ice in the Bedroom*.

'Brother Michael, what a lovely surprise, to be sure.' Father Brown fell into what he thought was Irish when the spirit came down upon him. 'I'd like you to meet Father Columbanus, who used to come from County Clare. This is Brother Hannigan, one of our young Turks.'

It was all right, Father Brown explained. They'd removed a little bit of bowel, and he had plenty to spare. Sister Xavier had assured him that he needn't worry about dying till he got to be old.

'God is good, always has been. I've seen plenty of it. The stories I could tell. This young one thinks he can write a bit. Dangerous thing that.'

Father Columbanus didn't agree. 'Saint Bernard and Thomas Merton, now there's two likely lads, if you please.'

'Of course, there's exceptions. Agatha Christie and the old Wodehouse. You be on' your way, Brother Michael, or you'll miss that train. And remember that you should enjoy yourself, even in Sydney, and that sin is in the eye of the beholder.'

Brother Hannigan left ten minutes later, after receiving a talk from Father Columbanus on the glories of Gaelic football and hurling and the evils of James Joyce, and being blessed by Father Brown, and then competitively by Father Columbanus.

At the top of the stairs he saw Nurse Moira Counahan walking away carrying a bedpan, and looking beautiful.

He dumped his case, light on clothes, heavy on improving books, and rushed after her. 'Moira, er, Nurse Counahan...'

She turned, with a pleasant, puzzled smile. 'I'm sorry. There's no Moira on this ward. Can I help?' She held the bedpan comfortably in front of her.

'Yes, no. Well tell Moira – no Nurse Hannigan, I mean Counahan – that Brother Hannigan sends his...Oh hell, it doesn't matter, thanks very much, sorry.'

When he stood outside Sydney Central station next morning, trying to sort out a bus to Sydney University, he felt a sense of liberation he could never associate with Melbourne's Spencer Street station. He wondered if this was because he associated Spencer Street with monastery arrival, Central with departure.

His first job in Sydney was to find a chemist's shop. Folded inside his copy of *The Little Office of Our Lady* was a prescription for his epilepsy medication, and a more tattered script for masturbation pills. He had been carrying this tattered prescription for nine weeks, the fruit of a visit to Father Superior's psychiatrist friend, Doctor Dainty. He found a chemist a block away from Central. He waited outside the small shop, while a gnome of a man coughed his way through reading the labels on bottles of cough mixture. It took a special sort of humility to ask for masturbation pills. At last the chemist shop was empty, with only God to watch and listen. He waited for the chemist to come out of the dispensing sanctuary. Hell! a woman. He expected her to exclaim in horror or fold her long body into laughter. But she merely looked over her glasses and said, 'Be a couple of minutes, Father'.

When the pharmacist was placing the four bottles of tables on the counter, the seminarian realised that a tall woman with red hair was standing next to him and looking carefully at his purchases.

'You on them, too, Father? Me, too. Do me no end of good they do.'

'Well,' he said, wondering whether to divert the conversation by disowning Fatherhood, and knowing that women didn't need masturbation pills, 'what sort of epilepsy do you have?'

'Me? Epilepsy? You gotta be joking, Father. There's nothing funny about me.'

He shoved the anti-masturbation pills in his pocket.

'No, it's me nerves, what with me back and me migraine and the Pope keeping me off the pill and...'

'Well, I've got a bus to catch and I've got to...'

'Of course, Father, don't let me stand here talking all day.

I'm sure you got better things to do, what with confessions and things...'

He was almost out of the shop but not quite out of the conversation.

'...and God bless you too, Father, you seem a nervy sort of chap, no wonder you need your valium.'

Conspicuous and embarrassed masturbator in his clerical hat and suit, he had to ask three times for directions to the Women's College. Once there, he registered for the conference with an air of a man who knew what he was about, but he was quickly awed by the people around him who seemed to know each other. And simply to know. He found his room in the west wing, and felt strangely at home, for Women's College seemed, *mutatis mutandis*, very like a monastery. True, the pictures on the wall of his cell were of James Dean, Marlon Brando, Clark Gable with Marilyn Monroe, and a pop group that he presumed were the Beatles. Largest of all was the picture of a man with fat ugly lips called Mick Jagger.

He unpacked his books: Lonergan's *Insight*, Karl Rahner's *Theological Investigations*, Graham Greene's *The Heart of the Matter* and Morris West's *The Devil's Advocate*. He hesitated about unpacking a last book, one given to him by Father Finnegan just before he had left.

Father Superior had summoned him to his room. He searched in the bookshelf that contained prominently the *Jerusalem Bible*, the *Summa Theologica* of Saint Thomas Aquinas, and Father Superior's own works of spiritual theology, *Christ's Kingdom of the Brave*, *Mary, Our Littlest Sister* and *Sin, Sex and Sanity*. Father Superior pulled out and handed to Hannigan what was clearly a Vatican paperback, in washed-out green, *De Masturbatione Seminariorum*, issued in 1938 when Pope Pius XI was swapping encyclical notes with Hitler. The Sacred Congregation of old men demanded the instant dismissal of masturbating seminarians.

Because he often worked in the seminary laundry folding

seminary pyjamas, and because he often had unkind thoughts, Brother Hannigan occasionally wondered how many seminarians might share his sinfulness. But then he would dismiss such uncharitable thoughts, insisting he must be unique in his sin, and that he couldn't distinguish between a urine stain and a semen stain anyway.

When he had tried, not very hard, to explain his real problems to Father Superior, he couldn't work out whether Father's problem of listening was because he didn't want to know or because he already knew too much.

'Well actually, Father, what I mean to say, it's not actually a problem of touching myself. Well, it is that, but well...'

'I know exactly what you mean. Enjoy yourself in Sydney, but not too much. God bless, Brother.'

He threw the book back into his case, and prayed. *Mary, mother of purity, keep my body pure and my mind holy. Gird me, O Lord, with the girdle of purity.* Then he started to read Graham Greene, glancing occasionally at Marilyn Monroe.

But he had more guilts on his mind than even Graham Greene. He removed his clerical coat and his clerical collar. He threw them on the bed next to his clerical hat. Then, in an act of daring, he took off his shirt and black trousers and sat in his underpants reading Graham Greene and feeling sinful. Father Master of Novices had often warned against any form of nudity, even in the hottest weather, and had encouraged the use of singlets when swimming. God apparently blushed at the sight of his own creation. And well he might in Brother Hannigan's case, as he was skeleton short-changed on flesh which seemed rather absentmindedly plastered over bones that stuck out at peculiar angles.

Although King's Cross was only a couple of miles away, and Marilyn Monroe a few feet away, his mind was on spiritual sins, which, as Aquinas noticed, were more serious than fleshly sins. The fact was that Brother Hannigan had been indulging in some lies of omission or 'mental restriction'.

Hannigan was not sure whether he had used purely mental restriction, which was not permitted, or broadly mental restriction, certain categories of which were OK with God.

For Hannigan knew who had torn the coverings off the statues in Breasted's *Ancient Times*. Just before going into hospital, Father Brown had asked him to collect a pile of books to return to the library. There were a dozen novels by Carter Brown and Mickey Spillane, none of which bore the monastery library stamp, and Breasted's *Ancient Times*.

'You know, I've been waiting fifty years for a good look, so I thought I was running out of time. Didn't do much good, though. Every time I tore off the covering, I tore off anything worth seeing. You take a look at the covers of those novels. Some pretty revealing stuff there.' Hannigan had surreptitiously returned Breasted to the library, and unfortunately had carelessly placed it on the shelves of the lives of the saints, where it was found by Brother Kiernane. He had kept the other books in his room, and so far had read *Ice-Cold Nude, Blonde on the Rocks* and *Lady is Available*.

But he had withheld this information from Father Superior. He also knew more about the midnight prowler than he had admitted. On the night he had met Brother Williams in the chapel, the last night of the retreat, Brother Williams had come later to his room. Hannigan had been reading through notes from a priest's book on marriage and contemplating the thought that *the longing of a woman for a penis is greater than that of a man for a vulva* when he was surprised by a knock on his door. It was Brother Williams.

'It's all right, I haven't got Father Superior's permission, but I don't need it any more.'

This was absurd. You always needed permission to visit a confrere. Permission was as important as prayer and Holy Communion. Obedience was the Weat Harts of religious life.

Brother Williams sat on the bed. 'I won't be here when you get back from Sydney.'

'You lucky devil. Where are they sending you off to? Not Rome is it?' This last question was rushed, as Hannigan himself had his eye on Rome, the focus of his humble ambitions.

'No. I'm going home.'

'Hell, is someone sick?'

In the spirit of Vatican II, seminarians were now allowed to go home to see sisters and brothers married and to watch parents die.

'No, nothing like that. I'm leaving. For good. Finish.'

Brother Hannigan was horrified. It was always like a death in the family when a seminarian left to join the world. Even if the seminarian was a pain in the neck, a misfit, it was at least like the death of the family cat. It was also a reminder that the world was out there beckoning, a reminder of one's own spiritual mortality.

At the thought of Tony Williams returning to the world, Brother Hannigan felt a sudden lurch of faith. Tony was going to be one of those priests whom they often read about, whom they occasionally met. Tony was going to be one of those priests they were all planning to be, especially at the end of the annual retreat: gracious, generous, confident in Christ, smiling on the world.

'Leaving? Don't be bloody ridiculous. Look, mate, you're going through a bad time. We all have them. Even me.' He surprised himself with the confession. Tony Williams wasn't smiling any more. 'For Christ's sake, Tony, we all screw up. It's not the end. Mate.' Hannigan paused to notice that his language deteriorated as his wisdom grew.

'Mike, thanks. You're supposed to be bright, but you don't see much.'

Hannigan hesitated, ready to argue the last comment but undecided which half was most arguable.

'No, you don't understand. I'm more of a monastery scandal than Brother Lynch. I'm not sure if I'll bother telling Father

Superior – perhaps I'll keep it for one of the many surprises he's going to get in the next life – but sure as hell, I'm leaving.'

Hannigan was starting to catch up. 'You mean all the fuss that's been going on lately?'

'Just that. It was me.'

Hannigan stood up and looked down at the balding head of his confrere. 'You can't put that one over. You see, Tony, I know.'

Williams looked up in surprise. 'You know. Hell, I thought you didn't notice anything.'

Hannigan walked up and down his room, pleased with himself. 'Yes, I know. How about that? I know. I've actually been told – confidentially, I can't reveal the name – who defaced Breasted.'

Williams laughed. 'Mike, you *don't* know what I'm talking about.'

'I do so, too. It was Father Brown. He told me very confidentially, it's top secret.'

'O Mike, I know *that*. He told me too. He's telling everyone except Father Superior and BA. I'm talking about something completely different.'

Hannigan sat down to regain wisdom. He looked up at the picture of the Sacred Heart, and the sight of Christ with his bleeding heart in his hand brought him back to the topic. 'Yeah, OK. But I can't believe that you would want to put the remains of a tomato sauce bottle in Father Superior's football boots.'

Williams, who had been fiddling with the tassels at the end of his sash, looked up in surprise. 'Tomato sauce bottle, was it? What brand?'

'White Crow.'

But Hannigan was not to be distracted from the enjoyment of confession. 'We all do silly things. If Father Superior knew some of the things I've done...'

'*Use every man after his desert, and who should 'scape whipping?*'

'God, you've got a funny way of saying things. But I have been lax about the discipline.' Hannigan passed on quickly, anxious to keep cracking the whip in his own style. 'Look at the attention I paid to that girl from Ringwood on the ecumenical day. You know, mate, I can't remember whether she was Presbyterian or Methodist, but I spent a lot of time wondering what her breasts were like.'

'Presbyterian. You told me three times. Mike, do you remember the night we went to the Passion Play?'

'Do I what! Jeez, mate, that was one of my agonies of decision. It was the Passion Play or going to see Essendon play Collingwood in the first round.'

Tony's eyes were patiently absent.

Hannigan blurted on, 'And remember, mate, nuns and seminarians got in for nothing, and we got to see Essendon as well. Tony, that proves there is a God.'

Tony sat statue-still on the horsehair mattress. He wasn't entering into the spirit of things.

'Well, Mike, that night I got a lift home with the McCarthys – you know, Father Provincial's cousins. Jim is president of the auxiliary, you know him.'

'And Monica makes the scones for the auxiliary afternoons.'

'Well, we dropped off at their place for a cuppa. Brother Lynch came too, and we did have some scones. Then we gave up tea, and started on whisky.'

Brother Hannigan turned to his confrere in relief. 'So that's it. Tony, you've got nothing to worry about. Once you're ordained, you'll have wine for dinner and tea, as well as before breakfast. In fact, I'm going to have a bottle of real whisky on the stage when we put on *The Cocktail Party* for Father Superior's feast day. By the way, how much of Celia's part have you learnt?'

'Mike, shut up and listen. You can forget about me for the play...'

'Tony, we're going to have real wigs. Father Bursar is going to hire them, not like the twine thing you had for Cecily in *The Importance of Being Earnest...*'

Brother Williams stood over him. 'Bloody well listen, for once in your life. That night Jim drove me home in the new Valiant. I offered to lock up the chapel. Brother Lynch was supposed to, but he wasn't feeling too well. I knelt and made a visit. I sat down on the steps of the altar. I'd never done that before, sat down at the altar. It's very lonely, you know, just you and God in the chapel in the middle of the night. Peaceful, the sanctuary light glowing, but lonely.' Tony Williams stopped talking and paced the small room.

'Yeah, I know what you mean. We're all lonely, it's the human condition,' said Brother Hannigan and the words clunked down.

Williams faced him. 'Damn it, it's not the human condition, Mike, Brother, it's the bloody monastic condition. Have you ever loved anybody...'

'Of course, lots of people.'

'No you haven't. Loved, made love to. Hugged, kissed, held someone close? Have you ever, really?'

'Well, once I...'

'Yes, that Madeleine, you talked guiltily about her for weeks. I bet you fucked her. Did you enjoy it?'

'No, not much.' Brother Hannigan looked down at his desk. 'I ran out on her.'

'That's what we do all the time, Mike, run out. On ourselves. On other people. They keep warning us against particular friendships; we're supposed to love all men and none; we're supposed to love God all the time, and women not at all.'

Tony Williams stood up in front of the window and spoke very softly. 'It's madness, Mike. We think we love because we do not hate. We think we love because we do not fuck. Or kiss or cuddle or tell ourselves to each other. You know, Mike, I felt so lonely that night, so close to the tears of things, as if I'd taken a vow of desolation. You know what I did, I wanted to console somebody. I went to the laybrothers' wing, I went to Brother Donnegan's room...'

'You what? Hell, Tony...'

'He's a kid, just out of the laybrothers' novitiate. He thinks he's dumb and he's frightened of all of us smart-arsed puppy priests. We've taken a vow never to tell someone we love them, never to hold them close. I stood and watched him sleep, the light from the cloister shone in his room, and he was beautiful and vulnerable, and sort of sobbing in his sleep. I once heard him crying when he was collecting eggs, and I was in the shed next door, plucking those eternal damn chooks.'

Brother Williams sat on the bed and was silent, meditating his memories. When he spoke again it was with a soft anger. 'Jesus Christ, Mike, God made people and things. Virgil was right. *Sunt lacrimae rerum.* I love that line. *There are the tears of things.* That's what we take out vows to, the tears of things. Our vow is never to cry. There are people out there who hold each other and cry to each other. This monastery is a desert of unshed tears. No wonder monasteries started in deserts.'

He now looked at Brother Hannigan and spoke slowly, emphatically. 'I wanted to hold Matt Donnegan, and tell him I understood about his father dying, about how he misses his little sister whom he hardly knows; that I loved him for his silly jokes and his good humour when Father Superior humiliates him, and for the way he picks up moths and says how beautiful they are. But I did a bloody stupid thing. I bent over and I kissed him gently on the cheek. Poor little bugger, he woke and yelled and yelled. I ran. I'm not sorry that I wanted to hold him, tell him that I loved him. Perhaps that makes me a homosexual...'

'Or perhaps it just makes you a person,' Brother Hannigan surprised himself by saying.

'Mike, you're learning. Remember your paper proving that

The Song of Songs is a love poem. You were right of course, but I thought it was just an idea to you. We love the idea of love. But we hate love and are afraid of loving. Remember that verse in *The Song: Stay me with flagons, comfort me with apples; for I am sick of love.* Of course, it means I am sick *with* love. But the Church is sick of love, scared of love. And I'm leaving. I want to be cured.'

They were both standing, facing each other.

'I expect you're shocked.'

'No. No. Not shocked. But, gee, mate,' Michael Hannigan wanted space to think about the unthinkable. 'No, Tony, not shocked. Surprised. I guess, yeah, that.'

Tony Williams smiled a sort of absolution. Then he gave him an idea, as if knowing that Michael was safer with ideas than with love. 'You know, Mike, the problem is not about believing in Christ and his incarnation, but imagining him. Knowing that he could feel what it would be like to hug John, the beloved disciple and Mary Magdalene, and hold them tight and feel the love in their bodies.' He put both hands on Hannigan's shoulders. Hannigan was scared. He hadn't been hugged and held tight for as long as he could remember.

But Tony was saving him with more ideas. 'Swap Jesuits, Mike. Give up Bernard Lonergan and take up Daniel Berrigan. When we sort out Vietnam, we'll be able to sort out the Gospels.' Then Tony Williams touched him lightly on the cheek and left him lonely and afraid.

Now in Sydney, the city of sin, Brother Hannigan paced his room in the Women's College. He wore white underpants, black socks and a dangerously cheerful heart. He sat down on the bed and contemplated his clerical hat. He put on his hat and stood in front of the mirror and sang, tunelessly, 'I Feel Pretty' from *West Side Story*. He faded on 'I feel pretty and witty and wise'. He had lost the words as well as the tune. Next door, Bob Dylan was singing 'Blowin' in the Wind'.

He hung his clerical suit in the cupboard, and put on the blue shirt and the blue trousers he used for seminary outings, known as 'stunts'. He de-frocked himself for the conference, under the impression that flared trousers were extremely fashionable.

He picked up his clerical hat and was about to put it in the cupboard when he paused to read some slogans pinned to the student's notice board: *All the way with LBJ is downhill, Support Bill White, Make Love not War.* He had heard of LBJ, and wondered if Bill White was a pop star or the student's boyfriend. With the defiance of the slogans, he crushed his clerical hat under his arm and walked nonchalantly downstairs and out the front door of Women's College. By the steps he paused at the rubbish bin. The few students passing by were happy and unnoticing. Summer had forgiven their year. He dropped his black hat into the bin and hurried back up the steps towards the college dining room, where the conference was getting its teeth into a Roman feast of cold corned beef and stras with flagon wine.

Brother Hannigan felt himself an outsider, though he noticed some modern nuns wearing just enough uniform to declare themselves for Christ. There was also a priest wearing full clerical attire and white hair and a full voice on the bits of Catullus you don't find in school texts. They all looked as though they belonged, along with the academics, wearing learned leather jackets and pipes. There were many more men than women, but that was a world he had been trained to believe was part of God's gracious design.

The nuns homed in on him immediately. 'Brother Hannigan, isn't it? Father Finnegan told us you'd be here. I'm Dorothy. And this is Philomena, the loved one. Good Greek word, even if she never existed, the saint I mean.' Sister Dorothy was a tall, middle-aged woman with peeps of grey hair coming from under her short grey veil. Brother Hannigan had never met a nun who owned up to her own unsistered name and to her own hair.

They laughed togetherly about the honoured saint, a virgin whose devotees wore a thin red and white cord around their middle, to remind them of purity, because it had to be wound tight. They laughed about the cord, and Brother Hannigan remembered the first he had owned, which had rotted after a year of unhygienic devotion. That skin-chafing reminder of purity had been the gift of his most-loved aunt. She was now dead, and he was sad for a moment for her, and for himself because he had not been allowed to visit her in her dying. He thought also of a Saint Philomena cord given to him by a very different kind of nun from these two, which lay in his cupboard at home, next to his rarely used discipline.

They laughed because the dear old Vatican had declared that Saint Philomena had never existed. And they laughed, looking over their shoulders to assure themselves of their privacy in the noise, because things were really changing, now. Weren't they?

If her patron did not exist, Sister Philomena certainly did, with blue eyes and red hair and no freckles. She was interested in talking to him, so he was about to walk politely away. Nuns always frightened him.

'Brother Hannigan, the MOMs have got missions among the Aborigines, haven't they? Don't you think the Aboriginal rights movement is exciting?'

He had no doubt that it was. It was just that he had never heard of it.

'One of our sisters went on the freedom ride with Charles Perkins. She said it was a very moving experience.'

He had no doubt that it was. It was just that he had never heard of it.

She tried again, waving her empty glass, looking for common ground. 'What do you think of Cardinal Suenens' *The Nun in the World*? Don't you think it's got something for all of us?'

He had no doubt that it did. It was just that he had never heard of it.

Brother Hannigan felt more alone than ever in the dining room of the Women's College, with its high, church-like ceiling. The room was busy with smoke and cheese and unconsecrated wine, busy with people who knew each other and with people who just knew.

He chewed on a piece of cabana, as conversation came to him in gobbets.

'Old McDonald's *Lucretius*. That's one book I'm really looking forward to. They tell me he's marvellous on the pluperfect...'

'Bombing the north is no solution...'

'...a new slant on the women in the Catullan circle...'

Sister Philomena had realised by now that conversation had to be drawn from a rather meagre table, but she kept trying. 'What say I get us both a glass of wine? What are you drinking?'

So far, nothing, but damn it all, God wouldn't mind and Father Superior would never know. Probably. 'Some wine would be lovely.'

'What sort?' She helped him. 'There's white and red.'

'Whatever you're having.'

When she was handing him the glass, the priest joined them.

'Sister Philomena, lovely to see you. I've been looking forward to this. I see you've changed the habit already. Jumping the gun a bit, aren't you? The bishops haven't approved anything yet, though I know it's in *Perfectae Caritatis*. The whole world's talking about the decree on religious life.'

He was one of those men who was often thought happy because his face was fat and red. He now looked across the gathering rather like a bishop claiming his flock. 'Great shows these. Always a good turn-up of nuns and brothers. Church's still active in Latin, at least, thank God...'

'Father Molloy, this is Brother Hannigan, a Marianite.'

'Glad to meet you. First time, isn't it?' rather accusingly, 'We've got to keep Latin alive...'

'Don't you approve of the mass in English, Father?' Sister Philomena wanted an answer rather than an argument.

The priest looked into his glass of red wine. 'I'm not sure about all these changes. *Festina lente.* Take it all very slowly, that's what I think Vatican II was on about.' Then he brightened up. 'Well, at least we won the election. I really admire the way Bishop Fox got up at the Christies at St Kilda and told them all to vote Liberal. About time. We've been getting a bit soft.'

'I thought he was interfering, actually, Father. And it's about time the DLP lay down and died, don't you think, Brother Hannigan?'

If he didn't know so much about so little, Brother Hannigan thought he would have agreed. Right now, all he could do was sip his wine and try to get used to the idea of a nun disagreeing with a priest on what was almost a matter of faith and morals.

Father Molloy was not disturbed. 'You've got to watch this one, Brother. She sometimes talks this feminist stuff, but she doesn't mean it. She only does it to bait me. She's as well aware as the rest of us that we can't have Arthur Calwell at any price...'

'Why not?' the nun interrupted. 'He's been a papal knight for two years.'

'See what I mean? She doesn't understand politics the way we do. What about getting me some cold meat and salad. There's a good girl.'

'Father, *the hungry sheep look up, and are not fed.* But you look as though you can feed yourself. Talk to you later, Brother.' Sister Philomena smiled at them both, and walked away with an easy dignity that Brother Hannigan knew came hard.

Father Molloy remained unruffled. 'Lovely girl. Bit head-strong. One of the main reasons I come to these dos is so the likes of her will know that the Church supports them in their teaching of Latin. She probably does have some silly ideas.

Wouldn't be surprised if she thinks that women should be allowed to use that damned pill. But she'll get over it. You know, I think I will go and get myself something to eat. Got to feed the inner man. By the way, I know old Ben Brown. I entered the seminary after he gave a mission in Tumbarumba. How is the old bugger?'

Before Brother Hannigan could tell him about Father Brown's approach to death, Father Molloy was making his firm way towards the food table.

Doing was better than standing alone and conspicuous. But being outside the monastery continually involved major decisions. He chose riesling, spilled some and then lined up for the food. Around him drifted floes from the pack-ice of the conversation.

'...Harpies and Heterae, the power of women in ancient Greece...'

'...I know it's been twenty years, but Marguerite and I were never suited...'

'...Cicero's metric in the Catiline...'

'...well of course, one doesn't come for the papers, they all look like bullshit. Of course, your paper on the women of the Catullan circle looks very exciting. I'm really looking forward to that...'

'...Daniel Mannix was right about conscription fifty years ago and he's still right...I know he's bloody well dead, but he's still right...'

'...and then Barry Breen kicks this wobbly punt, and I knew there was a God...'

Brother Hannigan put down his paper plate and plastic glass, and pulled out his pipe, a subversive gift from his sister, Bernadette. A Falcon, with a screw-in bowl, its metal gleamed with inexperience. He had smoked it only once before, a year ago, a guilty night.

A girl stood beside him; her short blond hair and her Levis and her *Save Our Sons* T-shirt, without the Marylike bra urged on his sisters by the nuns, all seemed too young for Latin. They swapped smiles and he poured her a glass of wine while he prepared his opening remark.

'Lo-re-tta!' A man wearing a brown beard and the last hopes of hair combed across a bald skull summoned her. At least she had a good Catholic name. 'Just so lovely to see you again. One forgets how too beautiful you are.'

Brother Hannigan stood superfluous, holding two glasses of wine.

'That PhD David tells me that you've got the goods on Tacitus. Hope you found that article of mine in *Antiquities Now* of some use.' He nuzzled confidently into her neck. 'They might let me examine the thesis – you look ravishing, but then you always do.'

Brother Hannigan resolved to get with it by looking up some back issues of *Antiquities Now.*

'Hello, Eugene,' she responded, removing his arm from her shoulder with the authority of experience. 'I'd love to talk to you about Tacitus. If you've got a moment. I mean, later, perhaps.'

For something to do, Brother Hannigan took a sip from each glass.

'Of course, we must, we simply must. Over dinner. Tomorrow, *carpe diem*, let's get away from all this and have dinner. I know just the place for us. Lovely little Cajun cooking spot in Balmain that hasn't been discovered yet.'

She accepted the riesling from Brother Hannigan without looking at either it or him.

'Thanks. Look, Eugene, I'm sure about the innovations in Tacitus, the ways in which that elliptical style is new. It's the modern parallels that I'm worried about. I've got to make it relevant.'

Brother Hannigan's mind had wandered to a thesis that Father Finnegan's favourite cardinal had written on the use of the subjunctive in papal bulls. He realised she had turned to him. 'Tacitus. He's terribly relevant, don't you think?'

Hannigan was working himself up to say 'yes', but Eugene was a couple of languages ahead of him. *'Sans aucune doute, ma chérie. Tempora mutantur, nos et mutamur in illis.* Meaning: we've got to get with it, kid. I've got some great suggestions, White and Hemingway. Let's get a coffee and talk about it.'

'You're full of shit, Eugene, but let's go and talk about it.'

Hannigan, who was not full of shit, but who was feeling scared shitless, quaffed his wine alone in the busy room.

For a moment, he found himself standing next to Father Molloy, whom he had watched listening in adverbs – 'Really?' 'Absolutely!' But now even Father Molloy had been disconnected from the concelebration. The two clerics stood beside the wine flagons, as solitary as two empty gumboots.

'I've just escaped Professor Boylan.' To Hannigan's surprise, Father Molloy added, suddenly man to man, 'He'd bore the barnacles off a bishop's bum. He's just discovered women. Only in Pericles' Greece, of course. Some of us have problems nearer home.' And he hurried off to do further battle with happiness.

Hannigan stood at the table, clerical Crusoe, nonchalant with his pipe, hoping it wouldn't die yet again. Voices focussed behind him, as if someone had finally found the station and turned the volume up.

'I know, it's a balls-up. I am sorry. In fact, I apologise. But the Nolans need that room. You see, it's got a double bed. And they're married.' The man's last statement came with the finality of a dogmatic theologian bemused by the Trinity.

'But you gave me the key. It's my number on the list. I've moved my stuff in. Besides, I'm married too. I might need the marriage bed as well.' The woman laughed in East-European. The accent was European-Australian, a purity of English, with tones and rhythms and grace that reminded him of the quickly acquired language of the misnamed 'Balts' he grew up with – and against – in the late forties and early fifties.

His pipe went out again. As he turned, probing for his

matches, he saw that her face was slightly older than her very young voice. The man pulled a sheet of paper from the back pocket of his jeans. It was Jim, the convenor – very Aussie, cultured, friendly and not-to-be-crossed. She was crossing him. His smile was getting lost in his dark beard. She stood before him, small, graceful and determined.

'I've put my things in. Just doing what I was told, like a good woman should.' Her laugh was amused, ironic, and it was winning.

Jim smiled, still friendly, bossy. His face was reddening through its charm. 'Look, you take my room. I'll swap it around. It's a much better room, in fact. Number thirteen in the west wing. That's it then, OK? I'll organise it.'

'All right, I'll forgo my rights to the marriage bed. Can I have some keys? Please?'

Jim walked off to reclaim control.

She moved along the table, to stand almost beside Hannigan. He lit his pipe again, trying to pretend he wasn't staring at her through the hurry of smoke. It was a firmly held belief among seminarians that they had originated and mastered the art of staring at women without being noticed. Living out this fallacy, Hannigan noticed high cheek bones, eyes of quick blue, a challenging, cheeky grace, that flowed through her sensuous, intelligent, anxious, over talking body. She brushed back her long blond hair, and acting on information received from his expert sisters, he looked at the roots of her hair to see if it was chemist-shop blond. That part of her, at least, passed his sisters' stringent tests.

'Another shag on a rock? My first conference. Yours?' She smiled at him warmly, now seeming confident, a lilt in her eyes, mocking gently. His pipe went out again. When it was making smoke again, she was talking to a man in yet another leather jacket at the end of the table. He too held a pipe in his hand and was fingering in tobacco from a leather pouch. Man and pipe and pouch looked confident and experienced.

Hannigan was startled as he watched her lean upwards – even on heels elegantly high, she had to stretch – and stare into the pipeman's mouth, proclaiming the bad teeth of pipe smokers. He tried, not very hard, to avoid looking at her buttocks firmly rounding in her cream pants. He could even see the outline of her panties. *Virgin Mother, keep my body pure and my mind holy, thou who wast immaculately conceived keep my purity intact, thou whose arse was alway modestly...*

The unlikely angel who saved him was a little man with deranged black hair and a corduroy jacket.

'That's Bernard Lonigan,' he said, thinking Hannigan was staring at the tall man with the pipe. 'Author of *The Catullus of Today*. I suppose you know it? Useful little book. Full of mistakes, but. I'm Bob Madden. Catullus is my field, as I expect you know.'

Catullus was also Hannigan's field, in which he sowed the seed for many of his confessions.

Without having read a word of recent Catullan criticism, Hannigan was inclined to agree with Madden. Lonigan was a youngish man, but balding, clearly growing a double chin and deeply engaging the attention of the young woman.

But Bob was talking about the lover named in the poems of Catullus. 'You're Michael, can't say I've heard of you. Well, Mick, I've worked out this Lesbia thing, you know. You must tell me, Mick, where your research is leading you. I'll get us some beer. "Lesbia" – we've always known that it was a nom de love, but they're wrong, you know. It wasn't that upper-class bitch, Clodia...slave from Cappadocia...fragment from the late Tibullus in the Bodleian...'

Hannigan realised he could safely listen in fragments while moonlighting with other thoughts. *Give me a thousand kisses,* that was his Catullus. Bless me, Father Brown, for I have had bad thoughts ten times and touched myself six – no, make that seven – times. And I've read 'Venus and Adonis' again. *Their lips together glu'd, they fall to earth. She seeks to kindle with*

[190]

continual kissing. Graze on my lips, and if those hills be dry, stray lower, where the pleasant fountains lie. Fountains? Fascinating. Adonis was a bit wet. He worried if his sinning was being taken seriously enough by Father Brown.

Bob was still talking about Lesbia. *Let us live my Lesbia and let us love. If old men mutter their protests, let's make sure we don't give a damn for their mutterings. When the light of our brief day is gone we must sleep through a night that will never end.* When shown the offending poem, Father Brown had commented that Catullus had a limited idea of Heaven, but had obviously heard the muttering of a few bishops. *O Virgin Mary, give me the grace to please Him always and in all things, and to live through the eternity of Heaven in the joy of your love.* That ejaculation carried an Indulgence of three hundred days.

She was still talking to the weak-looking man with the double chin.

Let us live, Lesbia. She was standing next to him, chewing a piece of cabana. *May the blessed Heart of Mary be loved among all peoples for all time. Amen.* Bob held a can of beer in each hand and was marching left-right through other groups.

'Clodia was having it off with her brother, Publius. Remember? Old Quintus Metellus, her husband...Cicero, in the *Pro Caelio*...'

'Let's see your teeth.' She surprised Hannigan, who was opening his mouth in the hope that some words might find their way out.

'There, see.' She turned to baldy, who had wandered up and was holding a defeated match over his grotty old pipe. 'His teeth aren't discoloured.'

Triumphant, Hannigan was pleased he had just shoved his pipe in his pocket so no one would guess that he was just learning to smoke.

'He's just learning to smoke. Bernie's the name.'

'This is Mick. Mick Hannigan.' Bob was shaking each empty beer can in turn with a slow suspicion of having been robbed. 'Someone seems to have finished this, Mick. I'll get you another one.'

The three of them stood, wishing words upon themselves.

Bernie was seized first. 'I've just escaped from one of those eternal rugby versus "aerial ping-pong" arguments.'

'My husband plays football. The real thing. Soccer.' Her smile wandered over both of them, and she had a way of making them feel important but not indispensable.

'Rather boring game,' said Bernie, whose face was admittedly handsome in a jumbly way, sort of. 'Not enough rough-and-tumble for my liking, personally.'

'I play a bit myself actually.' Hannigan felt he had come in out of the Greater Silence.

'Still plays, your husband, does he?' Bernie had picked up the soccer ball and was going to run with it.

'Yes, Eric's a full-back for Juventus.'

'Good team that. I always follow them for interest.'

Hannigan bet himself ten rosaries he knew more about soccer than Bernie, but he couldn't get onto the field.

'When I said boring, I meant to the uninitiated.'

'That's what Eric says.'

'Somehow, it's more real than all this,' and Bernie waved away the classical world with his pipe.

'That's what Eric says.'

The wisdom of Eric and Bernie came down among them. Hannigan decided to kick into the silence. 'I play on the left wing, actually.' He used the present continuous tense to cover a few games.

'Who for?' Bernie asked.

'Just a small team in the suburbs.' Brother Hannigan was getting pretty nippy on mental restriction.

'I play as a ruckman myself. University Blues. It'd be lovely to be married to a woman who takes football seriously.'

'That's what Eric says.' She laughed. 'I think it's all pretty bloody silly, actually. You were right before you changed your mind. It is bloody boring.'

She finished off her riesling. 'Can I be a good little woman and get either of you two gentlemen some wine. Or do you prefer a can of beer?'

Hannigan risked a pipe. When she returned with their wine, both men were puffing smoke into their silence.

'For my next edition,' Lonigan started talking, now that he had someone to talk to, 'I'm going to put in more about Lesbia.'

'She'll still be the bad woman in Catullus' poems for you men to get your thrills from.'

'No, not at all. Personally I don't find Catullus very erotic. You'd have to be pretty adolescent to do that, don't you think? No, I'm going to make her more central to my thesis...'

'Yeah, she's just a thesis, not a person.' The woman held her glass tightly, her angry hands warming the wine.

'Perhaps I could call the new edition *The Lesbia the Better*,' said Lonigan, at last realising that conference mateship was in danger.

'That's crass,' she said, and Hannigan had never seen such quiet, admirable anger, even though he didn't understand its source. 'Men can't forgive Lesbia because they want to fuck her. I hope your second edition doesn't have any jokes as crass as that.' Then she smiled at Lonigan, forgiving, but not retreating.

'It's going into a second edition, is It? Congratulations!' Bob was back, looking both unworldly and sadly sinful with his can of Toohey's and his roll-your-own and his small-boy smile on a been-there face.

'Well, nothing's definite, but I'm a great believer in keeping ahead of the times. That's what we've got to do with Latin.'

'Actually, I bought a copy the other day.' Bob turned round to the table and used an empty can as an ashtray.

'That's very good of you.'

'Yeah, I was lucky. Got it for a dollar. Remaindered.'

'It's a good book. I liked it.' She sipped her wine. Hannigan looked in surprise at a woman who knew her place in the world was wherever she decided it to be.

'It *is* a good book. I mean that.' Bob obviously could not wear his unkindness easily.

'Obviously I'd want to argue with you about Catullus' presentation of women.' She was clearly at ease with subjects that Hannigan only dreamt about.

'It's not important to me.'

'It was to him. It is to me.'

Hannigan found himself admiring her argument and her breasts. *Thou who wast a virgin in conceiving thy son, keep me as pure as you — as thou.*

Hannigan joined the conversation. 'I'll get us some more booze.'

Nobody said no. Nobody noticed. At the table, the flagons were empty. When he got back, she smiled ruefully over her empty glass. Around them, conference organisers were gathering glasses and ashtrays, the delegates were gathering goodnights and partners. Bob and Bernie were marooned on an island of arguments. Quintus Metellus. Clodia. Publius. Randy little shit, fucking his three sisters.

Brother Hannigan was shocked. By his ignorance.

They sparred with knowledge. Know my Cicero as well as you. *De Doma Sua. De Haruspicum Responso.* I won't mention the *Pro Rege Deiotaro.*

Perfectae Caritatis, but they were as heedless as God so he turned to the woman. 'I did play on the left wing.'

However, she was yawning, gracefully. 'But I bet you vote DLP. It looks like the party's over. Good night, professors.' They did not notice. She put her glass on the now sad table.

'Good night,' said Hannigan. No one noticed. As he moved off, he realised that she was still there, saying something about Catullus and Cicero, but it was too late to reclaim his goodbye. God was looking after him.

As he stood in the toilet drying his hands, he realised that he didn't know the girl's name. *Fuck me dead, send me to Vietnam,* said the graffito next to the mirror. He realised that he had failed to be a Christian Gentleman as described by Brother GC Davy, BA, Dip. Ed.: *The general rule is to introduce the inferior to the superior. A gentleman is always introduced to a lady. A lady is always introduced to a Priest, because a Priest is higher in dignity than a lady.*

Thou who wast a virgin after thy delivery, keep me pure. He was helped by Sister Philomena and Sister Dorothy who were looking for Father Molloy to arrange mass in the morning.

'Isn't it awful, Brother Michael. We've kept putting it off.' He didn't dare tell Sister Dorothy that the thought had never occurred to him. 'He'll probably want to say the votive mass for Saint Philomena again.' She drew herself up to a priestly voice: '*O God, who amongst other marvels of thy power, has given even to weak women the triumph of martyrdom . . . '*

Sister Dorothy interrupted. 'Perhaps he's in the Gents. Brother, would you be an angel and check for us?'

Standing in front of the one closed cubicle, he asked the door: 'Father Molloy, is that you? Sister Dorothy wants you.'

'No, it's the Pope, you stupid bastard. And Sister Dorothy'll just have to control herself and wait.'

When Hannigan came out, the nuns were talking to the girl.

'He's not in there. At least I don't think so.'

The nuns would blow his secret of his clerical status and God would be pleased.

But Sister Philomena was busy with another topic. 'Michael, I was just saying to Margarita that we must all get together when we get back to Melbourne. We met Margarita at a conscription rally just after Arthur was shot. She and I were the only ones who could sing the Red Flag right through . . .'

The toilet door opened, but it was Jim who faced them, his head resting against the 'Men's' sign that had been stuck on the door for the conference. He was amiably drunk. 'Jesus! I mean, hello all. Good night all, God bless, *Dominus vobiscum.*'

He drew them a careful blessing in the air and walked with distinctness along the corridor.

'Well, we'd better go in search of the other man of God,' said Sister Dorothy without enthusiasm.

'The story of our lives,' said Sister Philomena.

So Brother Hannigan was left *solus cum sola*. Alone with a woman on her own.

'Well goodnight, Michael, I have to find the west wing.'

'Funnily enough, so do I.' He did not add that he had already realised that his room was near hers.

They stood outside their doors, putting their goodnights on hold. He suddenly realised that a crumpled clerical hat sat in front of his door. He grabbed it and held it behind his back.

'Well, goodnight, Margarita. It's been fun.'

'Goodnight, Michael. Yes I've enjoyed it.'

Just as she was closing her door, he blurted out. 'I've got some riesling.' But her door was shut. He was putting his hat in the cupboard, when there was a knock at the door.

'You were offering some wine?' and she held up a tooth-pasty glass. He opened the flagon that had been suggested by Brother Lynch. It was moselle.

She sat on the bed and talked about herself and her four sons. Crossing his legs over his disobedient erection, Brother Hannigan felt safe with the mother of four, as he struggled to keep his eyes off her thighs and breasts.

'You're not married of course.'

'Well, not actually.'

'You must have a lot of fun.'

'Well, just a bit. I suppose you could say a bit.' He shrugged his shoulders to indicate an unspectacular bachelorhood. 'Well, I suppose you could say a bit of fun.' He filled their glasses to indicate that it wasn't too unspectacular.

'I envy you, no family responsibilities.'

He was losing control. He stood up and immediately sat his erection down again.

'Well actually, I mean to say,' and he could hear the grandness climb into his voice, as he confessed, *bless me, Mother, for I have sinned.* 'I'm a religious.'

She let his statement stand there alone.

He tried again. 'You know, belong to a religious order. Of priests. I'm a priest in training.'

'Oh, I know that. Philomena told me when we were registering.'

She leant back against the wall. On his bed. 'Tell me about it, celibacy and all that.'

'Well, it's not celibacy that's the hardest.' He knew this was true in some cosmic sense. 'We take other vows. It's the obedience that's a problem, having always to ask permission and believe your superiors are telling you God's will. And poverty, having to ask for a cake of soap and a new pair of underpants. Never having any money to spend.'

It was true and he felt quite moved, and only his erection disturbed the truth. She sipped her moselle. Her blue eyes were still chuckling, but they didn't seem to be laughing at him. Cornflower blue. There weren't any clichés in the spiritual novel that he was going to write, with Father Superior's permission.

'But it must be hard, mustn't it, being celibate? Not having sex and...'

'And missing out on the joys of family life. I know what you were going to say.'

'No. I was going to say, and masturbating all the time.'

'No. Not at all. No.' He paused to light his pipe. 'Well, yes sometimes. Fairly often, I guess. Especially for some. But as a matter of a hard fact, it's the obedience that I find hardest, for myself, personally. I can only speak for myself.'

He poured two more glasses of moselle.

She held up her glass in a mock toast. 'Here's to celibates and all others scared of the flesh.'

He had drunk half a glass before he got round to protesting.

'Scared. No definitely not. All that's changed. Especially since Vatican II.'

'I know nothing about that. Is it important?'

He was deeply shocked, and talked on against her yawns in great detail. '...and you ought to read the decree on the laity, *Apostolicam Actuositatem*...amazing recognition of the laity...'

But she was standing up and not really listening to the liberation of Vatican II – opening its windows, turning on lights, sweeping away the dust and cobwebs...

She put the glass on the desk and stood at the door, stretching, a small energy of grace. 'Well, past my bedtime. First paper at nine in the morning. You must have some prayers to say before you get your beauty sleep. First paper is on the power of the Senate versus the power of women in the years before Augustus. Sounds like your Vatican Council. Sweet, dry dreams.'

He was suddenly alone, in a room like a monastery room, deconsecrated by the presence of Marilyn Monroe, her white skirt blown up about her waist. As he sat down to read vespers, he glanced at Margarita's glass standing on the desk. Perhaps it would be charitable to return it. *Blessed Virgin, keep my body pure and my mind holy.* He read compline, praying for Brother Koenig, Brother Williams, Marilyn Monroe. His family. And Margarita. And Moira. And Madeleine. He prayed for himself, for a vigorous, humble priesthood that would be a light to all men. And women. At that point, he distinctly heard God stop listening.

As he finished reading the psalms in English, he thought of Father Brown, who insisted on reading his breviary in Latin, the language of the dead. He decided to write to him.

Dear Father,

Just a quick note. I'm sure you'll soon be better and out of hospital. I remember you in my prayers each day, and I know you'll do the same for me. (Know yours are better.)

I hope the doctors and nurses are treating you well, especially the nurses.

The Latin conference has got under way and seems very interesting. Some very nice people, including Father Molloy, who sends regards.

A few things I forgot to tell you. (1) Brother Williams is not going blind after all. Apparently he just had a lot of dandruff in his eyebrows. (2) The shorts for Schancks campaign is going very well — probably because of your prayers. (3) Re our discussion of the Blessed Sacrament — I'm sure you're right: it's a bit simple-minded to think the Eucharist was invented mainly for the consolation of Mary.

I'd better get to bed, it's late. No worries about chastity.

I enclose a poem I wrote on the way up in the train.

> *Mary, come and walk with me,*
> *and share the burdens of your mind,*
> *your father dead, your husband dead,*
> *your son has left you far behind.*

> *O Mary, let us listen,*
> *O Mary tell your pain,*
> *We will shield you Mary,*
> *You shall not weep again.*

There was a knock at the door. Brother Hannigan felt a sudden thrust of hope. When he opened the door, Father Molloy was standing there. Brother Hannigan knew he was in for mass in the morning.

'Michael, dear boy. I know it's late. Very late.' Father Molloy was dredging up his words slowly. He put his hand on Hannigan's shoulder. 'You know, you're a fine young man. Fine-looking young man. I think we're kindred spirits. I've got this wonderful collection of crucifixes I carry round with me. Would you like to come round to my room and we could go through them together.' By now there was a hand on each shoulder.

'Hell! No. I mean, thank you, Father, but no. I've got to say vespers.' It was a holy lie.

'That's all right, boy, I can wait.'

'Then I've got to get to bed. I need a lot of sleep. I've got epilepsy. And piles. And asthma.'

It was difficult to get back to Mary, but he felt he owed it to Our Lady and Father Brown.

> Mary, youngest sister, 'tisn't many days
> since you replied, 'Thy servant, Lord',
> the expected didn't come, God is not of us.
> Mary, giving is not its own reward.
>
> O Mary, younger than the dawning,
> and now so older than our pain,
> since that Bethlehem morning,
> when Jesus cried to be slain.
>
> You feel the darkness as Simeon
> is blunted with the truth
> and forgets a mother's crowded hope,
> the fears and wonders of your virgin youth.

(Just had a visit from Father Molloy. Most interesting chat. Crucifixes. Interesting and unusual man.)

> Tell me wondering Mary,
> all your sorrow, thought and pain –
> your boy not lost but walked away,
> no stars behind your sudden rain.
>
> Then he left you in his love,
> to live not for you but others.
> Did you feel, now lost and lonely sister
> a clamouring to spurn your brothers?
>
> But on a cross he owned you, mother,
> your glory has at last begun;

then he turns from you in agony,
and makes for you another son.

I mention only Our Lady's father. I couldn't fit Saint
Anne into the scansion. I presume both Our Lady's
parents were dead by the time of the crucifixion. There are
a lot of problems aren't there?
Anyway look after yourself, Father, and God bless.

Yours sincerely in Christ,
Michael Hannigan MOM

PS No problems with chastity.
PPS Not many women at the conference anyway.
PPPS Also pray for Brother Williams, as he also has
other problems as well as dandruff in his eyebrows. Bigger
problems.

He stood at the window and let fly with prayers. *Thou who*
wast a virgin when thou ascended into heaven, keep me pure. An
ejaculation every quarter of an hour, that was his resolution.

It was quiet now, as he looked out on the street, swished
clean by rain. He was mesmerised by the street lights planted
to scare the darkness. There was quiet, with noises mumbling
in their sleep. This was busy quiet, different from the Greater
Silence of the unlit acres of the monastery.

Sitting at the desk, he tried to think of the fruits of the
Vatican Council, the subject of his meditation notes for the
last seven weeks. The Church was God's two-thousand-year
reich and going strong. The problem with Hitler was that he
lacked ambition.

The fruits of the Council seemed a bit dry, so he turned to
his list of self-control points, a few of which he browsed
through each night.

103 I shall always go to sleep with my eyes towards Heaven
and my arms folded across my breast.

104 I shall always stand upright on alternate legs when doing up my shoes.

105 I shall not lick the jam from the spoon when cleaning up in the refectory after a meal.

106 I shall observe modesty of the eyes at all times especially in regard to women and their breasts and legs.

107 I shall avoid the use of condiments at table, except for those I do not like.

108 I shall not loiter in the toilet, but spend the time needed there making ejaculations to the Blessed Virgin.

O most excellent Virgin, obtain for me health and chastity of body.

He felt safe. He looked at Marilyn Monroe, standing where the Sacred Heart should have been, her mouth open in an ecstasy of surprise. The Virgin Mother keeps giving birth to love. *Thou art my mother, O Virgin Mother. Keep me safe lest I ever offend thy dear Son and obtain for me the grace to please Him always in all things.* Pride, and the loneliness of being another Christ, they were the problems. He felt contentment flow through his body. He looked up at Marilyn Monroe's lusciously opened-closing legs. He must go for a walk with Margarita some time during the conference and explain more coherently about life in the monastery and the fruits of Vatican II. It would still be *solus cum sola,* but it was the age of Vatican II and it would be out in the open, and not subject to the nasty misinterpretation of bedrooms. He knew his intentions were good. He smiled contentedly at Marilyn Monroe.

He was standing at her door, holding her toothbrush glass. 'Hello. I'd like to sleep with you.'

She was wearing a long and modest nightie, of a pattern his sisters had taught him to recognise as a Liberty print. Her mouth and eyes settled into a surprised smile.

It was a sin only in the mind, a sin of intention, because she was going to tell him to get lost, to smack his face, to tell him to piss off. To yell for help.

'You mean you want to fuck me?'

His astonished silence was yes.

She opened the door graciously. 'Well, you'd better come in, hadn't you?'

She lay on her bed, comfortable in granny nightie. 'Well,' and she was friendly, amused, 'what are you going to do about it?'

He approached the bed, then rushed over to the washbasin and put her glass in the sink noisily. He sat on the bed and kissed her with incompetent passion. He pulled her nightie up over her legs in a clumsiness of ecstasy. She was chuckingly unhelpful, but finally raised her arse. She was the first woman he had ever really looked at. He could hear his breath in gasping rhythm with a moth soft-pounding the light above him. He kissed her again and she led him with patient urgency into her mouth.

He hesitated for a moment, guilty, not for God, but for Madeleine, whom he'd failed to love. This time he was going to be loving, this time he was going to be joyous, he thought with determination.

Gently, she pushed him away. 'It makes it a bit more even if you're without clothes too.' She lay with her hands behind her head looking at him struggling against his belt as he stared at her breasts. He hesitated between untidy passion and neatness, decided against picking her nightie up from the floor, discarded his own clothes, till he stood naked in his black, to-be-washed-tomorrow socks. He bent down to kiss her.

There was a knock at the door. He knew they should have done it in the dark. Horrified, he watched her slip on her nightie. Horrified, he heard Sister Philomena at the door.

'I'm sorry, Margarita. I know it's horribly late. But I've started early. I didn't bring any pads. Could I bother you for one.'

'Of course, Sister. It's a pleasure.' Margarita pushed the door to, and rummaged in her case. She smiled across at him. Brother Hannigan smiled limply back. He noticed that his big toe was protruding through his left sock.

She went to the door, carrying a small parcel wrapped in floral pink paper. When she stood at the door, he could feel his horrified presence devil-dancing round the room.

'Here, take these. I've got plenty. Or would you prefer Meds? I think I've got a couple in my bag.'

'No, these will be lovely. Convent issue. Thanks so much. Sleep well. God bless. See you in the morning.'

She took off her nightie and lay down on the bed again, chuckling.

He worked up a laugh. 'What was that all about?' he asked, slipping off his socks and walking about the room.

'What do you mean? You don't mean...' She sat up. 'You really don't know, do you?'

He was sitting at the desk. 'Well, not exactly.'

She laughed with real amusement. But he also saw that something about him was being dismissed.

'Come on. Lie down.' He knew that sometimes her four sons heard those reassuring tones.

'Will I switch the light off?' he asked hopefully.

'No, I'm sure God meant fucking for the light, don't you think?' She held out her arms to him.

He started to kiss her, anxiously wanting his passion to rise again.

'Slowly. Enjoy it. I want to.'

He raised himself on his elbow. He stroked her blond hair, tentatively, waiting to be somewhere forbidden. 'You're not shocked are you? This is not the sort of thing I usually do.'

She laughed for him. 'At this point I say, according to the script, and I usually don't make love to strange men. But you're the one who's shocked.' She stroked his cheek patiently, kindly, then pulled him to her. 'I thought you wanted to fuck me, not talk to me. God won't hate you.'

He hesitated about talking about wanting to talk to her, about telling her that he respected her as a person. His thoughts got stranded on her taut, soft belly. He raised himself up again and finally put his hovering hand on her breast. Not bell-shaped. Melon, no. Pear, he couldn't see that. Breast-shaped, firm and soft when he started to suck and lick and bite and love into them. He almost wept with excitement and self-pity.

She stroked his penis. He had a joyous agony of memory, a vision of Father Smythe discussing in Moral Theology the problems of premature ejaculation. He rejected memories of Madeleine, and quick, uncaring lust.

She stroked his back and looked at him with warm intentness. 'I rather like you. Kiss me again.'

They kissed gently and he felt the passion rising from his tongue. Fumbling with folds of skin and flesh, his finger found its way into her cunt. He was surprised at her juice.

She was passionate and patiently instructive. 'Not there. Lower.'

'Sorry.'

'Yes. But gently.'

'Sorry.'

'No. Higher.'

'Sorry.'

'Gently.'

A week later, Brother Hannigan stood on the landing outside Father Brown's room in Saint Vincent's Hospital. He had already been to confession twice but he had always felt that Father Brown's absolution was a bit more potent because he was so much nearer to God than anyone else he knew. But he found Brother Lynch and, much to his surprise, Brother Williams standing at the end of the bed.

'He's asleep, is he?'

'No. He's unconscious. Father Superior has just been and

given him the last rites. He'll be back after golf. He'll be lucky if he finds Father Brown at the nineteenth hole.' Hannigan was surprised to see an uncharacteristic anger crouched in Brother Lynch's big, round-shouldered body.

They put together the desultory words that were, like all words, a shout against dying.

'Anything happen while I was away?'

'Brother Kiernane and Brother Forsyth are going to Rome.' Tony Williams was consoling. 'Don't worry, mate. You're better out of it. I suspect studying in Rome is as exciting as watching cornflakes dry or a bishop think.'

Hannigan could see his letter to Father Brown sitting on top of his locker. The old man stirred a little, his breathing became less laboured and his eyes opened a little.

'He's the best we've got, you know.' Dominic Lynch was being unusually explicit. 'He spent a life believing in the love of God.'

Father Brown opened his eyes fully.

He looked at them. 'God bless you, Brothers.' Then he stared beyond them. 'God, you can't let me die yet, after all I've done for you, you miserable old bastard,' he yelled.

And then he died.

Towards ten o'clock that night two young policemen entered the Champion Hotel in Gertrude Street, Fitzroy. The bar was strangely quiet. It was the first time in the hotel's long memory that the police had escorted from the bar three young men, dressed in clerical attire, who were much the worse for drink.

'Let us pray,' said Brother Hannigan to the policemen, young in their bewilderment.

Brother Lynch crossed Gertrude Street against the lights, and did an imaginary drop-kick down Brunswick Street towards Saint Patrick's cathedral. Impervious to the cars charging past him, he declaimed to all who would listen: 'Talking to God is like playing kick-to-kick with a kid who can't mark.'

'Brothers, let us spray,' said Brother Williams unzipping himself next to a lamp post.

Then he looked up to the sky and shouted, 'I'm going to be a priest, and bugger the lot of them! What are you going to do about it? Eh, what are you going to do about it? Or are you as scared as we are? Eh?'

1967

eight

*M*artha

I N THE LONG RUN, Father Superior was practising to be
a saint or a bishop. In the short term, however, he was
practising to win the clergy golf tournament. He had
come second two years in a row and, to Father Finnegan,
coming second was suspiciously un-Christlike behaviour. So it
was no surprise for Brother Hannigan to be standing on the
oval having Father Superior address both himself and a dozen
golf balls.

Father Superior was inviting him, in an ordering sort of way,
to join Carewarm. 'Carewarm is the chance of the laity to take
a lead. It's a volunteer organisation, counselling people in
crisis.'

Father Finnegan sliced a ball in the direction of the
monastery cemetery, said 'Hell!' and returned to people in
crisis. 'The laity can help them, you know. The laity can lead,
as long as they get proper direction.'

He explained how Mr Santamaria was the Daniel Mannix
of the laity, the Ben Hogan of the modern Australian Church.
Of Ben Hogan, Brother Hannigan knew nothing. Archbishop
Mannix was famous enough and dead enough for priests to
start making up stories about how well they had known him.
Mr Santamaria was famous enough to have a monastery
beagle named after him.

Father Superior fixed Brother Hannigan with the ancient-
mariner gaze of a liturgical reformer or a home renovator. 'A
Great Man, Mr Santamaria. Could almost have been Irish.
Could have been a priest. Even a bishop. It all shows the
mysterious ways of Providence and how the Christian

Brothers and the Jesuits can be trusted to balls – er, muck things up when they get hold of a promising lad. Mind you, no one admires the Christies and the J's more than I do.'

And he belted a golf ball straight down the oval, over the monastery cows and between the goal posts at the other end.

When Brother Hannigan returned after roaming the oval to collect golf balls, Father Finnegan proceeded to the cemetery. Here he practised his putting, because the graves were the smoothest stretch of lawn in all the monastery's twenty acres.

'So I want you to get in touch with Miss Wilson at Carewarm. It's the best, Carewarm is. Life Line and the Methodists are OK. They have one major problem, of course, they're not us. They think all this stuff was their idea. But we thought of it first. I mean God did, didn't He? The confessional, that's Life Line without a phone. Talking to a priest is a direct line to God. But Miss Wilson sounds quite intelligent for a woman, and someone who hasn't had our training.'

Father Superior just missed a putt in the hole he had got one of the laybrothers to make for him at the foot of Brother Alfonso's grave.

'So I want you to get in touch with Miss Wilson at Carewarm. She's a spinster lady, but does a good job for all that.'

When Father Superior missed another putt, Brother Hannigan decided that it was not the right time to discuss a worry about Brother Koenig that had been nagging him for months. At least the girl with stiletto heels was no longer clicking her way through the monastery grounds.

So Michael Hannigan met Martha Wilson, and was surprised that her fifty-year-old skin was as delicate as her kindness. She commanded love by giving it.

Martha was liaison officer for Carewarm, which meant that she comforted volunteers when crisis phone calls dumped them back into their own crises. She helped with the training of volunteers and kept the media informed about the modern

Catholic process of supporting people in crisis. 'Being in crisis' was almost a sacramental activity around Carewarm, and Martha seemed to be the only person without a crisis, but she didn't look deprived. Some thought she was a bit too pious, but she conveyed to the seminarian her sense of God as dangerous but friendly.

He knew that his reports back to Father Superior were being incorporated into a report to be given to a conference of Superiors on 'Seminarians in the Sixties: Sanctity and Sin in the Suburbs'. So he went to the Carewarm general meeting with a new Biro and Spirax note-book which he had obtained from Father Bursar, because he felt uncomfortable with his usual folder made from a corn-flakes packet.

He had got to like Carewarm, partly because it got him out of the seminary, partly because, in listening to calls from the lonely and the frightened and the deprived, he felt he was doing something priestly. Carewarm was for him a bit like a monastery that had got up off its bum. He was generally inept but Martha managed to make him feel that this didn't matter. And Martha could talk like a social worker and still sound like a person.

So he was pleased to meet Martha by the lift in the foyer before the annual general meeting. He suspected that the meeting would be a love-in, congratulating God on His good luck in having them do His work for Him.

Hannigan was wearing his clerical suit and hat. The hat made him feel stupid when he wore it, stupid when he tried to find something to do with it.

'First floor, here we go,' and Martha pressed a button and kept talking to him.

'Feeling slightly guilty, I am,' she said, straightening up her grey knitted twin-set with the red belt. 'Shouldn't be out enjoying myself,' and her smile disappeared somewhere inside. 'It's Mary's anniversary.' The lift stopped at the fourth floor. 'Got it wrong again, did I?' she said and laughed. As he manfully sorted out the button for their descent, Martha put her hand on his shoulder. She gave out a sort of professional affection, with a shimmer of sensuality. 'I miss her you know, Michael. That's why I put so much into this, I think.'

Michael Hannigan had heard often of Mary, in far away Dayton, Ohio. Martha and Mary had discovered theology in America in the fifties, before the clergy had discovered the laity. Mary had become a Carmelite nun and stayed in America; Martha had returned to Australia to help found Carewarm. Mary had died on the feast of the Betrothal of Our Lady, a year ago. Martha mourned her often and cheerfully, occasionally wondering if she hadn't died of disappointment at Vatican II. 'Not enough exercise, if you ask me, too much Jesuit theology and too many hamburgers before she became a Carmelite. Lovely person though, I miss her.'

They had made the return trip to the first floor and the lift doors snuck open against their privacy. But Martha was still talking. 'Too fat, she was, poor girl. I'm not going to die from a diet of hamburgers and Vatican decrees. Well, look at me. I eat well and I work well. Not bad for an old girl, eh?' She flared her body before him, with her large breasts, and a tingle of perfume that he noticed for the first time.

Martha had first told him about Mary on the one occasion on which he had met Martha outside the loving confines of Carewarm. And that had been with Father Superior's approval. Implicit approval, at least, for Father Finnegan certainly approved of Miss Wilson. Hannigan suspected this was partly because he had passed on to him the news that she had read PJ Finnegan's *Sin, Sex and Sanity*.

Hannigan had not mentioned to Father Finnegan that she had thought the book a bit of a wank, and had then to explain to Hannigan what wanking meant. Martha had considered the book slick, not tough-minded enough, and had shown him four articles in French theological journals which could have been called close sources for the thinking of the Superior of Saint Patrick's Monastery, Balwyn.

'He's a good populariser,' the seminarian had said weakly.

'Make a good bishop,' Martha had replied.

That occasion had been one of a chance encounter with Martha – a surprise interlude, a hint of friendship with a woman.

That day, as the other seminarians had started to move onto the oval for the afternoon's football, in a motley of football jumpers, Brother Hannigan had taken off on the privilege of his run outside the monastery grounds. He was recovering from a cartilage operation, after being driven into the ground by a large Franciscan full-forward during their annual friendly. He ran through the scaled-up English lanes of the surrounding suburb of Canterbury, enjoying the comfortable autumn trees standing guard over Peugeots and Rovers and the piles of leaves burning sweetly in the gutters. *Goldengrove unleaving.*

He had enjoyed himself that day. More often, lately, his share of the hundredfold seemed to be diminishing. He still looked forward to saying mass, to giving patient wisdom in the confessional, to placing the host on eager tongues. But too often, lately, God was *dearest him that lives alas! away.* The world wasn't charged with the grandeur of God; rather, creation seemed, too often, an achievement of magnificent carelessness, like managing to get a front-loading washing machine going with the door open.

'Why, Brother Hannigan, what a pleasant surprise!' In front of a green and brown terrace house, in the only row of terraces he had ever noticed in the eastern suburbs, there was Martha. She was trying to get a pile of oak leaves to burn. 'Michael,' she said, leaning on her bamboo rake so that it wilted, and surprising in jeans and gumboots, 'come inside and have a drink.'

A puffing parody of fitness, with knobbly knees and hairy legs, he regretted now that he had been a front-runner in the seminarians' 'Shorts for Schancks' campaign. In the sunlight, organised and subdued by the trellis, he admired her garden. *Long live the weeds and the wilderness yet.* Weeds are like opportunities of grace, he told himself, not knowing what he meant. Habit.

'Hells bells,' said Martha, 'just look at those bloody weeds, would you. I hate the damn things!' and she pulled the top off a piece of paspalum that was creeping up on a rose bush. 'Come inside and we'll do something sensible like have a drink.'

Her lounge room, first room off the narrow passageway, had been warm and surprising. Two leather armchairs stood before an open fireplace. One bookshelf was packed with green Penguin crime fiction. Another shelf had a translation of Aquinas' *Summa Theologica*, and works by Jung and Joyce, some Proust, even some Protestant theologians like Barth and Tillich. An opened copy of *Lolita* lay face down on a small table next to one of the chairs.

He had expected pictures of the Sacred Heart and Our Lady of Perpetual Succour, to whom Martha was known to be devoted. Having a genuine piety, which wasn't paraded too much, Martha went to mass each morning. In her office she had a gallery of posters, declaring 'Love is...' various things. She retreated to a convent in the Dandenongs each year and spent a week looking for lyrebirds and talking to God and to herself. This was the sort of thing he had gathered from chats over cups of instant coffee after a session on the phones – after a couple of hours listening, being responsive, being authentic, being frightened and confused.

But that day he had seen her walls smiling with ten years of Melbourne Cup winners, all neatly framed. Above the fireplace was a print of a Stubbs' painting of an English Derby winner, with horse, jockey and spectators all looking leanly thoroughbred. The mantelpiece was comfortably crowded with books on Phar Lap, Bernborough, horse breeding, betting, the history of the thoroughbred and of racing. At either end stood photos of Jim Johnson and Jack Purtell, looking pleased with their horses.

'You'd like something to drink?'

He was pleased at the thought of something like Fanta, a monastery indulgence on feast days, but Martha came back to the room with a tray of Black Label Johnny Walker and two glasses already poured. He laughed. 'Martha, I couldn't. I've never tasted it. Besides,' and this sounded weak even to himself, 'we're not allowed.'

'Come on, do you good. I'll give you some soda, though I never touch the stuff myself.'

'That hits the spot,' said Martha, falling back contented in her chair. 'Come on, Brother Michael, tell me about it. I've met plenty of priests, but I've always known them baked and put out to serve; I've never known one in the process of being cooked. We need some good priests, and of course it'll help when we finally get some women priests.'

He gulped down his whisky in surprise. Brandy, wine, and now whisky with a woman of wild ideas. He was really getting to know the world.

He fumbled through his thoughts and Martha listened well. The rigour of poverty, but no, you never had to pay a bill. The agony of obedience, but yes, it did make decision-making easier. The delirium of chastity, yes but there wasn't much in the way of relationships. Or children. Martha listened to the joy of administering the sacraments.

He didn't hear much joy in his voice and he was faltering into her silence when she stood up and said, 'God help us, you know I nearly missed it.' He looked back through the jigsaw of his pieties to find the missing piece. But Martha was turning on the transistor that stood next to *Lolita*. 'Got ten dollars on this – Gin-and-Bitters: seven to one.' The race was on.

'Good Catholic sport, racing,' he said.

'Probably why it's so crooked.'

Gin-and-Bitters was struggling against High Principle.

'Great race-caller, Joe Brown.'

'It's not Joe Brown. This is Rosehill.'

'We've got a parish at Rosehill.'

'Shush, I've got to hear my money go down the drain.'

Ken Howard was betting London to a brick on George Moore when a wail came from a machine that stood on the mantelpiece.

'Bloody hell, the bleeper,' said Martha and she got up and pressed a button that silenced the opposition to Ken Howard's voice.

'Well, did I win? What happened to my ten dollars?'

But Michael Hannigan hadn't heard either.

'Another bloody crisis. I mean my ten dollars.'

He waited as Martha rang Carewarm, talked briefly, then listened for a long time. She explained patiently that it was perfectly OK to give a homosexual the phone number of an advisory service; that, no, they didn't have to insist that homosexuality was a perversion.

As he had trotted home, prayerlessly, he thought that Martha was generous and interesting, if a bit of a worry. But then, she hadn't done a course in moral theology and therefore couldn't help it. And it was probably all right to send homosexuals off to an advisory service that helped them.

Now, nine months later, having come to recognise her as one of God's more intelligent smiles, he was glad of her company at the annual general meeting. As they got out of the lift, he was anxious to get to the meeting, as he hated the display of a late entrance. He scuttled after Martha over the lino tiles, feeling like a little boy, unable to keep pace without breaking into a run. Having heard her talk to her rose bushes, having seen her reassure the earth and soothe it, he was not surprised to see her carrying a bunch of roses, wrapped in the paper from some Christmas past. They were her annual offering of thanks to the director.

'I always look forward to this, don't you?' She smiled at him. 'There's some bullshit and some big-noting. But we do actually get together, and I feel at home here, with the people I love and trust.' She stopped walking. 'That sounds like a bit of bullshit too, but it is true, you know, Michael.' He had now caught up with her and by-passed his reply that this was his first general meeting.

Her legs were neat and crisp in her unexpectedly high-heeled grey shoes, her bum was broad and comfortable, and he felt guilty about noticing. She stood at the doorway, handed him her roses and took a Mason Pearson hairbrush from her large red bag. She looked at him, and smiled with that intelligent, sceptical trust in her blue eyes. As she pulled the brush though her greying, close-cut hair she said, 'I do like these get-togethers – seeing how we're all going, drinking cordial and eating scones.'

The auditorium was almost full of volunteers. On the stage stood three of the regulars at Carewarm celebrations, a couple of green plastic garbage bins filled with orange cordial, and the director in his dark brown suit, with a family of Biros in his pocket. Brother Hannigan felt smiles wash past him and onto Martha. She found two seats for them in the front row.

Roderick, the director, stood at the front of the room and was making beginning noises. 'I've got ten of eight,' conferring with his watch. 'You want that I should read the general report?' A year in California ten years ago had starred and striped his speech forever. 'Does everybody have himself a copy?' He held up the orange report with the Carewarm logo – a cross sprouting into a tree or a tree dying into a cross. Martha's artwork. 'So you want that I should read it?' Mistakenly, Roderick took silence for consent.

'Since we are now entering our third year of Carewarm's emergency phone service for people in crisis, we may do well at this point of time to take a reflective look at the quality of caring, the quality of our warmth, the quality of our loving kindness...'

As Michael looked across the room, he saw that already the faces had taken on the masks of patient boredom he associated with chapel and sermons.

'...twenty-six per cent call us because they are unhappy at home, fifteen per cent because of some psychiatric problem, nerves, depression, disturbed...'

'Mr Chairman!' A young man, redolent of points of order and wearing a black-and-red football jumper, had stood up. 'Mr Chairman,' he repeated with the authority of someone who had said it many times before.

Roderick, neat and dapper as a frog, looked as though he was about to jump away. But he worked himself up into patience. 'Yes, Frank.' Then he explained: 'A noo face.'

'We all have copies of the report. We all know that reports are boring,' said Frank.

They laughed a take-your-pick laughter, agreeing, disagreeing.

Frank picked agreeing. 'That being so, I move that the report be taken as read.' He sat down on a job well done. There was silence.

Martha looked at Michael Hannigan.

'Do something,' she pleaded. 'He so wants to read it.'

'I can't.'

'You mean, you won't.'

He almost smiled at this eternal Carewarm dialogue.

At the back of the hall, a little man in a three-piece suit of executive grey half-stood up. 'I second that motion, Mr Chairman, and just let me say this, I'm sure without any shadow of doubt that this report is not boring, and when I read it I'm sure I'll be proved right.' He sat down on his copy of the report, with the comfortable look of a man who had spent a lifetime seconding motions. The man was one of the few businessmen in Carewarm, and Hannigan remembered his name was Alistair, not a saint's name.

The report got tabled with the half guilt of arms half raised. Martha's hands threatened to reshape her plastic chair. Her face, moulded to smiling was re-fashioned into a frown, then a grimace. Roderick let the conversation swirl and eddy for what seemed to Michael a very long time, time to savour again the energy in the woman next to him. One part of her wanted to be the successful mother of the large family of human suffering, which had to be walked after, talked at, worried for. Another part of her recognised that loving her warring self was the hardest job.

'Could I, could I...' Roderick plunged into a hole in the talking, 'could we proceed to the next item, now that we have settled, buried, the report to everybody's satisfaction.' Smiling across the hurt world from Biafra to Balwyn, he then smiled down as though to welcome home his patterned shoes. 'The next item of business. The positions of secretary, treasurer and liaison officer are all vacant of course. I guess you want that I should get the easy one over.' Roderick was smiling himself back into loving them all. 'So let's start with the liaison officer, which, as you know well, is our important link between the volunteers, our backbone, and the professional staff. I think – a little birdie told me – that this is the easy one – like the last coupla times, if you take my meaning. I have a quarter after eight,' he said to his Seiko. 'Let's see if we can get this over by nine and then we'll have ourselves some fun.' They looked without longing at the bins of cordial.

'I'll call now for nominations for liaison officer – who is not the officer for organising liaisons,' beaming wittily. 'We do that ourselves.'

True, they acknowledged, as they handballed their laughter around the room, everyone reluctant to accept the pass.

'I nominate Martha.'

'I second that.'

'Me too.'

Roderick felt a speech coming down upon him. 'You all know that this most important position, which is filled by a volunteer, who is given an honorarium, an office and lots of love...this extremely important position,' Roderick was trying to track down his sentence, 'has been more than adequately filled by Martha for the last...' a struggle of memory and an embrace of a smile, 'let me think, well since Carewarm started, so do let us proceed...'

'You haven't called for any other nominations,' Frank interjected.

Roderick could respond to a joke. 'Yes of course, I take it that there are no other nominations.'

This time, Frank was standing. 'We all love Martha, very much, and we know she has done a splendid job. But she's looking tired. And, besides, a change is as good as a holiday.'

'Yes of course, thank you again, Frank.' Roderick's smile was stuttering. 'Well?' Silence. 'Well, that, that was easy, so I...'

Frank was still standing. 'Mr Chairman, I would like to nominate Brother Michael Hannigan.'

'God, no,' whispered Hannigan loudly as he looked across at Martha, before declining.

'Don't be a silly boy.' She was smiling at him and he didn't know what she wanted, or how much it mattered to him, or to her. He was distracted in shame by a vision of her office, a room of his own.

The new liaison officer drove Martha home to Canterbury in the blue, Our-Lady-coloured Holden. Again, *solus cum sola*, alone with her, not counting God and His Blessed Mother. Their silence was harassed by the Beatles lamenting 'Nowhere Man', and the Monkees declaring they were believers.

They were beneath the Skipping Girl vinegar sign before the music prompted Martha's first comments. 'Silly men, probably sentimental only when it suits them. Like Arthur Rylah weeping for the purity of his non-existent daughters. Not like Henry Bolte. He's going to hang Ronald Ryan, you know. No, you don't know.'

Outside her house in Canterbury, she put her arm around him and held him to her breasts. Inexplicably, he started sobbing, crying to someone else for the first time since his adopted mongrel dog had been killed by a car at Boolingalap when he was seven. His mother had hugged him and he had sobbed himself to peace. Now he grew quiet and began to kiss Martha's neck.

'I like you, too, Michael,' she said as she pushed him gently away. 'But lust is a self-hating sin. So is self pity. I still like you, though.' Her absolution was as powerful as Father Brown's.

Standing on the footpath, Martha looked up at the sky. 'Mary loved nights like this, when even the stars are warm. But then she liked the Rolling Stones singing "It's All Over Now" and Mario Lanza's "Ave Maria". Nobody's perfect.'

On her verandah she turned on the outside light and started searching in her bag for her keys. They were both startled when a girl suddenly stood in front of them.

She put her arms around Martha and sobbed into her shoulder. 'Oh Martha, thank God you're home at last. God, I've been all right, honest I have. For weeks I've been all right, but tonight, I don't know, I just needed someone. God, I needed you.'

Martha held her close. Somehow, almost without words, she stilled the girl's sobbing.

Brother Hannigan stood by watching, useless. Finally the girl looked up at him, dark eyes, dark skin, her face anguished. 'What's he doing here, Martha?' She kept staring at him. 'He's one of them. He comes from that monastery place near me. I've seen him. He stares at me. Tell him to go away, Martha.' She sobbed again into Martha's shoulder. Then, talking to him directly for the first time, she said, 'I'm sorry. You're probably OK. I mean, on the night that it happened, one of your blokes found me and took me home. He tried to help.'

Looking at her tear-stained cheeks, Hannigan realised that he was looking into the face of the girl in stiletto heels for the first time.

'Martha, why do I feel so horrible? It wasn't my fault, I was only working back late to get some money to go to Surfers. I always thought going through the monastery was safe. Martha, I know it wasn't one of them, but get rid of him.' She sobbed into Martha. 'I know it wasn't one of them, but get rid of him, Martha, please, please get rid of him. I hate all bastards in blue Holdens.'

Over the girl's shoulder Martha nodded him friendship, nodded him absolution, nodded him dismissal.

Brother Hannigan drove home, irrelevant, making irrelevant acts of contrition. On the seat beside him were a bunch of unwanted roses.

1968

nine

The Service
of the Bishop

*T*HE BISHOP was as gay, as innocent a man as ever walked a golf course. A tight waddle of a man, he hurried into breakfast with his usual brightness, which was the radiance of a Coke ad done by Murillo.

'Good morning, Fathers,' after he had made a very accurate sign of the cross and paused a blessing on his eggs and on the world.

The Bishop liked order at his breakfast table and he gave it lovingly to his Wangaratta diocese. He chased away his second frown for the morning: there was too much laughter among his priests. Then he remembered there was a guest at his table. When a guest comes, Christ comes. So he pushed away his eggs and accepted the Weet Bix and Weat Harts offered him by his visitor, Father Michael Hannigan. The Bishop hated Weat Harts, he hated cold eggs, but the boy meant well.

The Hannigan boy had gone off to join the MOMs when Bishop Mulligan had been parish priest of Wangaratta North. Bit of a waste, really, he thought as he swallowed the stodge, when the Church was crying out for diocesan priests. But they weren't a bad lot, the MOMs, more co-operative than some religious orders the Bishop could name, though he knew quite a few Jesuits who weren't too bad. And Joe Finnegan, who was good at God and good at golf, was always willing to send up one of his men to help out when they were undermanned in the diocese. At Father Quaid's request, Father Michael was doing some 'youth work' while he was in Wangaratta visiting his parents and his sister Bernadette. The Bishop was suspicious of 'youth work'. And he wondered if he shouldn't mention to Father Michael that Bernadette had stopped having children, in case he hadn't noticed.

Father Quaid and Father Hickey were now enjoying priest talk.

'Tom,' Father Quaid was saying to Father Hickey, 'you only backed Red Handed last year because it was a Catholic horse. If Cummings hadn't been training it...'

'That's bullshit, Gerry.' Father Hickey was righteous in argument. 'I often back Tommy Smith's horses and he's no Catholic.' He turned to the Bishop for confirmation. 'Tommy Smith, he's not a Catholic, is he?'

The Bishop noticed Michael Hannigan splutter as his surprised Weet Bix went down the wrong way. The Bishop understood. He didn't encourage swearing or gambling. But he understood them more than he understood the excesses of Vatican II. The Bishop sometimes had a flutter himself, acting on the advice that Jack McArdle always gave him in the confessional after receiving absolution. The Bishop's SP bookie was a devout Anglican and known to give generously to the Mission to Seamen.

The boy has a lot to learn, the Bishop thought, as he cut into his defeated eggs. The boy had served his mass that morning and the Bishop had resented the pause of surprise when he had started off in Latin, a luxury he allowed himself every Saturday. The Bishop still loved the rumbled mysteries of the old mass. He felt an ungainly guilt, but then they all carried their guilts. Gerry Quaid religiously watched Bob Santamaria on television but enjoyed 'Homicide' more. And Tom Hickey did explain rather too often the pastoral importance of his being chaplain-coach to the girls' basketball team.

The Bishop loved the old rituals and loved himself in the purple processional wobble from the back of the church to the altar on special occasions. And he didn't mind whom he said it to, though you had to be a bit careful these days even if you were a bishop: priests were getting too smart. Just the other week he had said, as a joke, that he liked the days when the Church had banned books. From what he had read in the *Advocate*, this Mary McCarthy woman was writing filth, and her with Our Lady's name and should have been a Catholic. Father Quaid had said, 'We should be like Hitler, and burn books.' And Father Hickey said , 'No, the popes had a better idea: they just banned them and ended up with a great library.' The Bishop did like a joke, but he couldn't tolerate frivolity.

'Well, I've got to pick up Hell-Hole Harry,' said Father Quaid, and he managed to straighten a chair and make a sign of the cross in one movement.

'And I've got to go and get pecked by the hens.' Father Hickey didn't even straighten his chair.

'What that means,' the Bishop translated, 'is that Father Quaid is going to the station to meet the Redemptorist missioner, and Father Hickey is going to hear the nuns' confessions.'

He had a lot to learn, this young man. Pleasant enough. Years ago, the Bishop had thought of him as attractive. Now he was just another eager young man, blue eyes permanently startled. And hard to talk to. The Bishop thought about asking his opinion on another premiership for Collingwood, but didn't want to shock him. 'How are the folk masses going these days, Michael?'

The boy smiled, uncertainly.

Nice smile, if only he'd let it off the leash.

'I've got a new tape recording from Sydney. Wonderful stuff. It really gets the kids in.' Michael Hannigan stood up. 'I'll bring down the tape recorder and play it for you, My Lord.'

'I'd just love to hear it, Michael.' Father Hannigan moved towards the door. 'Just love to. But some other time. I'm awfully busy this morning. Have to rush off now.' The Bishop poured himself another cup of coffee. 'Have some coffee. Mrs Tyler'll be in to clear away in a minute.'

The Bishop savoured his coffee, warding off the taste of the day.

'I knew Ben Brown, you know,' the Bishop said reflectively. 'I meant to get down to see him in Saint V's, but I never seem to get to Melbourne much these days. Not even to see Collingwood play.'

'Yes, he was a great priest, he helped me a lot.'

The Bishop noticed that the boy was hurting his way through his words and he understood the loss of a good father. 'Well, look, young Michael, he's better off in Heaven and I hear he died the death of a good priest.'

When Mrs Tyler came to clear away, Father Hannigan was still standing uncertainly in front of the coffee pot. The Bishop knew well her scorn for those who dithered their way to Heaven. He poured the boy a cup of coffee and told him to sit down.

'Does old Joe still tee off regularly these days?' The young priest hesitated. 'Your boss. Old Joe. Father Finnegan, your provincial Superior.'

'Oh. Of course. That boss.' Michael Hannigan was circling round for the right answer. 'Well, I mean, I don't know. I suppose. Probably.'

The Bishop stood up, blessing himself carefully before and after saying grace. 'Not good to forget your Latin, lad.'

'We've all forgotten it already,' said Mrs Tyler, who was busy at the table. 'Soon kids won't know what a zac is. It'll come to that, you mark my words.'

As the two men stood on the steps outside the Bishop's house, Hannigan gave a detailed account of a Latin conference he had attended in Sydney. The Bishop was impressed, and dismissed the young priest with good wishes for his folk mass. He was surprised when the boy knelt down to kiss his episcopal ring. He knew the boy was surprised when he found a hairy finger and no ring. A bit out of touch, young Michael, not up with all the changes of Vatican II.

The priest was rising in search of his dignity when a gleaming new mini pulled up.

'It takes a long time for the oils of ordination to dry,' the Bishop said irrelevantly. He turned to the tall man who had jumped out of the car. The Bishop was ever surprised that Edmond O'Neill didn't one day, in his life of bursts and bounds, leave his always-blue suit behind him.

'Ed, Mr O'Neill, I'd like you to meet Father Hannigan. He's a Missionary of Mary.'

O'Neill made a speedy reverence towards the priest, then turned his portly eloquence on the Bishop. The booming voice, coming from such a sliver of a man, always hit the Bishop with a shock. 'Hardly seven stone wringing wet, and half of that would be miraculous medals, sounding brass, that man,' was Mrs Tyler's view.

Ed was sounding off now. 'The Our Lady of Snow credit union, My Lord. That's top of the agenda, My Lord. After your spiritual worries, of course, My Lord...we need to have an overview looking after those matters which need to be done...Mustn't throw the baby out with the bathwater. In short, My Lord, we need proper cost accounting.' All the time his feet were stuttering up and down the steps.

John, the Bishop's weekly gardener, wheeled his barrow past, a shovel rattling against its sides. Ed O'Neill stopped talking to look at the man with the thick, careless body and the small after-thought head. He was still talking cost accounting when John wheeled his barrow past again, still in search of a load. Ed's busy, deserted eyes caught the blue catch-me-if-you-can of John's eyes.

He turned back on the Bishop. 'Some things have to go, My Lord. We all have to make sacrifices. The auditors will be in. Soon. And if you don't mind me saying so, My Lord, it's, well...it's a mess. Not my fault. And, of course, not yours. But we need to talk about an end-of-the-line, final, fallback position. They've thrown us in the deep end and now we've got to decide how we're going to cut the cake.'

The Bishop looked to the priest for help, but found no saviour there. The priest had noticed a small child getting out of the car. She was four, maybe five, years old. The Bishop wasn't very good on children's ages. She was a small swagger of a girl, fair, red cheeks, with a bubbling walk.

'Monica, get back in the car, or no Smarties.'

'Lovely child,' said the priest.

'Beautiful child,' said the Bishop, who was immediately scared of her.

She stormed the steps and fell over.

'There, I told you,' said her father. 'Now get back in the car, and then we'll pay a little visit to Our Lady and then we'll buy mummy's eggs and pantyhose and your Smarties.' He turned back to the Bishop. 'My Lord, it might seem impossible, even improbable that the deficit could be so lous...well, so escalated.'

Father Michael picked the child up. 'How about we get some flowers and put them on that statue of Our Lady?'

'I want to take them home.'

The priest looked down at her bleeding left leg. 'Would you like a band-aid? Or would you like to go home to mummy?'

'Band-aid. And mummy.'

The Bishop looked down at her with the benevolence of a WC Fields. Then he noticed that Michael had produced the miracle of one band-aid, and then another. The girl seemed happy with the crucifix of band-aids, and with the way the white handkerchief, touched with spit, cleaned up the blood.

'I think you ought to go home and show mummy, and all that,' said the priest.

'Yes, Father. Let's go, dad.'

Ed O'Neill paused in reluctance. The Bishop thanked God and the child.

'Well, My Lord, I don't want to harp back to a non-negotiable position that would mitigate against us, but...'

But Michael had placed Monica in the car and she was saying goodbye. 'You haven't got any band-aids in your dress, have you, Bishop? But that's a nice cross.'

As the mini burst out through the front gate, the Bishop put his hand on the boy's shoulder. He had felt comforted to have Michael with him. He had admired the grace of his control, and the confidence of the slim hands that had lifted the child into the car.

'Thanks,' he said. 'I mean, I can stand God turning up in most of his incarnations. God in gumboots, God with a guitar and those thong things, but when He turns up to present the accounts, and comes trailing a sample-size Mother Superior, then I wish to hell I'd never become a bishop. You think it's all sin and sacraments, but most of us end up being God's accountants.'

The Bishop could see that the priest didn't know what he was talking about. A nun came out of the church, unwrapping a Violet Crumble as she walked.

'Sister Bartholomew. Good value, though she's a bit cracked on the new liturgy.'

'Good morning, Bishop. Good morning, Father.' She took a bite into her Violet Crumble. 'I've come to do a reconciliation. You know, of the accounts.'

'God bless you, Sister,' said the Bishop as he realised what she was talking about.

'Well, I'll get on with it then. See ya,' said the nun and she went in the Bishop's front door without knocking.

'Great nun, bit casual mind, but a great nun. We'd be lost without the nuns, wouldn't we, Father?'

The Bishop started walking towards the church. 'Let's go and make a visit together, and then it's off to the desk for me. Better go over those accounts.' The Bishop took fast, fat strides. 'I've got to address Rotary on Vatican II, then a confirmation at Yackandandah, then a meeting on the Saint V de Paul waste-paper collection, then Father Deasy from

Barnawatha, curate there, wants to become a Trappist monk, quite a handy golfer...'

The Bishop stopped talking at the church porch, and allowed the priest to enter the church ahead of him. As Hannigan threw himself a sign of the cross and almost missed, the Bishop was suddenly reminded of another young man, a seminarian who had flirted with him twenty years ago when he was teaching moral theology. Nice lad, who had cheated in the exam on the sacraments. The Bishop had never been sure if he was sad for the loss of a good priest or the loss of a good smile.

Father Hannigan knelt with the Bishop beside a plaster statue of Saint Joseph, who stood patiently waiting with his experienced lily, snake at foot, for guests to arrive. The young priest touched the snake with his slim hand as he passed it on the way out.

They stepped out into the light, and found Mrs Moynihan shining on them.

'My Lord, what a pleasant surprise!' She was a graceful woman, and forceful. She closed off her sentences and her prayers with the decisiveness of a stapling machine. The Bishop was scared of her, even though he secretly agreed with her campaign to restore the public recitation of the rosary in church.

'My Lord, about that seminar thing on the place of women in the Church, I think the ladies should be asked to bring a plate.'

Father Michael smiled out at Mrs Moynihan, offered to discuss this matter with her and report back to the Bishop. Clearly this was something that needed a long discussion and His Lordship was pressed for time. He talked her away to the parlour of the Bishop's house. Nice lad. Nice woman, too, of course, though the Bishop found her dark nights of the soul had, like her clothes, a Pierre Cardin quality that was a bit too rarefied for him. The Bishop stood wondering why Fathers

Quaid and Hickey talked about Mrs Moynihan in that
vaguely lascivious way that graced the conversation of many
priests. Women were not a problem to the Bishop. At least,
not in that way.

Late that afternoon, the Bishop was sitting in his office
listening to the races. How shocked Father Michael would
have been at his worldliness. But a little relaxation was
deserved after a hard day. He had tried to explain a translated
Latin joke to puzzled Rotarians. They had been even more
bewildered when he explained Vatican II and the collegiality
of Bishops. They were enlightened by the analogy of a share-
holders' meeting, but then he felt perhaps that was rather
selling out the mystery of Christ's authority in the Church.
During his confirmation sermon at Yackandandah, two
children and the parish priest had gone to sleep, with two
babies crying all the way through. Even though the Bishop
had gone to great pains to refer amiably to one of those pop
groups – was it the Rolling Bones? – that Father Quaid had
told him about.

So, back home, he sought consolation in the radio. He
twiddled the dial, fleeing a group of young larrikins singing
blasphemously 'Mother Mary come to me'. He found peace
in the races, or cricket.

'...an immaculate stroke, this one.' Alan McGilvray, very
soothing man. Could be a Catholic name, though 'Alan'
made it a bit doubtful.

The Bishop sat at his desk. The high-rise papers before him
were bound by all sorts of cordage. Some butcher's string from
McMahon's, the Catholic butcher. A jackdaw collection of
black and brown shoelaces. A red and white Saint Philomena
cord, which the Bishop had years ago worn around his waist
when chastity was still a problem. Patron Saint of South
Melbourne. Young Michael would be shocked by such impiety.

The Bishop knew his weakness. He left his papers
untouched and twiddled his way between the races and the

cricket. 'Lowland has literally flown over the last furlong. Cummings the master has done it again.'

The Bishop answered the phone, the curate from Tenelong making his third enquiry, on behalf of a friend, about the Pope's new procedures for dispensing priests from their vows.

'McKenzie is really bowling an impeccable line and length.'

The Bishop gathered up his strength and used the Knights of the Southern Cross paper knife to cut the Saint Philomena cord. The engraving on the handle said: *The hundredfold is already here.* The Bishop glanced through the requests he had been avoiding. A couple who had just discovered that they were not validly married in God's eyes wanting to continue to live together, but as brother and sister, for the sake of their six children. A priest wanting to take the parish netball team on a tour of the Holy Land. Another priest wanting him to bless six pieces of the true cross. Another priest seeking his gracious permission...

'And Walters drives this ball with sweet authority.' The Bishop had a large whisky and then forced himself to read an article sent to him by a priest who had been foolishly, wilfully going round the diocese of Wangaratta declaring that the Pope would approve of the contraceptive pill.

'Chappell has taken a miraculous catch.'

At five o'clock Father Hannigan caught the Bishop pouring his second glass of Johnny Walker. The priest had come to ask if he could accept Sister Bartholomew's offer to play the guitar and sing at the youth mass tomorrow. The Bishop discussed cricket and contraception with him. Not an unattractive lad, when you looked at him, though the Bishop had once seen him picking his nose just before he had taken up the chalice to say mass. Mrs Tyler brought them coffee and fussed over them in a grudging way. The Bishop sat stirring his coffee as though dredging for something, then glugged the sugar bowl with the wet spoon.

When the Bishop and the three priests met for dinner, they found the breakfast joviality had died with the day. They ate loose-gut sausages and talked of the liturgy and sport, but antiphonally rather than conversationally. After dinner, the Bishop went over to the church to make the stations of the cross. Young Michael and the other young blokes probably thought this was all a bit old hat. The Bishop was himself a bit more express through the stations than usual, hesitating rather than pausing at each step in Christ's passion, slurring a genuflection in front of each image.

Outside the church, the glass-sharp shadows were gone. He walked across to the cemetery. He liked the companionship of the gum trees on the south side that leant tired against the darkness. He liked to say hello to Patrick Mulligan (1885-1951) and Maria (1888-1960), beloved wife of the above. He respected even the linked arms of the blackberry bushes on the north side, holding them all in place till the resurrection.

Sitting on his bed beneath the picture of Our Lady of Sorrows, inherited from his predecessor, he hurried through vespers and compline. He didn't touch his glass of whisky till he had said goodnight to God. He heard Father Michael singing down the corridor, on his way back from the shower. The Bishop was more aware of the lad tied into his towel than of the tuneless 'Ave Maria'. He got into bed and tried to decide which to read first of the books that Ed O'Neill has asked him to look at so that he could condemn them with authority. He tried *Lolita* but found it boring and therefore a bit disappointing. He had a go at *The Naked Civil Servant*, but found himself staring at his statue of a disapproving Little Flower, big with roses.

He rested the book on his belly. He was overweight, should be playing a bit more golf. He owed it to the diocese. He wondered if Joe Finnegan had taught young Michael to appreciate golf as a spiritual activity.

The Bishop loved God with an energetic compassion, but he did get a bit sick of doing all God's paperwork. From the wall opposite, a photo of a conference of bishops studied him, all of them suspicious, all of them committed to keeping God honest. But at least they had secretaries, all of them. Tom Quaid and Gerry Hickey laughed down the corridor. All very well for them, they could mess and mass their way through life. They didn't have his tomorrow. What with Kathleen Moynihan, Ed O'Neill, the priest who wanted to become a Trappist, the priest who wanted to become a husband. And Sister Bartholomew wanting to do readings during mass. All very well for Quaid and Hickey to be making smart remarks about the Church being an eternal bucks' night of spiritual fun. What did they know? The Bishop decided to drink his whisky and found the glass was empty. He needed a secretary, that's what. And young Michael Hannigan, he didn't know much, but he was keen. And he could handle Monica O'Neill and Kathleen Moynihan and Sister Bartholomew. Joe Finnegan would release him for a year or two. Joe liked co-operating with bishops. The Bishop needed someone keen around the place. Sister Bartholomew was young and keen, but the Bishop knew she was a woman and suspected her of having a taste for liturgical excess.

The Bishop got out of bed. He needed a piss. He hesitated before putting on his blue dressing-gown. Didn't usually, but should he run into Michael, the lad might be embarrassed at his sagging pyjamas. The Bishop always liked to show himself in purple, except to Tom and Gerry and they didn't count. The Bishop had a comfortable piss. Michael could get the filing in order; it needed it, God knew. Bugger Ed O'Neill and his little, accounting soul.

The Bishop walked down the corridor. From Gerry's room, a late-night radio host was being cosy and reverent about Hayakawa and his Tokyo Trombones. From Tom's room, Pete Seeger was singing 'There is a Time'.

In Michael's room there was silence.

'Michael, are you asleep?'

It was cold in the room. The Bishop's hands were shaking. They always shook when he was tired. The Bishop heard an ambulance hurry away with someone's death or fractures. The Bishop's pyjamas were sliding down over his large belly. He should have done them up properly.

The silence was awake.

'Michael, it just occurred to me, I was wondering...well, maybe you'd like to stay with me. I mean as my secretary.'

Back in his room, the Bishop found he was trembling. From the cold. Glad that young men were such sound sleepers.

ten

Melchisedech of the Mulga

*R*IGHT YOU ARE NOW,' Father Grady paused in the middle of a throaty spit into a tin half full of Fisher's wax.

Father Hannigan noticed the phlegm camouflage itself in gobs of polish.

'You'll take the car now. Here's the keys. You'll do just fine.' He placed the tin on a small bedside table, grabbed it again for a backwash spit, and then rummaged among breviary, Lifesavers, and empty glasses. 'Where the hell did I put those keys now? Did you have them for breakfast, Saint Aloysius?'

The young priest looked at the Alsatian, a sleeping eiderdown across the bed, licking its lips in its sleep, growling, then relaxing. 'Oh, the keys. Gosh, I'm sorry, Father, Miss Jamieson gave them to me last night.'

'Then you're right then.' The old man fiddled with the safety pin of his pyjamas and scratched himself carefully through his grey flannel. 'You'll be off then,' snuggling down under the sleeping dog.

The first mass was at the local Wagambie church. Father Hannigan was already late and ran down the path, his cassock swirling. He was clutching his breviary. It always made people feel he was busy with God. He braked into a dignified scramble as he neared the dusty station wagons and polished faces of his congregation.

Everything was a rush. He grabbed on the vestments, neatly laid out, violet-forlorn purple with fraying braid, not convent-clean as he was used to. Old Roman vestments, sandwich boards, derros from Latin masses, not the flowing Gothics of the Balwyn nuns; but somehow lighter and fresher because bought from Pellegrini's thirty years ago in memory of someone now forgotten. On the stage of the sanctuary, they would look impressive from the back of the redbrick church.

Because it was Palm Sunday, he handed out the bits of cypress pretending to be palms, pre-blessed and already brittle. With reverent speed and timing, he missed out the prayers that were supposed to follow the palms. He confessed to Almighty God on behalf of the community. There was a thud as a late station wagon bumped into another, and he shared their agony of 'whose?'.

'Glory be to God on High,' he began, and then withdrew the praise as it was Palm Sunday and no joy. He turned to the congregation and said, 'The Lord be with you,' a sincere and friendly God saying 'Hello, we're on the same side,' or 'G'day mate'. The latecomer arrived, making a merry-go-round with his brown hat and looking with terror at the only vacant seats – the three front rows. His confession: 'Bless me, Father, for I have smashed Mabel Moylan's car, it was double parked but.'

The Epistle. Saint Paul's letter to the people of Philippi. Where Caesar's ghost had appeared. He stressed *being of the same mind which Christ Jesus showed'*, wondering about the empty cowbail look on their faces. The same mind. Here all genuflect. The annual cacophony of Lenten confusion, when the rituals suffered changes to fit in with the celebration of Christ's suffering. The man reshaping his hat rushed to the front seat, as though taking advantage of half time. The priest paused at the few shuffles of those slow off the genuflection. Someone dropped the collection plate, which was really an old cheese box on a bamboo pole.

Turning to pray that their sacrifice be acceptable to God, he realised what a patient audience they were, here in the hills thirty miles beyond Mansfield. Their raggle-tailed response indicated that this was his show, that he was Christ in charge, proud and frightened. But they had patiently suffered the

Gospel of Saint Matthew. At least he wasn't back in the monastery having to sing it before a chorus line of musically alert
seminarians. He loved the Passion tale in Matthew's tart story-
telling. He liked the role of the priest as story-teller; he liked the
performance. But as an entrepreneur of sacraments and a
spruiker of grace and wisdom, he felt less comfortable. Now he
was aware of the reverence of their boredom as they waited the
Passion out, innocent bystanders, aware of their own guilt.

The latecomer with blond hair and years of summer
harvests on his face stood in the front row and looked at his
stilled hat. Down the back, near the hushed confessional
curtains, an old lady slumped in the corner of the seat
wrapped in the distinction of having fallen over during that
funny genuflection they have in the Palm Sunday Epistle.
'That old Mrs Flanagan, she's a character, she is. Must be
ninety if she's a day.' Nice, being noticed. Like being a priest.
And she could be excused standing at the Gospel.

The Gospel. '"*Art thou king of the Jews?*" *Jesus told them*, "*Thy
own lips have said it.*" *They said*, "*Barabbas. Jesus, who is the Christ,
let him be crucified.*" *Pilate sent for water.*' Poor bastard. Bit hard to
blame him, really. '"*My God, my God, why hast thou forsaken
me?*"' His voice caught a little bit here. '*Jesus cried out with a loud
voice and yielded up his spirit.*' Here all kneel. A shuffle of silence,
boredom and sadness. He had forgotten to clean his finger
nails. A timber truck broke through the silent prayer. He
finished the Gospel, and the congregation blew its nose and
reorganised its pants and skirts. He gathered up his sermon
notes and the priest turned to face his people. At ordination,
the Church had called him a priest according to the Order of
Melchisedech, the king of Salem who had blessed bread and
wine for Abraham. Some days he knew his priesthood con-
sisted centrally in consecrating the bread and wine. Other days
he had a lot of fun performing in the pulpit.

Today he was Melchisedech, king of the pulpit. 'My dear
people.' Pause, for the final settlement. 'Once I read a story.

And, on this Palm Sunday, I would like to share it with you. One night a family home caught fire. The father rushed through the smoke waking his children. He was gathering his family on the lawn out the front when he realised his fifth child was missing. Then he heard a small voice from a second-storey window. "Jump, son," he yelled. "Daddy, I can't see." "But I can see. Jump."' He had got the story right and was moved.

Using some good notes he had taken on the Epistle to the Hebrews, he preached briefly but with feeling on hope and on the humanity of Christ. 'He was just like us in everything but sin.' The priest demonstrated the meaning of 'just like us'. He did stop short of telling them what he had explained to the seminarians in one of his first sermons after he was appointed lecturer in philosophy at the Balwyn seminary. That Christ must have turned aside from his preaching to have a piss. That Christ must have suffered an embarrassed erection when Mary Magdalene anointed his feet with oil. But he was eloquent on his favourite topic, Christ becoming flesh just like us and hating Palm Sunday and all it led to. He was Melchisedech, king of the pulpit. He felt comfortably helped by the young couple standing at the feet of the statue of Saint Gerard Majella and swapping a pink-swaddled baby, bargaining about who should take her out into the sunshine. '*My God, my God, why hast thou forsaken me?*' He said it twice, because it was so moving. But he didn't comment on it, because it troubled him. '"But I can see. Jump." That is what Christ says to us on this day of sadness, that his resurrection has made into a day of hope.' The baby's father gloomily carried it out of the door.

As he rounded off the sermon, there was some subdued stretching, and the men exchanged their distress signals about whose turn it was to take up the collection. Back at the altar, he unveiled the chalice and then turned to interrupt the rustle of questions and *Advocates* to make some announcements he had forgotten. His own masses never seemed to have the smooth ritual flow of the masses he remembered from childhood. They would be pleased to hear that Father Grady would be back with them next Sunday. God willing. And he was grateful for their gifts and prayers. And the Fatima statue was coming over from Mansfield on Mr Schultz's truck (and they all had a lot to thank Mr Shultz for – or was it Mr Scholes? Mr Schultz, thank you, and the man with the brown hat in the front seat looked uncomfortable again) and the statue would be at Mrs Fitzpatrick's house next Sunday, Easter Sunday. And Miss Jamieson at the presbytery had three kittens to give away, two male, one female, all house-trained. They stared unsmilingly at his smile. Miss Jamieson seemed to be staring faraway at God.

He poured wine and a few drops of water into the chalice. He washed his fingers ritually. Should have had that leak before he started. There was no finger towel, so he talked a bit more loudly: *'With the pure in heart I will wash my hands clean, and take my place among them at the altar'*, and wiped his fingers on the front of the chasuble. He prayed out loud for the servants of the Lord, especially your Bishop, Patrick Aloysius. Funny old bastard with a heave of fat over his collar and a me-God look in his eyes. And all here present. And silently, he remembered his sister Bernadette, who was pregnant again. And Tony Williams, who had written to him from Trivandrum, South India. And Madeleine. And Moira.

The consecration always gave him pause. *'This is my Body.'* He enjoyed the deepening silence, the truce on shuffling, the attention on the host as he raised it with reverent dexterity. Holding long enough to adore quickly, but avoiding the theatrical. He always became conscious of his pipe-stained index finger. Here, as sometimes in the confessional, he felt real as a priest. Brushing a fly from the rim of the worn chalice, he mentioned the sacrifice of *thy great priest, Melchisedech.* He, too, was a priest according to the Order of

Melchisedech, and though he realised that his congregation knew nothing about this man who had offered sacrifice with Abraham, he liked the obscure connection with the Old Testament. The obscurity of the Order was part of his dignity as a priest.

At the prayers for the dead, he silently prayed for Brother Bernard and for Benito Alfonso, because he had died before he could become a priest. And for Roy McDougall, because he had lost his vocation.

The scuttle of communion time. The fleshy part of mass. Tongues. All shapes – spades, shovels, pencils, bulbs. All sorts of actions – resting, slavering, snaking, retreating, baulking. Some days it was a serene sacrament of completion. Today it was tongues – furry, cracked, blistered, nicotined. Would the host land safely, would he touch the tongue, would his fingers coat with spit? *'The Body of Christ. Amen...'* Hurrying it onto ridges, bumps, sandpaper. *Lord I am not worthy.* Tightening his grip on the ciborium. *'The Body of Christ...'* Swallowing, whispering, gobbling. *'...Amen.'* Occasionally disconcerting eyes open, then lips widen to smile before swallowing the host.

The tidying up prayers and the mass was suddenly over. That sense of relief after a performance.

'Would you like a cup of tea now?' He was in the sacristy, in only the white nightgown of the alb. Miss Jamieson seemed to be accusing about something.

'No thank you.' The alb eddied round him as he pulled at it. 'No, thank you very much,' as he folded the alb on the table and felt a little more dressed to face her. He smiled at her eyes that were clear and brown and shining, like imitations. But he knew her kindness was real. He resettled his collar, which wasn't anchored to his shirt because he wore only a singlet beneath his religious habit. 'I'm running late for the second mass at Windabadgery.' He refused reluctantly, because her Twinings was a luxury for him and her scones had a thick freshness.

'Father Grady always has one. That is, since they changed the fasting rules.' She showed up his ungraciousness and the weakness of the modern Church in one go, waving her missal that was a photo album of saints.

'I'd love one, really and truly. But all those palms – and thanks very much for them – have put me behind the clock. And we can't keep God waiting, can we?' The thought of her strong tea brought a flash of wistful longing for the toilet at the back of the presbytery next to the fowl pen.

'Well, the case with the hosts, the sacred vessels and the altar wine is in the car.' She waved her cypress at him. 'It's two female cats, and one male, it is.'

The FJ Holden was full of dust and barely absent dog and homeless seat springs. Saint Christopher shared the flat spot on the dash with some rubber bands and a packet of Marlboro. The saint had one arm missing and struggled to balance on his perch through a disheartened magnet. He dabbled his left foot in what Hannigan first thought was an inscribed prayer: 'Made in Japan'. Hannigan managed a dignified zig-zag through the parishioners, swapping smiles and waves. A small group stopped examining a crumpled mudguard when he drove past, as though they had been caught in an act of indecency.

Out on the road, he drove fast. Along the road to Windabadgery – the gumnut Nazareth, wattlebark Bethlehem. It was always embarrassing to start mass late, always seeming your fault, when it wasn't. Saint Christopher shivered on his foundations as if about to bail out. Of course, out here, they didn't actually blame the priest, they resented him deferentially.

Windabadgery was a post-office-cum-general-store behind a long verandah with a dying roof. The store was genuinely general, reminding him of his childhood in Boolingalap: shovels and shirts, petticoats and hobnail boots, grains and groceries. A school, pigwhite, No. 4967, 1921, leaned against its tankstand. Then the gum trees crowded back to the road, waiting for a procession that never came.

'Christ! I've passed the church.' There was not enough room to turn. Then, miraculously, the trees darted back and there were the church and a haystack facing each other across the road. Driving across the cattle grid, he felt more relaxed. He always preferred the second mass, as though he had got through a rehearsal. Now he felt comfortable among his congregation, eager and patient.

In the clean-scrubbed sacristy, he was forcing down his collar with the amice and dredging up the appropriate prayer. *Put on my head the helmet of salvation.* A girl came in after a gesture of a knock – about eighteen, dark brown eyes welcoming and only half reverent. 'Excuse me, Father. Would you mind terribly if you heard my confession. We don't get much chance here.' She smiled. 'It won't take long.'

He liked confessions. Mostly. He knew it was partly the pleasure of the priested voyeur; but he knew it was also his least shrivelled attempt to touch people, through a listening curtain, with the kindness of God and with his own kindness. Their faith, devious and frank, humble yet routined with guilt, exhilarated him with his power and his inadequacy.

He bustled on the amice and got the tapes twisted. He looked for something for her to kneel on. 'I'll see if I can find a cushion in the cupboard,' he said, wanting to make it comfortable for her and unable to visualise confession with her standing.

He fossicked through candlesticks, thurible, tins of Brasso. Nothing soft there apart from cleaning rags.

But she was already kneeling on the floor next to the green kitchen chair. 'Bless me, Father, for I have sinned.' Head bowed, she prayed her hands together and told her sins. 'A month, well about, since my last confession. Being unkind to my father. Missing my prayers. Telling lies, twice, perhaps three times.'

Her pause contained something beyond the formula.

'Anything else?' Gently he tried to offer her freedom and to push her. She looked up for the first time. 'It's not much, is it?' lapsing beyond the routine. 'I just like to go, I'm not sure why.'

'Is there anything else you want to talk about?' he asked kindly, trying to hurry her relaxation, tempting her to a quick freedom, as he heard the gather of reverence in the church and realised that he had not yet moved the hosts from the peanut-butter jar into the ciborium. But, as she kept looking at him, he fought against being a slush fund for grace.

'It's not much is it? I don't even manage good sins.' Scuttling the routine. 'Sometimes I wonder . . .' the smile drooping into her questioning.

Again he offered her the opportunity of her silence. He heard people move in the church and touch her silence.

She frowned. 'I worry about a hell of a lot of things. Sometimes I think I hate God and my dad. Dad's a bit funny. And, well, sexually . . .'

He felt the impulse to put his hand on her shoulder and bring her to talking.

'I think and feel all the wrong things.'

He ceased to feel a robot of salvation. Then there was a knock on the door and he allowed her to tell him how busy he was, gave her a quick absolution and a chapter of the first letter of Saint John to read for a penance. At least that was different, though he knew they sometimes worried about how carefully they had to read it.

There were two other confessions. One was really to have a medal blessed and to ask about the secret of Fatima. And an old man, in a blue suit burnished at the knees, had bad thoughts three times a week and was afraid of the wife who had brought him through thirty years of droughts, bad crops, bad markets and Sunday masses. The priest served up three Hail Marys for penance.

As he walked onto the sanctuary, his guts were tightly but comfortably intact, and not swirling for escape, as they sometimes were before the attack of a folk mass in Balwyn. He relaxed, a hundred miles of haystacks away from the loud majority of God's people. He placed the chalice in the shade of the hydrangeas. He realised the candles were unlit and raised two layers of skirts in search of matches. A man saved his dignity by offering him a box of Redheads. He handed out the pieces of cypress to a reverence of Sunday suits and best hats.

When he began mass, he felt the peace of the ritual movement away from cows and crops, from dishes and milk buckets, towards God and the neighbours and all the latest news.

He said mass with a speedy love, reverencing the tawdry miraculous sacrament. He slowed at the intersection of the consecration, not in show but in his daily amazement, humbled at his power to bring God out of bread.

'Let us give each other the sign of peace. Whatever way comes naturally.' This was part of the new liturgy and here the mystery came out into the open as a muddle. A son plunged a peck on the arm of his mother's glasses. Nods, wet handshakes and a grimace of grace between a potato inspector and a farmer. God sponsored a passionate kiss for a honeymoon couple. And the postmaster kissed a surprised young girl. The scramble of fraternal love over, the priest gave communion, this time a swift-tongued devotion. As he ritually washed his hands again, he thought again of his demanding bladder. The hymn, 'Hail Queen of Heaven', was a mishmash of tuneless piety. He wound up the ceremony with graceful haste, once again to the shuffle of newspapers.

He unvested quickly. He was in a hurry to get away, not simply because he was embarrassed by their reverence for him as God bumping into their lives. Now he wanted the salvation of a piss.

When he hurried discreetly to the back of the church he found the wooden toilet lying resignedly on its side. Some dock-weed peering out of the door indicated that it had been like that for some time.

He walked through the gum-tree saplings until the bush thickened. As he heaved up his religious habit, he heard a voice, 'No, not here, darling, later'. He could probably piss his way to contentment without the lovers noticing, but he froze at the vision of the mediator between God and men standing unzipped, with his skirts tucked up under his chin.

He found a path heading in the opposite direction and into thicker scrub. He pulled his breviary from his pocket and opened it at random. Saying the Holy Office made a priest look both businesslike and Christlike. When he felt certain the world was no longer with him, he threw the breviary in the dust and started a piss. Hissing, sweet short silence.

And then a hymn swooped:

O, Mother, I could weep for mirth,
joy fills my heart so fast.
O, could the transports last.

They didn't. As he turned towards the hymn he sprayed his breviary. He was unzipped, but modestly covered by his habit and fiddling with a shoelace when Mrs Fitzpatrick came hymning into sight. She was carrying a tray of scones and tea.

'Just fixing a shoe.'

'Got a nail in it, Father? Patrick'll fix it. He's wonderful with shoes.'

He remained genuflected, his religious habit covering his wetland.

'No, got a stone in it. Meant to take it out earlier.'

'Well, you should have, you silly man.'

'Well, a bit of mortification, self-control. Keeping the old flesh quiet.' His bladder was belting back at his kidneys. 'Anyway, I won't keep you. That tea'll get cold.'

'It's for you, Father. Come on now, or the Earl Grey will be cold.'

He followed her obediently, almost prancing with piss. Inside the sacristy, the agony was inspired.

'Now you must sit down, and I'll pour. Do make a good cup of tea, even if I say so myself.'

The rushing of the rich tea into the cup smote his loins.

Mrs Fitzpatrick settled the furrows of her back on the green chair and enjoyed her weekly spiritual talk, of pills and popes and pregnancies; of Vatican II and the good old Latin days; and of priests' socks. 'Stones in shoes, might be good for the soul, but they're hard on socks. You men are all the same. Terrible with socks. You drink up your tea now. Anastasia gave Patrick some dark purple socks for his birthday and he won't wear them. I'll go and get them for you.'

Mrs F went. Or almost. Father Hannigan was thinking of the ways under heaven of pissing, when she popped back in. 'By the way, Father, talking of Anastasia, I hope you gave her a good talking to when she went to confession this morning. Real little baggage she's becoming, she is. Causing Paddy no end of trouble. Probably told you some lies...'

'Mrs F, of course I can't discuss what I hear in the confessional. You know that perfectly well. As Saint Augustine said, *about those things which I hear in confession I know less than about those of which I know nothing.*'

'You're right, Father, of course you're right. I don't know what Saint Joseph of Cupertino will be thinking of me. I hope you put her right but.'

She rushed off to find the socks. The sacristy door could not be locked. There was no sink to piss into. He grabbed the bottle of altar wine, uncorked it, swigged down its remaining contents. Then he pissed ecstasy into the bottle. As the ecstasy frothed up, he realised that it wasn't going to be contained in one bottle.

He grabbed the other bottle of altar wine, half full. He was about to take a swig when the door from the sanctuary opened. It was Anastasia, carrying two vases of defeated hydrangeas.

'Hello, Father. Lovely sermon.' She stood, looking at him, as though wondering if he wanted to be talked to. He stood, wordless, the bottle of wine in his left hand.

She put the vases on the bench and left him to his silence. He shoved a prie-dieu against the door that led from the altar and leant against the other door, pissing his way to contentment.

He corked both bottles tightly and placed them in the case with the sacred vessels and the peanut-butter jar of hosts. Like God along the road to Damascus, Mrs Fitzpatrick was suddenly upon him, holding on high two pairs of socks and a triumphantly damp breviary.

'Look what I found, Father! What would you do without me? And what's more it's wet, would you believe?'

He closed the case as firmly as its one working lock would allow and sat undignified on it.

'Aren't you going to put this in the case too?'

'Well, no. Later. I haven't said lauds yet.'

'Of course, we mustn't forget lauds, must we.'

'Pity. I must have spilt tea or something on it. I hope it doesn't ruin it. My mother gave it to me.'

'The dear soul. Give her my regards. Is she still alive?' Unlistening, she gave him a plastic bag, in which three apples sat upon a pile of lamingtons.

'No, really, Mrs F.'

'No buts, thank you, Father. Eat something on the way home. You're as thin as a match with the wood shaved off. And here's a little bottle of something. We're all human after all.' And she went off laughing at the absurdity of it all.

He placed the case in the boot of the Holden. As he drove slowly out of the churchyard, he thought of ways of replying to Tony Williams' letter from Trivandrum. Tony was going to marry an Indian girl in the Church of South India, without the Pope's permission. Her name was Magdalena. Thirty miles on, he wasn't sure yet if he had anything to say to Tony. *But I can see. Jump.* Or to anyone.

He pulled in beside a creek. He took the case out of the boot. Ciborium, chalice, two bottles of piss, one bottle of beer and one of the almost-blood of Christ. He threw the two bottles of piss into the water. He was sitting smoking his pipe when a horrible thought occurred to him. He opened the case and checked to make sure he hadn't left a bottle of piss to be consecrated into the blood of Christ. He sat and listened to the confidence of birds chitchattering the news of the day.

He was still sitting next to the case, throwing bits of lamington upon the waters, when the bustling of the birds slowed as another car pulled up. It was the postmaster, looking for a fishing spot. He had a young girl with him.

'Hello, Father, going off somewhere, or just doing a bit of meditating?'

1968

eleven

Requiem for Minnie

*M*INNIE was the first person Father Hannigan helped die. He had just finished saying mass for the MAMs, the sister Order to the MOMs, when the call came. He was talking to Sister Margaret in the sacristy, standing half unvested. The cincture, the girdle of purity, was in his left hand and the gown of the alb flowed free. He was embarrassed when Sister John came into the sacristy. He was supposed to be disrobing prayerfully, and Sister Margaret was not supposed to be talking to him without a chaperone. In finding themselves alone together, Sister Margaret should call out 'Companion!', and one of her sisters would suddenly appear, rather like the Angel Gabriel all those years ago, when the Word became Flesh. Then they would be permitted to discuss liturgical reform or the convent cows as a threesome.

He thought on this occasion that Sister John was appearing to make up the numbers, but she had a message for him. His cousin Damien wanted him at Saint Vincent's Hospital. Damien's mother-in-law was dying and she needed a priest quickly, because she hadn't been to mass for years. He grabbed the holy oils from the convent sacristy and went off, nervously, to do his first anointing of the sick. The teaching staff at Saint Patrick's Seminary, Balwyn, were not much called on to administer the sacraments to the sick. Their priestly activities were generally confined to seminarians and to parish congregations on Sundays.

Minnie had broken both her legs in a fall while pruning her Judas tree. Pneumonia had set in after surgery to pin one of her legs. Damien, red-faced as ever, was grateful for the family priest and anxious for Minnie's soul. Minnie was famous for not going to mass.

'So good of you to come, Father Michael. Loretta and I are so grateful.'

Minnie watched them, her green eyes wary, her small body more shrunken than ever.

'I'll leave you two to get on with it,' said Damien. 'I'm sure you've got a great deal to talk about,' and he went to join three of Minnie's seven sons, whom Father Hannigan had heard discussing the Essendon-Collingwood match in prayerful whispers at the top of the stairs.

Father Hannigan stood at the foot of the bed, waiting for the words to come. He put on the violet stole and took refuge in the ritual of the anointing of the sick. *'Sprinkle me with hyssop, O Lord, and I shall be cleansed. Wash me, and I shall be made whiter than snow.'* He anointed Minnie's eyelids, ears, nostrils, lips, hands, asking the Lord's tender mercy on whatever sins she may have committed through these senses. When he pulled back the bedclothes to anoint her feet, he was confronted by her plaster cast, but nevertheless begged forgiveness for any sins she may have committed through walking.

Sister Xavier Herbert appeared in the room, holding a slice of wholemeal bread. She held it out to him. He didn't know what to do with it.

'Father, you wipe the holy oils from your hands with it, then I burn it.'

He took a long time wiping his hands, hoping rather than praying for inspiration.

Sister Xavier surprised him by kneeling down in front of him. 'I haven't seen you since your ordination, Father. I know the blessing of a new priest is especially powerful.'

He blessed, placing his hands on her shoulders at the end. Shoulders for women, heads for men. Priesthood had made him very aware of baldness, as well as other sins of the flesh.

Standing up, Sister Xavier said, without looking at Minnie, 'Well, I'll let you two get on with it then, I'm sure you've got a lot to talk about. We had to move out a Franciscan and a Jesuit.' Then she added brightly, 'But I told them it wouldn't be for long. It doesn't seem right to have priests out in the general ward, does it, Father?' She left without saying anything else, self-evident truth required no answer.

Father Hannigan had thought, guiltily, about asking for information on Nurse Counahan. But Minnie brought him back to his priestly present. 'It didn't work, Father Michael.'

'No, it didn't,' he said, looking at his oily hands, 'but don't you worry about that now, Minnie, I'll get some soap and water later.'

She smiled for the first time. 'No, I meant all that anointing. It didn't work. I'm still scared. I want you to hear my confession.'

He heard her confession, three times. Three times she confessed her unambitious sins. Three times he gave her absolution, vain with priestly power.

'I'm still scared,' she said humbly, her fingers probing hope along her rosary beads.

'But Minnie, I've absolved you from all your sins. I've heard your confession. God has forgiven you.'

He counted and prayed against the hours as the Saturday wore on. Sometimes, as family came and went, as Damien would stand at the door hovering pleased over Minnie's soul, Hannigan would hear snatches of football from a distant transistor, Jack Dyer mediating.

For most of the afternoon, Minnie kept silent. Towards evening, she went to confession again. Then she asked, confident of an answer, 'Tell me, Father, what's God really like?'

He told her in detail and found he did not know. He said the 'Our Father', repeating over and over again, *'Forgive us our trespasses as we forgive'*.

A smile had come home to Minnie's face and many of the lines disappeared. She smiled to herself but whispered to him as though she feared God's hearing. 'It's all right, Father Michael. You needn't be scared. I'm not.'

She smiled to herself again, forgiving him.

It seemed a long time before she spoke again, and then it was from a long way off. 'I won't go to Hell for missing all those masses, will I, Father Michael?'

'No, Minnie, I'm sure you won't go to Hell.'

'Absolutely sure?'

'Absolutely.'

'Well, not now that I've been to confession. I'll say my penance again, carefully,' and she said the 'Our Father' once more.

Half an hour later, he went to the toilet. When he came back, Minnie had died on him, still smiling to herself. He waved his hand through the air yet again, for that was how God blessed people with forgiveness. He thought again of Brother Bernard in his coffin all those years ago. Minnie looked more peaceful.

Opening the *Ritual*, he found the words: *'May Our Lord Jesus Christ, the Son of the living God, who gave to his apostle Peter the power of binding and loosing, in his loving mercy accept your confession and put about your shoulders again the robe of sonship, which was given you at your baptism. And now in virtue of the faculty given to me by the Apostolic See, I grant you a plenary indulgence and full remission of your sins.'* He gave another blessing and, too late, wondered if the Apostolic See had actually given him this faculty.

To be on the safe side, he added another prayer, that he knew he had the right to say. *May you never know the horrors of the outer darkness, the anguish of the flames, the racking of eternal torment.* Then he smiled, knowing that Minnie would not suffer an eternity of burning; hers had been a kind fire.

Before he took his words and sacraments home, he was blessed by Sister Xavier Herbert. 'What a wonderful job you

[265]

did, Father. Some priests I know would have just given the sacraments and gone off to the football. Though of course, it's the sacraments – isn't it, Father? – it's the sacraments that matter. I'll go and tell the priests they can have their room back. They have great theological arguments, those two, though the Jesuit believes in the Pill. The Pope will put the world right on that, and the sooner the better. God bless you Brother – er Father – Michael.'

He drove back to the monastery and prayed, *Dear God, don't let me make her death into a poem,* already pondering the first line.

Next morning, he heard confessions in the South Balwyn parish before the eleven o'clock mass. He often said mass here, and to extend his pastoral activities, he also coached the football team that the parish priest had founded to keep twelve-year-old boys off the streets of Balwyn.

It was easy, in the routines of priesting and being priested, to see humanity as the debris of divinity. As he sat listening to the routines of sinning, the humility of some contritions, the cunning of others, he kept thinking of Minnie and her large fears and little sins. The Church had found the words to bring God down to size. It was people that escaped the Church, frightened Her. Or at least they frightened Father Hannigan.

'Bless me, Father, for I have certainly sinned,' one woman began, 'but I don't want to go to confession. In fact, can't go to confession...'

He shifted in his chair and put his head closer to the grille, as he always did when he felt a more urgent need to bring God closer. On some days, he felt as if the pattern of the wire grille were embedded across his forehead.

'We can all always go to confession,' and he could hear the words 'my daughter' hiding at the back of his sentence.

'No, Father, you don't understand. I'm on the Pill, and the Church tells me I'm sinning, so...'

'Well, I have it on good authority that the Holy Father is making his statement any day now, and I also have it on good authority that the Pope is going to decide in favour of the Pill, so that's good news, isn't it?'

It would be too tedious to explain to this woman that the authority was no less than Father PJ Finnegan, MOM, now Provincial Superior and in charge of all Australian MOMs, who had recently returned from Rome via America. He had visited his old putting ground, the Balwyn seminary, bringing with him two copies of American *Playboy* for Father Smythe, the lecturer in moral theology, and the news that the Holy Father was about to decide in favour of the contraceptive pill.

'So you can rest easy,' Father Hannigan told the woman. 'Our Lady will open a window, you just wait and see.'

'It's all right, Father, don't worry about it. I just want you to bless this Saint Christopher medal for my brother Justin – he's in Vietnam. My name's Madeleine. The Church's not doing much about that mess either, is it?'

He blessed her medal, and told her he was a pacifist, which was almost true.

'Go in peace, Father,' she said.

He didn't have time to word-up his thoughts before the next penitent came. He liked hearing boys' confessions, because it seemed one way of scaring off the fear that still stalked through his own life. This boy, however, didn't seem to have heard of Hell. 'Bless me, Father, for I have sinned. I belted my sister three times. I masturbated four times. But she deserved it.' Blasé as he was, the boy was tugging at the confessional curtain on his side of the grille.

Father Hannigan paused over the penance. He disliked the fast-lane three 'Hail Marys', but found that his ideas for penance were not a popular success: Be kind to other members of the family for the next week; read the first letter of Saint John, prayerfully. I mean what sort of penance is that, Father? You don't know whether you've done it properly. They didn't want a dithering God and now Hannigan dithered. The boy clutched at the curtain, as the priest abandoned himself to three 'Hail Marys'.

The curtain fell. 'Shit, you're the coach of the under-thirteens,' and the boy scurried out.

'I absolve you of all your sins,' the priest said to the empty confessional.

The following Tuesday, Minnie went to mass for the first time in years, her own requiem mass. Father Hannigan said the mass and preached a short sermon about Minnie and the love of God. When he explained Minnie's statement about doing the best she could in her own way and not mucking things up, he knew they thought he was talking about getting into the sweet sherry and not going to mass very often. He was actually talking about her doing without priests, about her getting God right, at least in the end, and probably most of the time. But that was the sort of truth you couldn't say from the pulpit.

When they lowered Minnie into the grave, he apologised to her for not getting it right, and almost forgot to say, *'Eternal rest grant unto her, O Lord, and may perpetual light shine upon her. Amen.'*

When Hannigan got back from the funeral, seminarians and priests were standing around the cloister, cheerfully breaking the rule of silence. Most were looking excited. Father Smythe, however, was frowning in the way known and loved by seminarians who dared ask frivolous questions about mortal sin in moral theology lectures. 'He's gone and done it,' he said gloomily, 'he's gone and closed the bloody window.'

'Who has?' asked Father Hannigan.

'The Pope, of course. He's gone and done it. Banned the Pill. And to make matters worse, Bull Muldoon has said it's one step away from infallible, that it's forever unchallengeable. There'll be a fuss. Mark my words, there'll be a hell of a fuss.' It said something about the day when a prominent Sydney Bishop was nicknamed in front of seminarians.

There was such a fuss that the sportsmaster forgot to arrange the annual football match with the Franciscans. There were rumours that famous theologians, and even bishops in Holland and America, disagreed with the Pope's encyclical on the Pill. There was a confirmed report that four unknown priests in Canberra had published a letter in which they said that Catholics could prayerfully disobey the Pope with a good conscience.

On the Sunday following the encyclical, Father Hannigan again said mass at South Balwyn. He said nothing about contraception. Instead he looked a couple of days ahead to August the sixth, the feast of the Transfiguration of Our Lord Jesus Christ. August the sixth was also the anniversary of something else, but he couldn't remember what. He counter-pointed Saint Matthew's account of the transfiguration by showing the congregation that, even if Christ's face did on this one occasion shine like the sun, most of the time he was exactly like us. He proved it from Saint Paul and the Epistle to the Hebrews. He dazzled at least himself with the humanity of God made flesh, and left his sermon notes on the pulpit.

He had been rather distracted preparing the sermon because on the Friday he had posted a letter to the *Age*, saying that Catholics could make up their own minds on the Pill. He had shown it to Father Smythe, who had agreed with its contents, but not with publishing it. 'Anyway, you can't publish any-thing without your Superior's permission. Besides, all publishing is vanity,' he had added darkly, sounding like Father Gerard Manley Hopkins, SJ.

He had not shown the letter to Father Superior, or to Father Finnegan, who was still staying at his old monastery and was rather boastful that no MOMs had made fools of themselves in public.

On Tuesday, August the sixth, the Feast of the Transfig-uration and the anniversary of something or other, Hannigan recycled his sermon on the humanity of Christ for the seminarians and was rather pleased with his passion. The *Age* published his letter.

He was reading it in the Fathers' recreation room when Father Hartigan came in. He pointed to the *Age* spread out on the billiard table. 'You've done it, Michael, you've really done it this time. Father Provincial is after your blood this time. Here, I want you to kneel down. I've got this relic of the Little Flower I got when I went to Lisieux after the General Chapter in 1948. It's done a lot of people a power of good. And you need all the help you can get right now.'

Kneeling down next to the billiard table, his right hand absentmindedly rolling a red ball to the end pocket, Father Hannigan was blessed by a certified third-class relic of Saint Thérèse of Lisieux. He was still kneeling in front of the *Age* when Father Finnegan came in.

'Kneeling down in front of your vanity are you now?' Father Finnegan seemed taller than ever, his hair still mainly red, his face red with anger. 'What nonsense is this, Michael? What in Heaven's name, in God's name, got into you, man? Who do you think you are? Unqualified to talk on matters of moral theology...'

'But, Father,' and Hannigan thought it was better to talk standing up, 'I've just finished seven years training.'

'Good grief, man, that just qualifies you to talk to the laity, not to write letters to newspapers. And what about your vow of obedience? Whatever happened to that? When did that go out the window?'

'But, Father, I wasn't asking people to disobey the Pope. I was just saying...'

'I'm not talking about the Pope. I'm talking about obeying me, your lawful Superior.'

'Well, Father, if in our training we argue that sometimes you have to make up your own mind about obeying the Pope, or the bishops...'

'*You* argue, just you. Nobody trained argues...'

'But Father Crotty, he's trained...'

Father Hannigan was arguing for the first time with a superior and the superior was hardly noticing,

'Bishops, that's another thing,' Father Finnegan was striding around the billiard table, straightening up another cue in the rack each time he went past. 'The Bishop of Wangaratta – I've had a complaint from him about you. He says you snubbed him when he enquired if I'd let you do some work for him. We MOMs have always been very faithful to the bishops. Very.' He straightened up two cues this time.

'But Father, it's a bit more complicated...'

'And another thing, Father Hannigan: I've heard from Father O'Gormon in South Balwyn that you're always going on about the humanity of Christ.' He paused in front of Father Hannigan and spoke more gently, 'That's all very well for theologians, but lay people get confused. So do you, obviously. I put you back here in the seminary for a few months to teach the first-year students logic till I can find something useful for you to do, and it all goes to your head.'

Father Finnegan walked to the door. 'I'll have to find something else for you to do. I think this is the worst thing that has ever happened to the MOMs since Father Galvin eloped with a nurse during the war, and that was twenty-three years ago.' Father Provincial was about to walk out the door, when he reflected, 'It was actually twenty-three years ago today. Exactly. God help us all.'

It was an anniversary, of sorts, but Hannigan was sure it was not the one he had been trying to remember. Priests who gave up their vows were forgotten with vigour and mentioned only darkly during retreats to make the seminarians meditate on the unthinkable, a lost vocation. On the other hand, the anniversaries of priests who died loyal were listed on the notice-board outside the chapel so that the seminarians could pray for different ones each day. The names of God's loyal servants needed to be brought to His attention. It was an article of faith among the seminarians that when some priests did leave, unknown men in the distant past, there was a woman mixed up somewhere. The war and women were responsible for a lot of damage.

Father Hannigan was shocked that it had come to this with Father Finnegan. He also wondered if, by getting all worked up about something like contraception, which wasn't eternal, he had destroyed forever his hopes of playing soccer with Indian boys at Our Lady of the Snow College, Trivandrum, South India, and through soccer, of introducing them to Our Lady and Vatican II.

He stood alone in the recreation room, rolling the white down the billiard table.

Father Finnegan appeared at the door to have one last word. 'Besides, Father Hannigan, I'm not sure that you told me all you knew about who put the glass in my football boots. God alone knows the whole story of who put the glass in my football boots,' and his face seemed transfigured at the mystery of it all.

Father Hannigan skipped breakfast, without permission. For want of something useful to do, he played himself at billiards and lost. He was surprised, when he went upstairs to his room, to hear the noise of talking coming from the refectory. That usually happened only on Sundays and when there was something special to celebrate. The Transfiguration was too small and too dangerous a feast to celebrate.

In the quiet of his room he remembered how much Father Finnegan used to emphasise that the Greater Silence reflected the presence of God. He realised, for the first time, that on this at least Father Finnegan was right.

He tried to read Newman's *Apologia pro Vita Sua*, thinking that Newman's arguments about individual conscience would be useful in the theological arguments that lay ahead. It dawned on him that the theological arguments lay behind him, in ambush perhaps, in ambush still, but behind him.

He abandoned Newman and his conscience for *The Gospel According to Peanuts.* Charlie Brown's friend, Schroeder, was right: to play a Beethoven sonata on a toy piano with the keys painted on does take a lot of practice. He had been practising obediently for fourteen years and perhaps the truth was that he had no ear for music. Or maybe there was no music. Only words.

He thought of Minnie's funeral. He thought of his father's pleasure in the thought of his son saying his requiem mass. But he had a feeling that Minnie's was going to be his last funeral.

O most excellent virgin, obtain for me the grace of fear. At least one prayer had been answered.

He felt descending upon him the dark peace that preceded a seizure. He was surprised, for he had not had a fit for a long time, and besides, he'd had to stop having fits before the bishop could lay his ordaining hands on him and take him up into the Order of Melchisedech. He thought he heard the noise that always took over his head before darkness seized him. But perhaps it was only BA Santamaria barking in fun at the far end of the cloister.